# "So, um, I suppose this is awkward," Meg began.

"I suppose," Charlie returned, wondering if it would be less awkward if she weren't quite so nervous. Or maybe drunk sex just always made things awkward afterward.

He sighed. At himself. At the situation. At...life. "You know—"

"I'm pregnant," she whispered.

He leaned closer, sure he'd misheard or misunderstood. "I'm sorry. What?"

"I know you don't have any reason to believe me. We don't know each other well. It never should have happened, but the very fact of the matter is, the only person I've been in any potentially compromising positions with is...you...and my doctor confirmed a positive pregnancy test. So..."

He leaned back. Away from her and words that didn't make sense. He was thirty-five. He was a vice president of... No, not anymore.

He was an unemployed thirty-five-year-old being told the drunken one-night-stand he hadn't meant to ever let happen had resulted in...

"I didn't mean to just drop it on you like that." She skirted the table of her booth, and that felt like a purposeful distancing. He was on one side, and she was on the other.

Pregnant.

With his baby.

Dear Reader,

Four years ago, I decided to write a book about two farmers and a farmers' market. When I wrote that first chapter, I was determined it would be a stand-alone book. So many people on Twitter were complaining about series, and I was going to write just *one book*.

But the heroine, Mia, had a really interesting sister in Cara. Okay, so maybe, given the chance, it'd be a two-book series. But *that* was it.

I very purposefully gave the hero, Dell, a brother whose name and temperament did not appeal to me at all. Or so I thought.

The funny thing about writing books with complicated family dynamics set in vibrant communities...you can't help *wondering* about the people in the background.

I never meant to make Charlie a hero, but the more I wrote about Dell and his complicated relationship with his father in *All I Have*, the more I had to know what made Charlie Wainwright tick.

Much like Cara, the heroine of *All I Am*, it took me a few tries to find Charlie's match. But when tattooed, goat-farming Meg popped into my brain, I knew no one better could help Charlie find exactly who he was meant to be.

I hope you enjoy this final trip to the farmers' market!

*Nicole Helm*
www.NicoleHelm.Wordpress.com

# NICOLE HELM

—

## All I Want

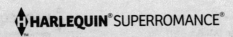

Recycling programs
for this product may
not exist in your area.

ISBN-13: 978-0-373-61002-0

All I Want

Printed in U.S.A.

**Nicole Helm** grew up with her nose in a book and the dream of one day becoming a writer. Luckily, after a few failed career choices, she gets to follow that dream—writing down-to-earth contemporary romance. From farmers to cowboys, Midwest to *the* West, Nicole writes stories about people finding themselves and finding love in the process. She lives in Missouri with her husband and two sons and dreams of someday owning a barn.

### Books by Nicole Helm

#### HARLEQUIN SUPERROMANCE

***A Farmers' Market Story***

*All I Have*
*All I Am*

*Falling for the New Guy*
*Too Friendly to Date*
*Too Close to Resist*

#### HARLEQUIN E

*All I Have*

Visit the Author Profile page at Harlequin.com.

To all the readers who've reached out to tell me how much they loved this series. It's been a joy.

# *CHAPTER ONE*

CHARLIE WAINWRIGHT STOOD at the entrance to his brother's vegetable barn, phone in hand, many, many curse words in his head.

He was about to send his third *where are you?* text in fifteen minutes but then saw Dell's head appear, along with a much smaller, darker head leaning against his shoulder.

"You ask for my help and now you're late? See if I help you again," Charlie called, keeping the curse words in his head only for his niece's benefit.

"Mia's not feeling great. She was going to watch Lainey even so, but the terrible twos are alive and well." Dell approached, and Charlie had to admit the guy looked exhausted.

"She isn't two yet."

"Close e-da...darn-nough." Dell handed the little girl off to Charlie and then opened up the barn.

"Hey there, Sugar Snap," Charlie greeted his niece. Maybe he said it quiet enough so Dell couldn't hear, because *maybe* Lainey had climbed under every last tough-guy facade he'd ever had since the day she stopped spitting up breast milk.

"Chawie." She slapped him on the face, her greeting of the moment.

"Lovely," Charlie muttered, bouncing her till she giggled while Dell loaded up his market truck with vegetables for the day. "So, what's Mia down with? Not flu season. Sure she's not just sick of you?"

Dell grinned as he shoved the last pallets of vegetables onto his truck bed. "Nope. Not nearly sick of me."

Charlie grimaced. His screwup younger brother's happiness and business success over the past few years were a little salt on the wound right now. He could deal with being wifeless and childless, usually, but with the company he worked for being bought out and rumors that layoffs would happen next week, well, work and success were all Charlie had. The very real threat he could lose them was...terrifying.

But he wouldn't lose. Couldn't. *Didn't.* He was the best man for the job, even if the company buyout meant cuts were coming. Most likely to people as high up as he was.

Not thinking about that today. Today was helping Dell at the farmers' market. He'd worry about work at work.

*Right, you're so good at setting boundaries like that.*

He flipped Lainey upside down and she screamed

with delight. When he brought her back upright, Dell was grinning at him. "What?"

"Nothing. Just never expected you to be Mr. Doting Uncle. Good thing, though, as you're going to be an uncle twice over soon enough."

Charlie's eyebrows shot up. Dell had been married for almost four years now, and his and Mia's farm business was booming. It shouldn't be a shock, but even with years to tell Charlie otherwise, he'd still been of the mind-set that he was better off than Dell.

Charlie had attended a challenging school, escaped their tiny farming community hometown. He was a vice president of National Accounts, the youngest one his company had ever had. He lived in an expensive apartment, drove a nice sports car and had a solid retirement plan. He had *investments*.

But for the first time, maybe because he knew his job and all that success he'd worked so hard for was on the line, he looked at Dell and realized his brother had come out on top.

"Blank stare all you got?"

"No." Charlie forced himself to get over his own problems for a minute. "Man, congratulations. Really. Although Mia's the one doing all the work. Don't know why I should be congratulating you." Gotta get a dig in, right?

"Same old Charlie," Dell said, shaking his head as he took Lainey back into his arms. "I'm going to take her to Mom. You want to start up the truck and meet me out front?"

"Sure." He took the keys Dell handed him. "Number two, huh?" Three years younger, many years wasted and Dell was way out in front.

Christ.

"We haven't told the folks yet, but God knows Mia's blabbed to Cara and Anna, so it's my turn. Cara's pregnant too."

"No sh—" At Dell's finger-to-neck motion, Charlie changed where he was going. "No way." Mia and her sister pregnant at the same time. Every person he knew who hadn't made much of himself until long after him, happy and procreating.

Dell rolled his eyes. "She said the F-word the other day," he grumbled, ruffling Lainey's feather-fine hair. "Clear as you please. Right in the middle of the grocery store. Needless to say, I was not hailed as a hero that night."

"Right," Charlie said, feeling uncharacteristically tongue-tied. "Well."

"Babies everywhere, man. Watch out. It's in the air and it might be catching." Dell slapped him on the shoulder before heading up toward their parents' house.

Charlie climbed into Dell's truck and turned the key in the ignition. The feeling weighing down his arms, twisting in his chest, it was all very new.

Something he'd never experienced before, so it was hard to pinpoint, hard to label.

His career was being threatened. He had no wife, no serious girlfriend, no chance for kids anytime soon. He had things, but the intangibles, success and love and contentment…well, if he lost his job, they would all be missing.

His chest squeezed tighter, arms feeling heavier. He had a bad feeling it all meant one thing.

Charlie Wainwright was a failure. And that was something he'd never been.

MEG CARMICHAEL IGNORED the heavy grief in her chest and set up her table at the Millertown Farmers' Market. She chatted idly about the weather with the woman to her left, who had a table of colorful jellies and jams set out. She pulled out brochures, breathed in the scent of lavender and smiled despite the tears pricking her eyes.

Lavender had always been her grandmother's favorite.

With a deep breath Meg plastered a smile on her face and looked at the display she'd put together. Baskets of soaps boasting different shapes and scents. The Hope Springs Farm name and an illustration of a poppy and a goat graced her signs, brochures and labels.

*Look at all you've done.* It was Grandma's voice, because that was the voice that had guided her since she ended her last stint in rehab. She'd been clean for eight years now, sober for six. She had a business, and a life she was proud of, to show for it.

And Grandma was gone. Meg had to keep telling herself that was okay, *that* was life. Getting high wouldn't change the fact that her sole familial supporter was gone. Dead.

Nothing would change that, so what was the point in throwing away her life again? The pain wouldn't go away. She'd have to be her own positive force. Her own support.

That wasn't scary or overwhelming. It was *empowering*. Or something.

Meg repeated the word *empowered* over and over inside her head. Willing herself to believe it as the morning went on. She was *powerful*. She was *strong*. Breathe in. Breathe out. Smile. Charm. Sell.

The market was busy, which made it easier. Though her booth that boasted no food products wasn't as popular as the vegetable stands and the honey and egg stands, she was having a pretty successful morning for herself.

Because she *was* successful, empowered, strong.

An older woman with a little white dog passed, ignoring her greeting on her way to the organic dog treat table a few spots down. Not to be deterred,

Meg greeted the next passerby. "Mother's Day is just around the corner!"

As she'd hoped, that caught the attention of a man who appeared to be in his thirties, alone and the type to be too busy to remember Mother's Day. Meg had a knack for recognizing those types.

"We've got lots of scents and shapes. Owls, foxes, pretty designs. Perfect for any mother who likes nice, usable things." She smiled broadly. He couldn't be much older than her and was only an inch or two taller. Sandy-brown hair that looked carefully styled, the kind of five o'clock shadow that looked cultivated rather than accidental.

He was...actually kind of hot. Which was weird, because she wasn't usually attracted to men who looked like they belonged in the world she'd grown up in. Except for the jeans. Her mother never would have approved of *jeans*.

"Owls, huh?" He stepped closer, squinting at her baskets of soaps.

"Owls are scented with lemon verbena. Very cute and fun," she said, pointing to the appropriate basket. "Goat milk soap has great antiaging benefits—not that I'd mention it to the recipient."

"No, I don't suppose I would either."

"You can buy by the soap for three fifty a piece or a gift basket of five is fifteen dollars."

"Fifteen dollars for soap?"

He wasn't the first person to balk at her prices,

and he no doubt wouldn't be the last. Still, her repeat customers didn't seem to mind. "I promise the recipient will be a convert and won't blink an eye at the price. Goat milk soap is *that* good."

"Well, you're quite the saleswoman." He gave her a sideways glance, his expression changing as he took in her bright and colorful arm of tattoos. "I'll give you that," he added, looking away. But she read the expression all the same. Judgment.

Once upon a time, the judgment had bothered her, fueled her. She'd used that judgment to prove the world didn't understand. She was above the world, its rules, everything. She sought out that judgment.

These days…well, she figured it didn't really matter what some stranger thought of her choices.

"Mix-and-match gift basket?" he asked, running a long finger over the face of an owl.

"Yup. Name your five, and I'll even package them up all pretty." She went behind the table and pulled out one of her gift bags, complete with the Hope Springs logo on the front and a pretty red lace ribbon to tie it up with.

She waited for him to pick the soaps he wanted, but he just stared at her wrist. "Is that…"

"A goat?" She held out her arm to emphasize the tattoo at her wrist—the only one she'd gotten post-rehab. A little goat with a poppy, sitting beneath the cloud design that took up most of her forearm. Her fresh-start goat. "Yup, it's a goat. I love them."

"I see that." Finally he shifted his gaze away from her arm and started looking through the soaps, picking out one of each kind and handing them to her so she could package them. He then pulled his wallet out of his pants—his very expensive-looking leather wallet.

"Don't want anything for yourself?" she joked.

He glanced around her table of pastels and bows and flowers. Girly to the extreme. "Why not? Not getting any younger. Maybe I could use some antiaging soap. I'll take the goat to remember you by." He picked it up with a grin that said he knew he was charming. The kind of grin that usually made her roll her eyes and stick a finger down her mouth in a gagging motion.

His didn't quite have that effect, though. His made her grin back.

He plopped the goat soap into her palm and she blinked for a second before remembering the routine. Wrap it up. *Get yourself together, because you are not sixteen.*

"Well, I certainly appreciate your business."

"I can't resist a good saleswoman."

A little flush crept into her cheeks, totally against her will. Oh, he was too charming and he knew it. Somehow, it didn't dilute her reaction at all. "Keep me in mind for all your soap and lotion needs." She plucked a card from her table and handed it to him, trying not to cringe at how ridiculous that sounded.

"My..." He cocked his head, gaze running from her table back to her.

His dark eyes met hers, and one side of his mouth quirked up. "I don't have a lot of soap and lotion needs, but I'll still keep you in mind."

He was flirting with her and it had...been a while. Her life was pretty isolated these days. Not so much by design, but necessity. Running a goat farm all by herself was hard work, and she didn't know a lot of fellow thirtysomethings as interested in cloven-hoofed creatures as she was, aside from the occasional satanist.

He pocketed her card and took the bag of soaps. "I'll see you around."

"I'm here every Saturday." Oh, brother. That was just lame. But he smiled and nodded, and she let herself stare as he walked away.

*Really nice butt.*

*Designer jeans.*

Couldn't win them all. The fact of the matter was, cute and flirting or not, he was the type of guy she'd known all too well growing up. The nice clothes and expensive watch, that serious business resting face.

He was a type—a type she had no interest in.

Oh well. It didn't hurt to look, especially when

the chances of him returning were slim to none. When her phone chimed in her pocket, she stiffened. The text from her mother wasn't unexpected, but it felt cruel. Mom surely considered it efficient, but the timing, the brevity…

The funeral will be Thursday.

Grandma was gone. Meg hadn't been allowed to be in the hospital for fear she might "upset people." Even though Grandma had been the only one to stand by her. Even though Grandma had set her up with the farm after Meg got out of rehab, and even though Grandma had supported her through every setback.

As though that hadn't been bad enough, every offer of help with arrangements had also been rebuffed. Because it was what *they* wanted. No one in the Carmichael clan was thinking about what Grandma wanted. Would have wanted. All they could think about was appearances. What people might *think*.

It had been drilled in them for generations, Meg figured. This strident need to show only perfection and success.

To them, Meg would always be a failure. Always be imperfect.

Meg blinked away tears and forced her lips to curve upward as two women passed. "Good morning! Goat milk soap has many skin benefits. Can I offer you a brochure?"

*Suck it up. Smile. Pretend nothing is wrong.* Mom would be so proud.

# CHAPTER TWO

"OBVIOUSLY WE'LL OFFER you a reference as this isn't a reflection of your abilities."

Charlie sat in the cushy chair of his new boss's office, which had been his old boss's office, but now...

He blinked, trying to make his thoughts follow a straight line. This wasn't out of the blue. He'd known this possibility existed. But now it was here and he somehow couldn't wrap his brain around it.

"We'd like you to stay on for a few weeks, ease us through the transition. You'd be compensated, naturally. Alisha here will go over your severance package once that's done." Mr. Collins nodded toward the human resources woman Charlie had never met because she'd come from this new company.

It didn't matter who she was or what she went over, he was being let go from the position he'd worked his ass off for. He'd poured ten years of his life into this company and what did he have to show for it? A severance package?

"I'm sure you'll land on your feet. You're sharp. I'm sorry we couldn't keep you, but you know how these things go."

Mr. Collins held out his hand, the same dismissive gesture Charlie had extended to others in the past. But always for performance reasons. He'd never had to lay off a member of his team just because.

But Charlie had been businessman professional too long not to smile politely, take the offered hand and let Alisha usher him down the corridor to her office. An office that had belonged to Marissa, a mother of three, not that long ago.

This new woman's office was spare and efficient, absent of a million hand-painted drawings with goofy magnets along the edge of the filing cabinet. No giant bowl of hard candy at the edge of her desk either.

Things like this had been happening for weeks, and he was shamed to realize how it'd failed to hit him until *he* was the one getting the ax. Change usually meant a person's life was being upended. The changes that had been sweeping through the office hadn't been voluntary or easy for most involved.

But he'd been too wrapped up in himself, in how much he deserved to stay, to notice how it was affecting people, and that shamed him too, deeply.

There was paperwork to fill out. Alisha spoke in gentle, patient tones, so he nearly felt like he was back in kindergarten, complete with her escorting him back to his office.

His *office*. His.

"You'll want to start notifying your clients," Alisha said in that elementary school teacher voice. "Before they hear from anyone else."

Right. Work to do. Clients to notify so the company that was firing him—no, *laying him off*—didn't lose any business. He would need to prepare everything to turn over to his replacement, whom he'd meet tomorrow. It didn't matter that he'd been let go, there was still work to do.

For the afternoon, he worked as diligently as he had the previous ten years. Making sure clients understood nothing would change, readying files and binders. He efficiently and methodically worked to make his job something he could simply hand over to someone else.

It was a long day of continuous surrealism; none of it really sank in. Because he had a few weeks ahead of him, of training someone else to do his job. He had weeks of making sure things were "in order."

So, at the end of the day, when he shut his laptop down, he thought this would feel the same too.

Instead he stared at the blank screen. His usual next step was to snap it shut, slide it into his briefcase, check his phone one last time for emails or messages and then walk out. Most Thursday nights he ate dinner with his parents. It wasn't a day to stay late in the office, like he did every other night.

But the IT Department had asked him to leave the computer so they could prep it for his replacement. He didn't know how to walk away from this extension of himself that was going to be handed off to someone else.

His replacement.

He looked around the office that had been his for almost two years. He wasn't a knickknack kind of guy. There were some awards on the wall, a picture of the Wainwrights from Lainey's first birthday on his desk next to his Stan Musial–signed baseball.

It would take him ten minutes tops to erase himself from this office, and he didn't know what that said about him, or his job, or his life; he only knew it felt like it meant *something*—something not particularly good.

MEG PACED THE SIDEWALK outside the church trying very hard to breathe through the sobs that racked her body.

She couldn't hear what was happening inside, and she wasn't sure she wanted to. She didn't want the prayers or priest's words telling her Grandma was in a better place. What better place was there than *here*—at Meg's side?

Meg tried to mop up her face, but she'd neglected to bring tissues, so she had only the collar of her dress and the backs of her hands. And she just kept crying, so it was a completely useless exercise anyway.

She might not *want* to be in there, but she knew she *should* be. Grandma would want her in there, would consider it the right thing to do.

But she also wouldn't want a scene, and if Meg tried to get in a second time…

The broken sob was impossible to swallow down. How could they turn her away from the funeral? How could they ban her? Grandma wouldn't have wanted that. Grandma had always loved her.

No matter what.

Meg knew, in a way, this was her fault. She hadn't planned well and the black sweater she figured she'd throw over her tattoos had boasted a giant hole in the armpit when she pulled it out of her closet.

Meg had spent ten frantic moments pawing through her closet trying to find something acceptable to her parents that would also cover her arms and match and be suitable grieving colors and she'd just…given up.

What was the point of scrambling through your

closet when your grandmother was gone and your family was going to snub you anyway? To her parents, the tattoos were the visible slap in the face of all Meg had thrown away, all the shame she'd brought to their doorstep. In the world of her parents, appearances were everything.

So she'd accepted that Mom would sneer at the simple black dress that allowed some of her tattoos to be visible. She'd accepted that she'd probably have to sit alone, maybe even toward the back of the church.

But she'd never imagined it possible, not in a million years, that her parents would bar her from her own grandmother's funeral.

The church bells tolled and Meg felt like she was eight again, alone outside this church, not understanding what was wrong with her—why her parents would rather pretend she didn't exist than hug her.

She'd run out of church one Sunday, determined to just *run*. Because the priest could talk all he wanted about God's love, but it hadn't been infused into her parents. All they'd ever cared about was what their friends might have said behind their backs, or to their faces. The deals Dad might have lost if certain business partners found out he couldn't control his daughter. The Carmichael *name*.

"I won't go back there," she muttered aloud, no

doubt looking like an insane person. But surely this couldn't be the worst behavior anyone had ever seen at a funeral.

The stately church doors opened with a groan, and everyone began processing out. Red eyes, tears, handkerchiefs. Some people didn't look twice at her. A few of her distant relatives touched her arm briefly on their way to the cars that would take them to the cemetery.

But everyone knew not to stop and talk to Meg. Meg the addict. Meg the failure. Meg the giant black splotch on a proud and old-moneyed family.

When Mom approached, her eyes held more fury than grief, and all Meg wanted to do was leave to find a drink. Find oblivion. It had been a long time since she sincerely wished for something else to take her away, but that wish was so deep, so big, it was all she could think about as Mom bore down on her.

"You are not wanted," Mom hissed.

"You made me miss the service, but you cannot bar me from the cemetery."

"Yes, I can, because *I* care about how this family looks. Do you really think your grandmother would want you here reminding everyone how you've continually thrown your life away?"

Meg wanted to speak, wanted to yell, *Yes, she would want me here. I know she would want me here.* But she couldn't form the words, not in the face of her mother's righteous fury. Meg's decisions as a teenager had been a betrayal to the Carmichael name that Mom would never forgive.

"You are not welcome, Margaret," Mom said, before smiling at an elderly couple who walked by them.

Margaret. Meg's hated given name. "All I want is to say goodbye. I will stay out of your way," Meg said, trying to be strong.

Dad stepped between them, easily clamping a hand over her mother's elbow. "That's enough."

For a brief, blinding moment Meg actually thought her father was standing up for her. All the grief and confusion, for just one second, felt bearable. Like she could handle it if one of them stood up for her.

But then his icy blue gaze landed on her face, and his mouth went into a firm, disapproving line. "You've done enough to upset your mother. You ought to be ashamed of yourself making a scene like this."

"I…" But she couldn't finish the denial. She didn't want a scene. She didn't want to feel like she was fifteen and emotionally bleeding all over the place in front of them while they sneered and pushed her away again, but here they were, making it happen anyway.

Blaming her. Looking down their noses at her. When she was theirs.

"She'd want me here. You know she would," Meg managed, trying to firm her chin enough to lift it, trying to find strength somewhere deep, deep, deep down. Grandma's strength.

"Well, we do not," Dad returned, pulling Mom with him as they walked toward the sleek black car that would follow the procession to the cemetery where nearly a century of Carmichaels were buried.

In the end, Meg couldn't force herself to go. She didn't know how to fight them. She never had. She might be an adult, but they could still make her feel as though she was nothing—or worse.

There'd only ever been one way to get rid of that feeling, and she wasn't certain she could fight it anymore.

# CHAPTER THREE

"YOU'LL LAND ON your feet." Mom pulled Charlie into a firm hug at the front door of the aging farmhouse he'd grown up in.

How the hell had this happened? This whole day was a warped nightmare. First having to *hear* the words he'd been let go, having to go through the day with the knowledge he'd poured so many years into that company. Outselling every junior salesman, climbing the ranks by sheer force of will and determination to succeed.

"It's a good severance package, son. And I'm sure you'll have a new job lined up in no time."

Charlie tried to force a smile. He appreciated his parents' support. More than he could fully feel in the numb aftermath of today. But he'd been lucky to grow up here, to have this family, even for all their problems.

Unfortunately he wasn't in the mood for support and hugs. He wanted to yell. He wanted to punch something.

"Thank you for dinner," Charlie managed to

say with some semblance of a normal voice. "I'll see you on Saturday."

He knew he didn't fool his mother at all, but she let him walk out into the night, knowing as she always did exactly what he needed. Which wasn't support or coddling.

With stiff, heavy limbs he climbed into his car. At least it was paid off. Money really wasn't an immediate concern. While he splurged on occasion, growing up the son of a struggling farmer, he'd been too practical to waste money. A nice car, a nice watch, a nice place, but he wasn't like his friends, getting an expensive car every few years, eating at expensive restaurants every night, filling every inch of their lives with stuff.

Money and even finding a new job weren't the issues. He'd have headhunters calling him next week. It was his pride that lay bruised and bloody on the ground, not to mention the sneaking suspicion he'd somehow failed before he'd even lost his job.

What good was success if it could be unfairly ripped out from under your feet?

Christ, he needed a drink.

Normally that would mean heading back to the city, meeting friends. But heading back to the bustle and lights and his still-employed friends sounded a lot more painful than heading to an old New Benton townie bar.

Maybe he'd be able to remember how good he had it surrounded by people way worse off than him. He drove away from his parents' house, past Dell's warmly lit cabin, dissatisfaction uncomfortably digging deeper and deeper.

By the time he got to the Shack, an aptly named dilapidated building with neon lights that only half still worked, he was ready to get so drunk he wouldn't even know his own name. Something he'd never done, not even in his college days.

Because he was Charlie Wainwright. He followed the rules. Did what he was supposed to. All so he could succeed.

*And for what?*

Those words kept haunting him. All day. Over and over. *For what?*

He walked through the smoky bar, low strains of old-time country music twanging in the air. The room was mainly filled with old men in overalls, older women in ill-advised leather and a few people who probably looked a lot older than they'd ever actually be.

He strode up to the bar, ordered two doubles of their best bourbon, which was not very good at all, then situated himself on a barstool.

It might not be the practical, sensible, *Charlie* way of dealing with a problem, but what did it matter? The practical, sensible, *Charlie* way of dealing had gotten him here—with nothing to show.

*You're pathetic, Wainwright.*

Not something he was particularly proud of, but he'd give himself this weekend to wallow. Indulge in a few un-Charlie-like things. Monday he'd nip all this self-loathing, self-pitying in the bud.

But for tonight…tonight he was going to wallow. He knocked back the first drink, and then the second, before gesturing to the bartender that he wanted another. Once that third drink was comfortably downed, he looked around the dimly lit barroom.

The blonde in the corner caught his attention, first because her hair was a kind of honeyed blond, not the near white of the cougars in leather. Second because her arm, just barely visible, was streaked with color.

Hey, he knew that tattoo. Yes. He got off the barstool and made his way over to her, plopping himself down at her table.

"I know you," he said, pointing at her. "Goat Girl." Oops. Probably shouldn't call her that. That wasn't very charming.

Fuck charming. He didn't feel like being much of anything.

"I prefer Capra Crusader for my superhero goat name," she replied, unsmiling, though he was pretty sure it was a joke.

She was wearing a black dress, which made the colorful arm all that more bright and noticeable.

Her forearm was the oddest antithesis to this bar. A sunny blue with white puffy clouds. He couldn't make out what was above her elbow because the sleeve of her dress cut it off.

In the past he would have made a joke about the tattoos. Maybe not to her face, but at least in his head. *I-don't-want-a-job tattoos.*

But her job didn't require the level of respectability that his did. Oh, wait, he didn't *have* a job. "Buy you another?" he said, gesturing to her glass.

She stared hard at the remnants of whatever her first drink had been. Then stared equally as hard at the bar behind him. "You've bought my soap, might as well buy me a drink," she said eventually. "Can't go back anyway," she muttered.

He didn't know what that meant, but it didn't matter. He meandered back to the bar, got two drinks, belatedly realizing he hadn't asked her what she wanted. So he ordered four different drinks. Couldn't hurt.

He carefully carried the four glasses back to her table, only sloshing a little over his fingers.

"I bring variety," he announced, the heat of the liquor quickly spreading from gut to his extremities.

A nice feeling all in all. Kind of numb and tingly. No heavy failure constricting everything. He felt light and fluid. Very nice indeed.

"So, what on earth are you doing here?" she

asked, pulling one of the glasses close to her. "Don't tell me you actually live in New Benton?"

"No. I don't." He sipped his bourbon, studying her. Her eyes were almost the same blue as the sky of her tattoo. Wisps of blond hair framed her round face. She didn't look like she wore makeup except for the slight smudge of black under her eyes.

"Let me guess." She linked her fingers around the glass. Long, elegant, but with blunt nails painted black. She was quite the contrast. "Central West End?"

"No. Downtown."

She snorted, taking a big, long gulp of her drink. "Yeah, you're that type."

"Type?"

"Mr. Super Yuppie. That's *your* superhero name."

Perhaps sober, practical Charlie would be offended, but relaxed, inebriated Charlie found it funny. And true. It was like this day had separated him from his life and he saw what a joke it all was.

So he laughed and polished off that fourth drink no matter how irresponsible it was. How would he get home? How would Goat Girl, er, Capra Crusader, get home? Eh, he'd figure it out. Later. "Super Yuppie. Well, at least I'm super at something."

She waved a hand at him. "Oh, please, I'm sure

you're super at everything. Like I said, I know your type. Silver spoon, right? Private school. Mommy and Daddy paid for college. Oh, I know *all* about your type."

"If I'm all those things, how did I end up solo at a New Benton townie bar on a Thursday night?" Because for as much of a yuppie as he might have turned into, nothing was handed to him on a silver platter.

She finished off the drink in a quick gulp, put the glass down with a thud and then leaned forward. Her dress was modest, but still, the leaning and the way her arms were crossed under her breasts meant he had a decent view. Meant he wondered if she had tattoos in other places. Meant he wondered...

"My eyes are up here, sir."

He closed his for a second. "Sorry. Can I blame booze for my lack of manners?" When he opened his eyes, training them on her face, she was smiling.

"Manners are kind of a turnoff for me, so you're absolved." She pulled another drink toward her like one might hold a treasured object. "So, how *did* you get to a New Benton townie bar alone on a Thursday night? Decide to slum it a bit?"

"I grew up here."

Her eyebrows drew together, her nose wrinkled. "Oh."

"On a farm."

Then her eyes went wide. "I…can't picture you on a farm."

"No, I don't suppose you can."

"So, you hated it?"

He shrugged. "*Hate* is a strong word. I didn't love it. My father, the farmer, really didn't love it. So I worked my butt off to do something better with my life."

"My farm is the best thing that ever happened to my life," she said vehemently, reminding him much too much of Dell.

"Yeah, well, different strokes and all that." How had they gotten to talking about farms of all damn things? He didn't want to talk about farms. "Why are you here? What sorrows are you drowning?"

"My grandmother's funeral." She pointed to her modest black dress. "I got kicked out."

"Oh. Well, you win."

"Don't I just?" She downed the shot, exposing the slim column of her throat, a blue light casting an eerie glow to her pale skin. "What are you drowning?"

"Hold on. How…how does someone get kicked out of her grandmother's funeral?"

MEG KNEW THIS was all wrong. Grandma would not approve. She wasn't popping pills or snorting anything, but alcohol had led to drugs on more than one occasion. Not that someone like Mr. Super

Yuppie would have any idea how to get his hands on illegal substances.

So, really, what did getting drunk matter? It was the lesser of two evils, and if she didn't have something loosening the tightness in her chest, she was afraid she would just…stop breathing. Drown on land.

How had she gotten kicked out of Grandma's funeral?

"Apparently daring to show my tattoos was grounds enough to be told I couldn't be in the church. Then I was informed I was deeply upsetting my mother, you know, by existing. So I couldn't go to the burial site. At least not without causing a scene and…that wouldn't be right. They aren't right, but neither would that be." It wasn't anywhere close to the full story of her parents' disdain for her, but she didn't have years, and this man wasn't her therapist.

She stared at the drink. Three in. She didn't feel numb or light or any of the things getting high used to do for her. She just felt heavy and sad and she couldn't erase the look on her mother's face, the hurtful words from her father.

Their little failure. She meant nothing to them. A stain to the Carmichael name, the worst thing two proud, conceited, powerful people could produce.

At thirty-two she should be over it, and on the day-to-day she was, but the fact they couldn't take a break from protecting their precious image for her grandmother's funeral…

It made her feel like nothing and, considering that was what had shoved her into the drug scene in the first place, considering she was sitting here getting trashed, was just pathetic.

"So, what's your story?" she demanded of the man in front of her.

"Not as bad as yours."

"Good. I want to hear all about it. So I can feel less pathetic. Spill. Every lame detail." Even though it was wrong, she finished off the second drink and pulled the third one toward herself.

"I got fired. Sort of."

"*You?* You look like a guy who spends Saturday night responding to work emails." Just as her father would have been doing twenty-some years ago.

"Something I would do, yes. It wasn't… I mean, I shouldn't have been let go. But the company I worked for was bought out and I was axed to make room for their staff. Since I'm high up on the food chain so to speak, there wasn't really room for me anywhere else."

"Yeah, I definitely win."

"If it helps, I'm having kind of a premidlife crisis over it."

"That does help, actually. Tell me, Super Yuppie, what's so terrible about losing your job? If

you're so great, don't you just get another one?"
Anytime Dad had bought out some mom-and-pop,
he waved away the damage. *Oh, those people will
find jobs if they're any good.*

"Well, jobs at that level don't just sit around.
But you're right, I'm not too worried about unemployment."

"So why the crisis?"

He took one of her empty glasses, clinked the
melting ice around before crunching a piece in
his mouth.

She watched his throat move. He was dressed
up in his yuppie best from the waist up. Striped
polo short-sleeved shirt. Though his hair looked
less perfectly mussed tonight, and the five o'clock
shadow looked a little more accidental.

"Let me get one more. You want?"

She nodded, watching him head back up to the
bar. She had no idea why she was attracted to
him. The square jaw? The brown eyes with flecks
of lighter brown and maybe gold? Or maybe the
way he smiled without showing any teeth, like he
was always holding back, which made her want
to make him *not* hold back.

Or maybe she was just lonely and any guy
would do. With alcohol thickening in her limbs,
she didn't care about the answer.

He returned with two drinks instead of four this
time, which was good. She was going to need to

call a cab to get home regardless, but anything beyond one more drink might lead to passing out.

Or other really bad choices.

"All right, you have your drink, tell me your sob story," she demanded. Maybe whatever his lame crisis was would make her feel better about hers.

"That company, that job, it was everything I'd worked for. One more promotion and I would have been exactly where I wanted to be to start focusing on my personal life. You know, the wife-and-kids thing. Now I have to start all over, and I'm thirty-five. I've worked my whole life…for nothing."

Even though it wasn't as bad as losing her grandmother and being kicked out of her last chance to say goodbye, Meg did feel sorry for him. Because for all the ways he surprised her by not falling into type, he'd obviously wrapped his identity in his job, and he'd lost it.

She understood that. She'd wrapped her identity in being a screwup. She'd never lived up to her parents' exacting standards, so why not thumb her nose at said standards at every turn? That had been the hardest part of getting clean, finding her real self, not how other people viewed her. "We're pathetic."

"So. Much."

She looked around the smoky bar. It was getting late and a lot of the sturdier crew had disappeared a while ago. "You got money for cab fare?"

"Um. Sure. If we can catch New Benton's one and only cabdriver."

"I'm sure we can flag Dan down. Eventually. Let's go," she said, grabbing his hand. "I want to show you my goats."

And that was only a little bit of euphemism.

## CHAPTER FOUR

CHARLIE WOKE UP praying to every available god that he would not throw up. Or maybe he was praying that his head wasn't going to roll off his shoulders and *then* throw up.

Why did it smell like…he didn't know, but not his apartment, not the farm, not any smell he was familiar with? Kind of flowery, but not quite floral.

What had he *done* last night?

Gearing up for the onslaught of pain, he slowly squinted his eyes in a semiopen position. Then, despite the headache slicing through his skull, he opened his eyes completely, because he had no idea where he was.

Something moved next to him. He jerked, cursed at the sloshing of his stomach, eyes involuntarily closing again. He took a deep breath and let it out, willing the nausea away. And then opened his eyes to the woman next to him. In what he assumed to be her bed…

Goat Girl. That colorful arm of hers a shock of memory. The bar. The cab. They'd…

He rubbed his hands over his face, trying to remember, but everything was so blurry.

Goats. He remembered goats. Feeding them? Christ.

He took another deep breath and tried to focus. The important thing, the *most* important thing, was that he still had pants on. And Goat Girl still wore the black dress she'd been wearing at the bar.

So, hopefully, whatever idiocy their drunken selves had been up to, it wasn't sex. Because surely if they'd had a drunk hookup, he'd (a) remember, and (b) not have pants on. *Surely.*

"Damn."

He dropped his hands, glanced sheepishly at… God, he didn't even know her name, did he? Had he asked and forgotten? Surely they'd at least exchanged names?

*But you didn't have sex, so it's fine. It's totally fine.*

Tell that to all the panic hanging out with all the ill-advised liquor in his bloodstream.

Her blue eyes met his gaze tentatively. She shook her head and covered her face with her hands, repeating the F-word approximately ten times.

"Please tell me you're not swearing because you remember something I don't."

She peeked at him through her fingers. "What do you remember?"

"The bar. The cab ride. Goats. I remember goats."

"I remember kissing."

"In the cab?"

She nodded.

Yeah, he kind of remembered that. Kissing and laughing in the back of old Dan Riley's cab. He really hoped that didn't get back to his mother. Making out with some tattooed goat farmer in a cab.

Actually Mom would probably get a kick out of it. Dad, not so much. And Dell or, possibly worse, his little sister? He'd never hear the end of it.

"There was some…bra removal on my couch and subsequent…touching," she added, her face all wrinkled up.

"But…actual…" He made useless hand gestures, not at all sure why he couldn't spit out the very simple word.

"Sex? I don't remember any. Do you?"

He shook his head, too hard, and had to take another few deep breaths to settle his stomach.

"Okay, and you have pants on. And I…" She patted herself down. "No bra, but underwear intact. Surely if we were so drunk we don't remember, we wouldn't have had the wherewithal to put our clothes back on."

"Agreed."

She let out a long breath. "So we didn't. And…"

She pressed a palm to her forehead. "God, I need some water and a time machine."

"I need to get home."

"Right. Yeah. Totally."

He gingerly slid off the bed, then stopped in his tracks. Ohhhhhhh, shit. "Um, I don't suppose you keep condom wrappers on the floor for fun?"

Their gazes met from opposite sides of the bed. She looked about as crestfallen as he felt. She skirted the bed, then started swearing again.

"On the bright side, we used a condom?" Which was not much of a bright side. He certainly didn't pride himself on drunken sex he couldn't remember with women whose names he didn't know.

It was sleazy. Irresponsible. So not him.

"You're right. If we used a condom and don't remember it and…stuff, then, really, it's like it never happened. Right?"

"Right."

Right. They would just pretend it never happened.

"I should probably find my shirt, then."

"Yeah. Yeah."

SHE WAS PRETTY. Even the morning after a bender, her skin a little pale and her hair all rumpled, she was pretty. What he could remember of their night had been, well, maybe not fun, but easy. Companionable.

But she wasn't his type. Not even a little bit. Tattoos. Goat farming. He was getting to be the age where he couldn't casually date anymore. He needed to find the right woman to settle down with.

There was nothing about this woman that fit his idea of that. Nothing. So he took his shirt from her outstretched hand and pulled it over his head. "I should go."

She nodded, then put her palm to her head again. "Yeah, you need some water or anything for the road?"

"No. No, I'm good." He could practically hear his head and stomach laughing at him, but he was starting to feel panic set in and he didn't want to stick around for it to blow out of control.

Control. Ha. What a joke. "Um, shoes?"

"I think outside, maybe? I feel like we…"

"Danced barefoot on your porch."

"With a goat."

He started laughing because he could kind of remember that, in a fuzzy unreal way. But it had been real. He'd gotten drunk, danced barefoot with a woman whose name he didn't know, a goat at their feet, then apparently had forgettable sex.

This was a pretty epic premidlife crisis if he did say so himself. In fact, if he told anyone who knew him any of that, they wouldn't believe him. Not for a second.

He followed her out of her room, through a little hallway and into a bright kitchen. It was full of stainless steel equipment, spools of ribbon and herbs hanging from the exposed beam rafters above.

The house itself looked cozy and well lived-in, but a little worse for the wear, much like his parents' own century-old farmhouse.

She opened her front door and stepped into the bright sunshine of the morning. She used her arm to shield her eyes as she stepped outside and he followed, already squinting.

He found his shoes and tried not to lose his tenuous grasp of his volatile stomach as he bent over to pick them up.

From the front of her house, he couldn't see her goat operation, but he could hear their sounds in the distance.

So. Damn. Weird.

"Well, you know, thanks for the commiseration."

"Yeah, yeah, you too."

She still had her arm over her face. Against his will his eyes were drawn to her chest; the fact that she wasn't wearing a bra was quite obvious.

Seriously how could he not remember having sex with her? Maybe they hadn't. Maybe the condom wrapper was a fluke. Maybe…

He pushed the thoughts away. Didn't matter. Last night was the fluke. His one and only foray into self-pity and irresponsible behavior. It was a blip, had to be, and he needed to be on his merry way.

He patted his pockets, then remembered he didn't have a car there. It was still sitting in the Shack's parking lot, along with hers.

"Huh," she said, clearly realizing the same thing. She let out a gusty sigh. "I guess I'll call Dan so we can go get our cars." She moved to step back inside, the storm door squeaking in its frame. "I'll get you some water. And some toast?"

"Toast sounds…edible."

She nodded and disappeared. Charlie stayed on the porch, taking a seat on the railing and slowly pulling on his shoes.

So he had to have the awkward morning after without even remembering the sex. Cruel and unusual punishment. And a really good reminder that he was not the kind of guy who got rewarded for being irresponsible.

He only ever got punished for it. Of course, he'd been punished by responsibility too. And with a hangover threatening to kill him, he didn't have the energy to figure out what that meant.

MEG JUMPED WHEN the toaster popped, then cursed because thirty-two-year-old Meg was a total wimp when it came to hangovers.

She was about 65 percent sure she was dying.

And 35 percent sure she was going to die of embarrassment if she had to serve…so and so…toast on her porch.

She didn't even know his name.

Hanging her head in shame, she pulled the toast out of the toaster and dropped it onto the paper plates she'd retrieved. It would be at least half an hour before the cab got here.

Bully for her.

Unfortunately she had to face the guy. She brought the plates of toast out to the porch, handed him one, then put the other on her swinging love seat. Another trip to the kitchen and she retrieved two bottles of water.

"The cab should be here in about twenty. Hopefully."

He nodded. "Thanks. For that. And for this." He held up the toast and then took a careful bite. She guzzled some water and they sat in silence, only the sounds of insects and goats in the air.

A pretty spring morning, and she needed to get to work before the cab got here, but first she had to feel human. Or at least like her head wasn't going to explode every time she moved.

After an awkward silent breakfast, Meg forced herself to stand and smile. "Um, so, I need to go milk the goats."

"Milk the…? Right."

"You can come watch if you're curious." She

wasn't sure where the offer came from. It would have made more sense to ask his name. But he hadn't asked hers. So either he knew it and she was the sole uninformed participant, or he didn't *want* to know hers. Which meant she didn't need to know his. In fact, the less she knew about him, the better.

*Fantastic idea inviting him to watch you milk the goats, then, yeah?*

"Sure."

She tried to smile at his agreement and not hate him for following her. Although *hate* was too strong a word. She didn't hate him. Surprisingly she didn't even hate herself. Sure, this was embarrassing and uncomfortable and stupid, but she'd done a lot worse. And in about fifteen minutes it would all be over.

Or so she hoped.

She went inside while he waited on the porch. She sped through changing into jeans and a sweatshirt and tried to ignore that *that guy* existed. But the sooner she got her goats milked and him out of here, the sooner that could be accomplished.

She went back outside, and there he was. She walked down the porch steps, realizing she hadn't grabbed socks, but was too tired and nauseated to care. Besides, he was following her; there was no way she was turning around.

She collected the containers from her sanitation

station outside the barn, then shoved her bare feet into the work boots she kept outside the doors.

Her stomach was still sloshing, her head still pounding, but the goats didn't care. That was why she loved them. They needed her to be responsible. To do something the same way every day. It kept her on the right path. So, even with last night's slipup, she hadn't totally screwed herself and her life over.

She entered the barn with a shadow for the first time ever. What was she supposed to call him? Ugh, she didn't want to call him anything. So she talked him through the process of milking: bringing the goat to the stand, offering it grain, cleaning, milking.

He watched, asked a few questions, and it was almost comfortable. Despite the awkwardness of the situation, talking about goat milking and the soap she made tabled some of the weirdness between them.

Just as she was loading up the containers to be refrigerated, a honk sounded from out front.

"If you go ahead and meet him, I'll be there in a second."

He nodded and she took the milk to storage, then hurried inside her house from the back to find some socks and shoes.

She walked to the cab, sliding her purse over her shoulder. A few more awkwardly silent moments and this would all be over. She would probably never see the guy again, and she could maybe even convince herself it had been a figment of her imagination.

Fall down seven times. Get up eight. How many times had Grandma said that to her? And yes, Meg was pretty sure she'd exceeded seven, but as long as she kept getting up, she'd be okay. Getting up was the only option.

Besides, she had some people to prove wrong. People who'd never have to know about this lapse in judgment.

# *CHAPTER FIVE*

As Dan's cab idled at the stoplight, Charlie could feel the man's stare. He knew what had happened, and he was going to say something. Oh, not to Charlie's face, but probably within earshot of someone related to him.

It was amazing—truly—how life could turn you around in a complete one-eighty. No warning, no clues how to handle it, just here—your life isn't what you thought.

*Now what are you gonna do?*

He'd always known the next step. Since he'd been a kid. He'd known the exact next step to take to get what he wanted, to do what was wanted *of* him. He'd always known.

Now he didn't have a damn clue, sitting here in a cab, after some bizarre one-night stand with a goat farmer. With tattoos.

He couldn't decide what next step to take. The only thing his mind seemed capable of doing was recognizing the smell of lemon, on her skin, in her hair.

"That'll be twenty-eight fifty," Dan said through a mouth of chew.

The woman dug through her purse, some fringy thing that looked completely out of place against the jeans, ratty sweatshirt and frayed tennis shoes she was wearing.

"Tell you what, Meg, you just put together a nice soap basket for wifey and we'll call it even."

Meg. So she had a name. Meg. A simple name for an incredibly complicated moment in his life. And now that name would probably haunt him for years to come. Lovely.

"That'll be fourteen twenty-five." Dan's eyes met Charlie's in the rearview mirror as Dan brought a bottle to his lips and spat some chew into it.

Charlie's stomach turned and he had to close his eyes to keep from losing it completely. Still, he dug into his pants, pulled out his wallet and handed over a credit card without meeting Dan's accusing glance.

Dan wasn't known in New Benton for his kindness. Small-town cab work wasn't for the faint of heart. He'd had more than one brawl with a man over cab fare, to the extent that most knew not to mess with him. He might've been getting on in years, but he'd as soon bash you over the head with the Louisville Slugger he kept in the passenger seat as he would offer you a smile.

But he'd called this woman Meg and offered her a barter and a smile. Charlie was beginning to think she was a fictional creature. Like some kind of siren or goddess.

It'd make this premidlife crisis a hell of a lot easier if she was. But he was too practical to even allow himself the fantasy. She had a name. She was real.

Dan returned the credit card. No receipt offered, but Charlie started to push the door open anyway.

"Oh, and, Charlie?"

Charlie raised his eyebrows at Dan's pleasant tone. "Yeah?"

"Added tip for ya."

Tip probably meant doubled the fare. Charlie couldn't bring himself to care, so he nodded. He'd consider this penance. He closed the door of the taxi behind him, breathing through the dizziness and blinking against the bright sun. His car was parked in the corner lot, the Shack looking particularly worse for the wear in the daylight.

The only other car in the lot was an old truck. No, not just old. Antique. But it was more recently painted a bright blue, the words *Hope Springs Farm* painted in red, with an illustration of a goat.

Seriously. Alternative dimension he'd fallen into.

It wasn't one he wanted to face. He didn't want to look at *Meg*, or offer a lame goodbye or lamer apology. He wished he'd never heard her name. He only wanted to go back to his downtown apartment and find normal again.

But as mixed-up as his world was, if he had anything left in this new version of his life, it'd at least be that he was a decent person.

He was a decent person, right? Maybe he'd been a little ruthless at times, a little hard, a little unbending, but…

"Well, it was certainly an interesting turn of events," she said.

When he looked up, she was already inching toward her truck, forcing her mouth into some approximation of an awkward smile.

"That it was," he replied, following her lead and taking a few backward steps toward his car.

"And, um, good luck with the job thing. I'm sure you'll land on your feet."

"Thanks. And I'm sorry for your loss." Odd to find it wasn't just a rote thing to say; he meant it. She was nice enough, and loss was always hard.

"Thanks," she replied, her voice tinged with surprise. But then she lifted her hand in a little wave and turned away from him.

He found himself watching her. The confident way she walked to her truck, the way the tasseled, beaded colorful purse shimmied and glinted in the sun. She was a conglomeration of things that didn't make sense.

He turned to his car but then just stared at it. Funny, it didn't seem to make much sense either. It fit the man he'd thought he was, but wasn't anymore.

Charles Andrew Wainwright. Oldest child. Successful businessman. Always in control, always responsible and always serious.

That felt like another person. A stranger. But he didn't know what to do with that feeling when it *was* who he was, who he'd always been.

So all he could do was go home and hope the feeling would pass.

MEG WORKED HERSELF to the bone. She ignored her aching muscles, her pounding headache and her rumbling stomach and worked with the soap molds until she'd lost the light.

She'd made up more than a little basket for Dan's wife. Part embarrassment, part because Meg was one of the few people who knew Dan's wife was going through chemo right now.

Which oddly made Meg wonder about Charlie. *Charlie.* So odd to hear a name after the intimacies they'd shared if not remembered.

He didn't look like a Charlie. Of course, he didn't look like a Charles or Chuck either. She wasn't sure what he looked like; she only knew that watching Dan scold him in a roundabout way had made her even more curious about him.

A man who so obviously belonged in her father's world but had been born into this one. She didn't know people like that. Her family, the people she'd grown up with, they'd all been the same kind. They hadn't all been bad people, though she'd desperately held on to that belief as a teenager. It just had been a world she couldn't get comfortable in.

Cleaning up her workroom, she frowned. Was it the world, or was it her? What was it about her family that kicked her back to a place where she'd lose herself? She wanted to blame them, and she couldn't count them blameless, but she was too old to ignore her own role in this.

Grief and pain were hard, but that was life. She could build this goat farm and build her business, and grief and pain would still touch her. But if she allowed it to fell her every time…well, things could quite easily get worse than a bender and a beyond embarrassing one-night stand.

She couldn't let things like loss do this to her, or she'd lose so much more. What was the point, really, when she could mourn Grandma in her own way? She didn't need the Carmichaels' permission for grief.

She didn't need anyone's permission to feel or act. It was easy to forget that when Mom was so intent on crushing her like a distasteful bug. Mom would never understand that Meg was made from a different mold; she'd always hold Meg at fault for her inability to shape herself into what a proper Carmichael was supposed to look like.

Meg was too old to let that knock her down, too far into recovery, into rebuilding her life. She had to be better than this, and she would be.

Workroom clean, she grabbed the fancy basket of soaps she'd made up for Elsie and decided not to wait to deliver it. The world was dusky, but it was early yet.

She forced herself to grab an apple so she'd at least have something in her stomach and ate it as she drove into town. Though she was embarrassed by the reason for needing to pay off Dan in soaps, she was glad for something to do tonight that would hopefully keep her mind off what she'd done *last* night.

When Meg arrived, Dan's cab was in the drive and he opened the front door with his version of a smile. He ushered her in, and Elsie eased off the couch, where she'd been watching TV, to ooh and aah over the soap basket.

Meg realized she needed to do more of this. Not just sell, but give. Not just build, but enjoy the moments of joy and simple pleasures.

Elsie fussed over her, though she was bone thin and gray. Meg did her best to allow some of the fussing, and curb some of it. She tried not to think too hard about what it might have been like to have parents like this.

"Now, Elsie, you're worn to the bone."

Elsie huffed out an irritated breath. "Get a little cancer and this tough rock of a man turns into a fawning worrywart."

"It's important to keep your strength up, though. I so enjoyed visiting with you, Elsie." Meg patted her knobby hand, knowing Elsie looked and probably felt much older than she actually was.

Life was oddly harder here. None of the comforts of what Meg had grown up with. None of the luxuries. Dan and Elsie looked like they could be her grandmother's age, but she was pretty sure they were only in their early sixties.

"I'll walk you out, Meg," Dan offered as his cell phone bleeped. "You get in bed, Elsie, so I can take this fare, or you're going to be in big trouble."

Elsie muttered something that sounded like a creative string of curses, but she took her basket and eased her way into the dark hallway.

"She seems to be in good spirits," Meg offered as she walked outside their seen-better-days tiny postage stamp of a house.

"That's my Elsie."

Meg smiled. Dan was a crusty old codger, but the love for his wife always shone through and that warmed Meg's heart.

"You know much about Charlie Wainwright?" Dan asked, his segue less than smooth.

Meg tried not to blush, but she couldn't manage it. Though she'd been in far more embarrassing situations and faced them with don't-give-a-crap aplomb, something about Dan and Elsie and the way they'd taken her under their old, withered wings in this tight-knit community made this humiliation burn through her.

"He's slick, but he's not a bad kid."

Kid. Meg wanted to laugh. They were adults and people still called them kids.

"I like the Wainwrights," he continued. "Good family."

"Okay."

He shifted, then spat. "But if he ever gives you any trouble, if anybody does, just know, Elsie and me, we got your back. Got it?"

Meg didn't know why it hit her so hard. Maybe it was because he was mostly a stranger, an odd little friendship built because he thought his wife might like her soaps. "You've always been so nice to me," she managed, her voice more than a little raw.

Dan shrugged, looking out into the starry evening. "You know Cornley House?"

Meg stilled. It wasn't the recovery center she'd been in, but a friend of hers had ended up there. Was she that transparent? After all these years?

Still, what did it matter if Dan knew? If everyone knew. It was part of her, and she was healing. "Yes."

"Our daughter is there now." He nodded at Meg's shoulder where a bright orange-and-yellow sun poured light onto the blue sky and white clouds of her forearm. "She's got that same sun thing, but on her back, and her hair used to be just your color." He shrugged and spat again. "You remind Elsie of her. But last time she was home she trashed the place, took all the cash we had on hand." He let out a breath. "Elsie's had a rough life. I think it's good for her to see you and think Hannah's got a chance. She needs some hope."

Meg swallowed. So much pain and grief in the world. And people like her who did it to themselves, and their families—at least the people in them who cared. No, she wasn't going to fall back into that. "I'd like to come visit once a week. Bring some soap, maybe some food. What day would be good?"

Maybe she couldn't make up for anything she'd done, and she couldn't completely eradicate the feeling she was worthless, but she could put some good out into the world. She'd start here.

# CHAPTER SIX

"You better get it together before Mom calls a therapist."

Charlie tried to grin and bear it, but it was hard. His acting skills were failing him. Hell, what wasn't?

He'd been unemployed for a month. He'd grown a beard. He felt like a ghost of himself, and his family was tiptoeing around him like he had some kind of communicable disease.

But he didn't know what to do. Who to be. He'd finished out his last two weeks at Lordon, ever the dutiful employee working to ease the transition for all those who got to keep their jobs.

He'd been offered interviews by a few head-hunters. There were companies interested in his experience in sales, in his years as management.

He couldn't muster up the energy to make the calls. A decade ago he would have jumped at the chance to move to Chicago, California, Denver. But sitting in the middle of his niece's second birthday party, he thought relocating was the last thing he wanted to do.

The whole love of the farm thing might be Dell's shtick, and Charlie might have moved downtown to get out of the small-town atmosphere of New Benton, but that didn't mean he didn't love his family. He wanted his mother close enough to make him dinner and tell him he'd land on his feet. He wanted to watch his niece grow up. He wanted to be *here*.

Lainey was running around dressed up like a princess. His baby sister was talking intently with Mia's baby sister. Except Kenzie and Anna weren't babies anymore. Both had graduated from college, Kenzie was going on to get her master's and Anna was taking over her father's dairy farm operation. Mia and Cara were fussing over a table full of cupcakes while Dad, Cara's husband, Wes, and Mia's dad were standing around the grill. Dogs ran all around the spacious green yard, yipping happily.

He liked this. This right here.

"Dude, seriously."

Charlie slanted his brother a look. "I'm reevaluating my life."

"Reevaluate faster. You stay unemployed much longer, Dad is going to have a stroke and Mom's probably going to sign you up for one of those online dating things."

"I've had offers," Charlie muttered.

"So take one."

He let out a sigh. His relationship with Dell hadn't always been an easy one, and it'd certainly never been one where they shared much of anything too deep. It would be easy to clam up, to say something snide and walk away.

But Charlie didn't have the energy for that either. "So far the only jobs I've been offered are lower positions, less money, and…require relocation."

"I'm guessing that means…far?"

"Yes."

Dell was quiet for a minute. "And you don't want to move?" he asked as though he'd chosen each word very carefully.

"I'm certainly not going through the hassle of changing my life for a job that isn't up to my standards." He sounded like a douche. He *knew* he sounded like a douche, but he didn't know what this thing inside him was, just that it'd been there for a long time.

It was like he'd built armor over his real self, a shell the outside world, and even his family, could see, but it was impenetrable. He could only give people what they expected, because underneath this shell…he really wasn't sure who he was.

Maybe he *did* need therapy.

Suddenly he thought about leaving. Ditching the party. He could go to the Shack. See if *Meg* would be there, still drowning her own sorrows. Why was that a fantasy? It wasn't like he remembered much of what they'd done together. It wasn't like he *knew* her.

He'd certainly made a very careful effort to avoid the market the past month. So, why did he still think of her at all?

"We'd miss you, if that's what you decided to do."

Charlie looked at his brother. They hadn't always gotten along. In fact, there'd been some times they'd probably both felt they hated each other, but something about Dell having a kid had smoothed a lot of that over.

Still, the sentiment surprised Charlie, and maybe that was on him. So he'd offer some honesty even if it made him uncomfortable. "I don't want to move. I'm not in dire straits quite yet."

Dell gave a nod, looking over where the Wainwrights and Pruitts mingled in the yard. "Good. I mean, I'd offer help, but—"

"I'd tell you to shove it."

Dell's mouth curved. "Exactly. So…" He gestured to where Lainey was trying to ride one of Wes's dogs. "I better get in there."

"You're lucky, man." It felt odd to admit it aloud, to let some of that envy show. He'd spent so much of his life convinced he was better off than Dell, never made any bones about Dell's choices being beneath him.

But Charlie had been wrong, and it felt imperative to say it. Out loud. To Dell.

Dell stared at him, a kind of deer-caught-in-
headlights, who-abducted-my-brother look. But
then he glanced back out at the yard, daughter
and wife with another kid on the way. Then Dell
simply shrugged. "Yeah, I am."

"How'd you do it?" Charlie said, knowing it
sounded like a crazed demand but not being able
to help it. He wanted to know. What steps did he
need to take? How could he build his own version
of what Dell had?

Eyes still on the yard, Dell seemed to consider
the question. "I figured out who I was. Who I
wasn't." His smile went soft as Mia approached.
"And I let the unexpected happen."

Mia took the stairs of the porch before Charlie
could answer. She fisted her hands on her hips and
glared at them. "Are you two going to come help,
or stand here and gossip all afternoon?"

Dell's arm slid around his wife's waist easily.
"Just talking about how lucky I am."

She rolled her eyes. "Sure."

"He's not lying. We were," Charlie returned.
Seriously, probably way too seriously.

Mia cocked her head, looked at him, then Dell,
then back again. "Well, that's…nice. I'll feel a
whole lot luckier if I can get something into my
stomach before I feel like puking."

"All right, let's get you some food, sugar." And they walked off, but not before Charlie heard Mia murmur to Dell, "Is Charlie okay?"

No. He wasn't. Because he didn't know who he was, or how to find out. And he certainly didn't know how to let the unexpected happen.

MEG WOKE UP in a cold sweat. She grasped around in her bed for…for…what? She stopped, realizing she had no idea what she was trying to reach. She had no idea why she was breathing so heavily or why her heart was pounding.

"A dream," she said aloud. "Just a dream." It felt steadying to hear her own voice in the pitch-black of her room.

Three nights in a row. Ever since the little niggle of worry had sprouted in the back of her head. Every night it had grown, every night the dreams had grown more vivid and more disturbing.

Stress had always brought on nightmares for her, long before she'd understood what stress was. But now she understood, and she couldn't keep pretending that idea wasn't looming in the back of her mind…waiting.

She couldn't put it off any longer. She couldn't keep hoping it would go away. It wasn't going to go away, and her psyche was going to drive her absolutely bonkers until she sucked up all her fear and acted.

She forced herself out of bed and into the little bathroom. She'd shoved the offensive box under the sink after running errands in Millertown yesterday. She'd been so determined and hopeful it was unnecessary, and that the moment she purchased the test and brought it home she wouldn't have to use it.

But if she was going to get *any* sleep before milking the goats, having breakfast with Elsie, followed by an afternoon meeting with a local store that might want to sell her soaps, she had to suck it up and do it.

She pulled the test out of the box with unsteady hands, read the instructions and then followed them to the letter.

She waited the three minutes feeling exactly as she had upon waking up. Shaking, heart beating too fast, breath coming too hard. It just couldn't be.

Except when the timer went off...there it was. *Pregnant*.

Her breath whooshed out of her. Pregnant. *Pregnant*. She had fallen not just off the wagon, but utterly, completely. The condom wrapper either a false promise, faulty or possibly drunken user error.

It didn't matter. The results were the same. She was pregnant with a stranger's child. All those years she'd punished her body for some foolish insecurity inside herself, but she'd kept herself out of this kind of trouble.

Clean and mostly sober, for years, and now, at thirty-two, she'd made this mistake too.

She swallowed at the nausea that swam up her esophagus. But it wasn't a mistake, was it? It was a life. She'd created it in bad choices, but that was hardly the thing growing inside her's fault.

Meg squeezed her eyes shut. Dear Lord, she was pregnant.

Needless to say, she didn't sleep. She tried, lying there, staring up at the ceiling in the dark, but then her alarm went off and the goats needed milking, and dawn slowly rose on a new day.

A new day in which she had to start facing the consequences of her actions. That was scary, because all the options felt wrong and hard and overwhelming.

She got ready to go to breakfast with Elsie, determined to keep her problems to herself. Elsie's chemo was showing promising results, but she was still weak and frail. The reality of the situation was Meg had come to rely on the company probably more than Elsie did.

Funny, Meg thought she was finally getting her life together, and now it felt unraveled and pathetic.

But she was going to keep that to herself. She would be cheerful and encouraging with Elsie.

She ordered their food at Moonrise, took the bags from the waitress and smiled the whole time. She was fine. She could handle this. Tonight, when she got home, she would figure out what she was going to do. Alone.

Because she was alone.

When Elsie opened the door, Meg burst into tears. Elsie didn't hesitate, didn't ask what was wrong; she bustled her onto the couch, took the bags of food and plopped a box of tissues next to her.

"Eat, please, eat, while I get myself together," Meg croaked, trying to breathe, trying to cope.

Elsie pulled out her foam container of food, and then she handed Meg hers on the little TV trays that more often served as a dining table for Dan and Elsie than their actual kitchen table.

"Now, I'm not taking a bite if you don't spill what's troubling you."

"That's mean."

"Darn straight it is. I'll use a little meanness to get my way."

Meg swallowed, tried to manage a wobbly smile. "Take a bite and I'll talk."

Elsie gave her a suspicious look, but she unwrapped the plastic cutlery from the bag and cut a bite of pancake before lifting it to her mouth.

Meg waited for her to chew a few times, and then she knew she had to be honest. When she was honest with Elsie, Elsie was honest with her, and Meg liked to believe it had helped at least a *little* in these weeks Meg had been visiting with her.

"I… It's…"

"Spit it out, child."

"I'm pregnant."

Elsie's eyes widened and she set her plastic fork down. "Well, didn't know you was seeing someone."

Miserable, Meg shook her head. Her own pancakes made her stomach turn, and she didn't think it had anything to do with pregnancy. It had everything to do with Elsie being disappointed in her.

She wanted someone to be proud of her. Someone to look at her and see success instead of failure.

Maybe she should stop failing.

"Now, I don't condone getting the sheets sweaty with someone who you ain't married to, let alone not well acquainted with," Elsie said primly. "'Course, I can't exactly judge either, as I'm not a hypocrite."

Meg wanted to laugh—leave it to Elsie—but it just came out like more of a sob. "What am I going to do?" she asked in a hushed whisper. Elsie pursed her lips and studied her sternly. "Don't have any people, do you?"

Meg swallowed. It sounded so *harsh* when she put it that way, but it was true. Even her friends who'd gotten clean had a hard time being around each other; it dredged up memories of how they'd wasted their youth. And then, of course, her family pretended she didn't exist, and it had been hard to make new friends with the hours she poured into her business.

Charlie Wainwright was the most non-business-related interaction she'd had—besides Dan and Elsie—in years.

And now she was carrying his child.

"Well, you're my people now."

Meg shook her head, afraid she'd cry harder. "You have so much on your plate already."

"That may be true. But if my daughter was crying on some other old, sick woman's couch, I'd hope she'd do the same. Now, first things first, you should tell the father. Unless he's not a good sort."

"I think he is. Not bad anyway."

Elsie nodded. "Then you tell him."

"Tell him what?"

"The truth. Easy as that. You give him a chance to have half a say—half, mind you, as you're the one doing the carrying and the laboring."

Oh. God. Labor. "But…what if I don't know what I want?"

"Doesn't matter, honey. You got a life growing inside you."

That she did, and while there were options in that regard, options she'd supported a friend through when they were only teenagers, Meg didn't think she had that option in her as a solvent adult. A solvent adult who'd always wanted to be a mother someday—in some abstract world when she had it all together. But...maybe she was never going to have it all together. Maybe she had to jump in, not quite ready. More than a little scared that she'd be terrible at it.

Which meant she had to admit something exceedingly scary for someone who'd failed at almost everything until her farm had come along. She'd have to admit she wanted to do it, and that she was scared of screwing it up. She'd have to admit a lot of things she usually faked her way through.

"You need to call yourself a doctor, honey, and then the Wainwright boy."

Meg jerked her head to face Elsie, who merely shrugged. "Dan's got no secrets from me." She then reached over with a frail hand and patted Meg's knee. "But we'll keep yours, sweetheart. Don't you worry about that."

*Don't worry.* Yeah, she didn't think she'd be able to follow that advice anytime soon.

# CHAPTER SEVEN

CHARLIE WASN'T HAPPY to be at the market. It wasn't that he minded helping Dell. Especially after Lainey's birthday party when things had felt… Well, he'd been a mess, but it had been nice that his family and Dell had voiced some kind of concern over him leaving.

It was a starting point to this new life he had to figure out. He wanted it to be here. Well, not *here* here. He could take or leave New Benton and Millertown, but St. Louis and the areas better suited to him were only a forty-five-minute drive from home and these people.

So it wasn't the loading and unloading of vegetables, it wasn't even the forced smiles, it was that when he stood in a particular spot, he could see Hope Springs Farm's booth and his gaze seemed to drift that way no matter what.

Which was stupid. If he was still thinking about the woman, the least he could do was ask her out. Just because they'd had an awkward, drunken one-night stand didn't mean it had to stay that way. Maybe, despite all outward appearances, they would be compatible while sober.

It was possible, and maybe if he at least tried, all the guilt dogging him over that incident would finally go away.

It had been weeks, though. Over a month. Maybe it wasn't that out of the ordinary for her. Maybe the guys all blended together for her and she wouldn't even remember him.

Of course, then her embarrassment and awkwardness that matched his own didn't make sense, but he needed to move on. Figure out his life, not where he stood with his one and only ungentlemanly drunken exploit.

He needed to stop looking down the aisle, hoping to catch a glimpse of her. Except the next time his eyes drifted that way, despite his brain's express admonitions not to, there she was. Walking toward him.

He straightened. Maybe she would walk right on by. But before he could duck out of sight, she stopped in front of him, a completely unconvincing smile on her face. "Hi, Charlie."

It was the first time she'd said his name, and he definitely had some kind of internal reaction to it.

"Hi. Meg." It was a name he'd likely said before in his life. He knew Megans. Yet saying her name felt…weighted.

Yeah, therapy, that was a thing he really needed to look into.

"Well, well, well," Dell said under his breath, and damn Meg's timing because there were no customers to keep Dell's attention off whatever reason Meg had for coming over here.

When Charlie made no effort to introduce anyone, Dell stuck his hand between Charlie and Meg. "I'm Dell," he offered, the I-know-how-to-piss-off-Charlie grin firmly in place.

Meg smiled. It occurred to Charlie that she had a unique one. That it always seemed to light her up with a mix of mischief and joy, even when there was sadness behind it. Or nerves, as there seemed to be today.

"The Naked Farmer. Yes, I know. You're…" Her brow furrowed as she looked between him and his brother. "Related," she said, sounding weirdly put off by that.

"He'll try to tell you his brother isn't the Naked Farmer, but he'd be lying," Dell said. "Hope Springs is yours, right? My wife loves your soaps. Do you do any fun shapes for kids?"

"Um, well, we have a few animals. Owls, goats."

Dell nudged Charlie. "Lainey'd love that. Why don't you go pick some out for me."

The not-so-subtle verbal nudge was no more effective than Dell's physical one. And Meg's clear nervousness was off-putting in its own right. Charlie wasn't sure he wanted to find out the source.

*And are you a timid coward or a grown man?* "Sure." He shoved his hands into his pockets, because for the first time in his life he didn't have a clue what to do with them. He didn't know what to say, or how to manage this situation.

What an incredibly odd feeling for a man who'd prided himself on always being in control, or if not in control, well on his way toward it.

"So, um, I suppose this is awkward," Meg began, twisting her hands together as she walked next to him on their way to her booth.

"I suppose," he returned, wondering if it would be awkward if she weren't quite so…vibrating with anxiety. Or maybe drunken sex just always made things awkward afterward.

He sighed. At himself. At the situation. At life. "You know—"

"I'm pregnant," she whispered so quietly he leaned closer, sure he'd misheard or misunderstood.

"I'm sorry. What?"

"I know you don't have any reason to believe me. We don't know each other well. It never should have happened, but the very fact of the matter is the only person I've been in any potential compromising positions with is…you, and my doctor confirmed a positive pregnancy test. So."

He leaned back. Away from her and these words that didn't make sense. He was thirty-five. He was a vice president of... No, not anymore.

He was an unemployed thirty-five-year-old being told the drunken one-night stand he hadn't meant to ever let happen had resulted in...

"I didn't mean to drop it on you like that." She skirted the table of her booth in what felt like a purposeful distancing. He was on one side of this frilly, feminine table, and she was on the other.

Pregnant.

With his baby.

"I only meant to set up a time to talk, but it just..." She waved at the air around her, pacing under the tent that shaded her inventory of soaps.

He couldn't think of anything to say, or do. He couldn't wrap his head around this at all.

Someone cleared their throat—an older woman, looking between the two of them as if she could read between the lines.

How could she? He couldn't even read the actual lines here.

"You have a customer," he managed, when it was clear Meg hadn't noticed.

She jerked, and for the first time in the ticking minutes between her dropped bomb and now, he finally saw something he recognized.

It was a look that accepted life was not what

you wanted to be, and the acceptance you had to move forward anyway.

He'd seen that look on the face of just about every person he was related to, except maybe Kenzie. God knew he'd never seen that look in the mirror, because when life didn't give him the things he'd wanted, he'd forced himself to want something else.

He'd never accepted that things might not go his way. Never rolled with a punch, knowing or accepting he was felled. No, he'd kept punching. Kept fighting. Kept fooling himself into thinking he was exactly where he wanted to be.

He'd called all that strength. Sense. *Determination.*

But it wasn't. He could see it so clearly as he wordlessly watched Meg help her customer, dull smile firmly in place.

He didn't know her. Had very few clues about the life she led day in and day out, aside from milking goats. But he could tell the acceptance— worried and freaked-out as it might be—was far stronger than the fight.

Far, far stronger than pretending failures didn't exist, or were only steps leading you where you wanted to be.

He didn't want to be here, now, with this information, but nothing could change the fact that he *was*. He couldn't keep moping around, acting like some version of a whiny teenager, with or without a child. A child.

That'd never been him. He met challenges. He crushed them. But this wasn't one he could carefully maneuver around or through. It involved people. It involved a child. His child.

Single. Drunken one-night stand. Tattooed goat farmer. He felt more than a little dizzy over the whole thing, and the next time he glanced at Meg, she was looking at him, big blue eyes solemn, but there was also something in them he didn't understand.

"I've had some time to think about it. You should take some time too."

"To think about it?"

"Yes. How involved you want to be. *If* you want to be involved. Like I said, I've had time to think about it, crunch the numbers. I can raise a kid." She said it almost defiantly, chin raised, just daring him to argue with her.

But why would he argue with her? What did he know? Clearly he knew very, very little. Life had decided to finally show him just how little.

"So, if you're not interested, that's your choice. But it is *your* kid, so I wanted to give you a choice."

"A choice."

"Yes."

"In how involved I want to be. With my…" He couldn't form the word. Not with his mouth, not so it echoed down the aisle of a crowded summer afternoon at the farmers' market. He didn't belong here. He took a deep breath. It didn't matter. Nothing about the self-centered pity party of the past month really mattered, not when he was faced with this.

"It's a lot to process. Take some time, and when you're ready…" She offered him a card, which he stared at without taking it. Because she'd handed him her card before. He fished his wallet out of his pocket, flipped it open and thumbed open the crease.

There was the card. He hadn't been able to throw it away. So it had sat there. In his wallet. Like a very weird omen.

"I've got it," he said, his voice sounding rusty and out of place.

When he looked up from the card to her face, her lips were curved. But she didn't say anything, just gave a little nod.

"Moonrise," he blurted, shaking his head at the total lack of finesse he was doing this with. "What time could you meet me at Moonrise Diner?"

She glanced at the delicate watch on her wrist. He'd held that hand, had sex with this woman—made a child, and he only remembered bits and fuzzy pieces. He'd been struggling to accept that before, but now?

"One thirty? But I'll only have about half an hour before I need to get back to the farm."

"It'll be a start."

It would have to be a start.

MOONRISE DINER WAS one of Meg's favorite places in New Benton. While she'd had this picture of idyllic small-town life growing up in well-to-do suburbia, New Benton hadn't lived up to most of it.

It was old and run-down, and a lot of the people weren't sweet, quirky characters from a sitcom. They were rough, they were hard and they didn't much give a damn who you were or where you came from.

But Moonrise was like something out of a movie. A diner still firmly planted in the past that did a bustling business to locals and very little else. The waitresses weren't overpolite, more harried than charming, but she stepped into the bustle and felt like she'd found something.

Community, in a loose way. The waitresses knew her name. Some of the ladies would ask her about her goats or her soap. If she saw Dan, she always bought him a cup of coffee, and while she didn't feel that sort of warm bloom of instant belonging she'd hoped for when she set out on this road, she didn't feel like a stranger either.

So much of her life had been about feeling like

a stranger. In her own home, to herself when she was high, to the friends who didn't want out of that ugly cycle and to the friends who didn't want to look her in the eye because they might remember and want a hit.

Meg blew out a breath as she slid into an empty booth. Between Grandma and pregnancy, all the old crap was getting stirred up and she needed to get a handle on it.

It hit her then, like a bolt of lightning straight through the diner roof and into her chest. She'd lost Grandma and created a life within the same week.

She placed a hand over her belly, where everything she read told her what was growing inside her was barely larger than a speck.

She'd lost one light and been given another. She had to believe that. It solidified her resolve, the choice she'd made. *And if you're a girl, your name will be May.* Which was more than likely getting ahead of herself, all things considered. But it was only right. It had to be right.

She blinked at the tears, hoping to have them under control before Charlie arrived. She was going to have to come to terms with the fact that tears would be part of the next eight months. That was okay, but for the next however long Charlie wanted to talk, she needed to be in control.

She didn't know Charlie. The kind of man he

was. If he'd want a piece of this responsibility. She thought it might be easier if he didn't, but that was easier for her and she understood that some of the choices she was going to have to make in the next few months were about her *child*—not her.

She had a responsibility to protect both of them. It had to be the mantra she held on to while she navigated some really tricky and unknown waters. She wouldn't let that spiral her back to where she'd come from, and she wouldn't let a few mistakes break her down.

She had to be calm, rational and above all…a mother.

A mother.

*Better than my own. I will be better than my own.* She would love this child no matter what he or she looked like, or acted like, or wanted out of life. She would always love them so much more than she cared about her reputation or image. Always.

If that was the thing that kept her going, so be it.

She glanced at her watch, trying to calm her nerves and her worries with the prospect of the business at hand. It didn't surprise her that just as the second hand hit the twelve to make it one thirty exactly, Charlie walked through the front door.

He seemed like that kind of man. Prompt and responsible and *dutiful*. At least in business. Her father's ethics and morals had lacked plenty, but he'd never been late to a meeting. Never shirked a business responsibility.

She hoped against hope that Charlie was a better man than her father.

He gave her a slight nod and walked to the booth, all seriousness.

He *was* handsome. The nice jeans, the preppy fashionable sneakers, the T-shirt he'd probably bought from some high-end department store—none of it detracted from the way his face was put together. Strong jaw, sharp nose.

He didn't ooze charm like his brother had at the market, but there was something attractive about his self-assurance. The way he moved like he knew exactly where he belonged.

It disappeared the moment he sat down, and she found that endearing too. Because God knew she was working with a big old question mark. The least he could do was feel the same.

"Hi," she offered.

"Hi. Are you eating?"

She glanced at the counter, where Mallory was chatting with some customers. "Maybe."

He gave a slight nod.

And then there was nothing but silence.

Meg waited, searching her mind for some way of bringing up the pregnancy in a way that would be fruitful instead of "what the hell are we doing?" and "how did this happen?" Because her brain had done enough of that, and she was ready for the part where they moved forward.

"It's a lot to take in. If you need more time—"

"What are your plans?" he asked, and she might have gotten offended by the demand in his voice if he hadn't winced after he said it.

"My plans?" she repeated, because even with the wince she wasn't quite sure what he was after.

"I mean, insofar as you've had more time to think about this than I have, what is your current plan of action?"

Plan of action. She wanted to be calm. She wished she were the type of woman who could hide the look of disgust that passed over her face, but it was a part of the reason she'd never fit in her parents' world. She didn't have a poker face. She didn't have a coat of armor to put on over herself when the vultures were circling. Everything she was or thought was there, and she didn't know how to hide it.

"So you haven't thought that far ahead," he said gently.

A gentleness that made her stomach turn. It reminded her of the teacher in school who assumed she was dumb. *You just don't understand. That's all right.*

No, she understood. She understood this better than him. She had a plan of action, but it was her own and her own way, and hell if she'd let a stranger wreak havoc on the sliver of confidence she'd built for herself.

"The plan of action, *Charlie*, is to spend the next eight months growing a life inside me. And then push it out my vag—"

He held up a hand, the expression that passed over his face so very much like her father she really thought she might puke.

"That's not quite what I meant," he continued in that frustratingly even tone. "I meant—"

"I know what you meant, and what *I* mean is that this is the plan. To have this baby. That is *my* action plan. That is the *only* plan of action. This isn't some kind of business merger we're going to bang out the details to in a few calm and prepared meetings."

Charlie didn't say anything to that. He sat opposite her in the booth, his expression blank and a little hard.

She didn't know him. She didn't know him at all. She'd created a child with him, but she didn't *know* him, and that hurt.

# CHAPTER EIGHT

HE'D COME TO Moonrise prepared with a million little speeches, a million little plans, but as he stared at Meg across the old, chipped table, all he could think was, this woman was a stranger.

She was carrying his child and he didn't know or understand a thing about her. That wasn't how it was supposed to be. That wasn't how you were supposed to start a family.

It wasn't part of the *plan*.

"What can I get you two?"

He glanced up at Mallory, who'd been a waitress at Moonrise for at least the past ten years. She met his gaze, then looked at Meg, and though she was obviously filing away the information of the two of them together, she didn't say anything.

"You know, I think I'll have a piece of cherry pie."

"We've got the house stuff, or Cara's Local Pies for a buck more."

Meg smiled, the kind of smile that could almost make him forget she'd looked at him like he'd suggested harvesting her organs. Horror, disgust, complete with physical recoil.

All because he'd asked about a plan. It wasn't as though he'd judge her if she didn't have one. This was quite the wrench. He'd only asked in case she did.

And because if she didn't have a plan—which she didn't seem to, not a real one—he had one. And it would solve everything.

"Charlie, you want anything?"

He refocused on Mallory and managed a smile of his own. What would be good for a pregnant woman to eat? Probably protein. And some vegetables. He felt like maybe she was ordering pie to somehow poke fun at his mention of having a plan, and he simply wouldn't allow that.

Something in his gut felt a little off at that point, but he wasn't planning on listening to his gut when so many important things were at stake. He had to listen to his brain. "I'll have a grilled chicken sandwich. Whatever steamed vegetable you've got on the side. And a large glass of water." He'd try to get her to eat some before she dug into the pie.

"Oookay," Mallory mumbled, marking it down on her pad before she walked away.

When he returned his gaze to Meg, she was scowling. It was an odd expression on her. He'd seen her sad and nervous. He'd seen her smiling and flirtatious. Irritated and possibly a little angry didn't suit her. It didn't seem to naturally fit her.

He needed to continue to be reasonable. Reason always won. If he laid out his plan, explained it, she'd have to realize it was a good one. If she had a few caveats to add, he'd be happy to listen.

There was a lot of compromise that lay ahead, and he was willing to bend when necessary. Okay, maybe not always happily, but he wasn't going to be unreasonable.

"So, listen," she said. "Let's just take this one step at a time. I think plans of action are a little premature."

"A plan is never premature."

This time she rolled her eyes and he had to bite back the irritation. Because this *was* irritating, but he was going to accept it, handle it, deal with it like a responsible adult. Like a *father*.

That was the point. Not that they hadn't planned this, but that it was here and they were going to deal with it. As parents.

"I realize we don't know each other very well," he continued. "And yes, this is a surprise, but there's really only one solution I can think of that makes any sense."

She leaned back in the booth, crossed her arms over her chest. For a second all he could think was he'd created a child with this woman and he didn't even remember what she looked like naked.

But for a fleeting second he thought he could remember the feel of her skin under his palm, the sigh of her breath against his neck and something uncomfortably like belonging.

But that was some figment of his imagination—or the alcohol's imagination.

"Okay, so what is this only solution?"

He knew she was determined not to like it, and that made him hesitate. Maybe he should be broaching this subject somewhere else. Somewhere more private. After more discussion about what her plans were.

But she'd made it clear she had no plans for the future; everything she'd talked about was centered on just getting to the point where the baby was born, and there was so much more to worry about. So what was he supposed to do? He knew this was the right plan. The right course of action. He couldn't keep it to himself.

"We should get married."

It had to be his imagination that the entire diner went silent, that all eyes were on him. Really, it was just Meg's two eyes. Big and blue and amused. She actually laughed.

"Is something funny?"

She choked, coughing a few times. "Oh my God, you're serious. You're *serious*?"

"Of course I'm serious. It makes financial sense, and it'll offer everyone a sense of security."

She laughed again, so hard she had to wipe her eyes. Charlie found none of it amusing, but he'd as soon let her get it all out before he tried to speak again. Maybe he could attribute this whole response to hormones. To the shock of the situation.

"I'm sorry you're irritated," she said after taking a deep breath. "And I know this *looks* like the fifties, but we live firmly in the twenty-first century. I don't know you, Charlie. I only know your name because *Dan said it*...after we had sex and woke up not remembering said sex." She grew more and more serious and angry with every word. "I've got all the *financial* sense I need, and I can handle my own damn security. What we're talking about here is how much you want to be involved in this *child's* life—not mine. I've had my fill of self-important businessmen who think they can plan everything into the ground."

It was a wonder that it hurt, because why should something said by someone who was essentially a stranger bother him? But it did. It cut, the same way Dell's dismissals of his offers for help years ago had cut.

When all you wanted to do was help, and people couldn't even take that seriously, or got offended by it, how could it not hurt?

But why should she see how sincere he was? She didn't know him. He didn't know her. It was an old familiar feeling all in all, and one he knew just how to deal with. Give them what they wanted.

He stood. "Maybe we should meet to discuss this at a time when you're more willing to be reasonable."

She laughed bitterly. "You would be an asshole, wouldn't you?"

If that was what she wanted to think of him, did it really matter what the truth was? He shrugged and fished one of his old business cards out of his wallet. He took the pen out of his pocket and crossed out everything except his name and his cell number.

Setting it on the table with a twenty, he slid it toward her. "You can contact me when you're ready. But if it takes too long, I will contact you. Because I do want to be a part of *my* child's life. You'll hear from me one way or another." Then, because he couldn't help himself, he added, "And eat the sandwich and vegetables when they come."

And because there was nothing else to say, he turned and walked right out of Moonrise, to his car, and got the hell away from New Benton and all the ways it'd never understand him.

THE FEELING SHE'D been wrong dogged Meg all afternoon.

It shouldn't. Charlie had been so ridiculous, so *familiar*. She'd wanted to reach across the table and bash him over the head. With what, she didn't know, but reasonable "action plans" always made her want to rip her hair out.

And he *had* been a jerk, so she shouldn't feel one second of regret over calling him on it.

But it was something in his expression after she'd said it, a kind of weary acceptance, one she recognized from her family simply refusing to see her. Eventually, you just accepted they weren't going to.

Everything about that last minute with Charlie burrowed under her skin and she couldn't itch it away or ignore it. Something was off, and she had a terrible feeling the fault rested with her even though he was the one insane enough to propose marriage.

A proposal. Ha! It was a stupid suggestion and she hadn't been wrong to scoff at it. But she didn't feel right about the way she'd treated him.

What had happened to doing what was best for her child? Being a responsible, mature adult? There hadn't been a lot of that going on at that table. She'd reverted into old familiar patterns that weren't particularly fair when it came to Charlie.

He was involved in making half this kid's DNA and it seemed as though he was interested in being a part of the kid's life. She had to find a way for that to work, *marriage* to a stranger aside.

So he was traditional. Either that or he didn't

have a high opinion of marriage and thought *easy peasy, we'll get married*. She didn't know, because she hadn't listened enough to find out.

She'd been too busy freaking out, because what man in his right mind proposed marriage to a stranger?

"And you can keep going on and on in this idiotic mental circle or you can call the man and find out yourself." She stared down at the herbs she'd been processing and took a deep breath.

Part of growing up—part of getting clean—had been realizing she needed to own up to her mistakes. Accept them, and then learn how to move on from them. But that was all *her*, and the thing about being pregnant, even if she was the one dealing with all the growing and laboring and whatnot, was that she hadn't gotten here alone.

She had to deal with the father of the baby, had to be bigger than her knee-jerk reactions. She had to be the reasonable one if he wouldn't. He may have been calm and sure, but he was *not* reasonable if he was proposing marriage.

So she couldn't get nasty about it. She had to show him he was wrong. This would be the first step in learning how to be parents to the same child even though they obviously all but lived on different planets.

She grabbed her phone out of her back pocket, and his card that she'd crumpled into the front pocket of her jeans. She dialed the number before she could talk herself out of it, hoping the scent of lavender would keep her strong.

When he answered, his voice was skeptical and wary and she couldn't even work up any irritation for it.

"Hello?"

"Hi, Charlie. It's Meg." *Mother of your child, some way, somehow.* "I think this afternoon kind of spiraled away from us."

"That's a way of putting it, yes."

Oh, that measured, reasoned way he spoke was *so* grating. But she would rise above it. She would. "So, I was wondering if we could try again. It's pretty important, after all."

"Yes, it is."

She bit her tongue for a few humming seconds, literally held it between her teeth just to the point of wincing pain so she wouldn't say something snippy.

"Are you free this evening?" he asked.

She blew out a breath. "Yes, are you too far to come out here? It might be easier to do in private, and I can't really leave the goats alone that long without more notice."

"The goats. Right. Um, no, that's fine. I can come out to your place."

"Okay. So…"

"I'll bring some dinner. That is, if you'd like?"

She narrowed her eyes, allowing herself the snippy expression, since he couldn't see it. But like the chicken sandwich order and telling her to eat it, she wondered. "Why are you offering to bring me dinner?"

"Why do I feel like the truth might actually get me into trouble here?"

She softened a little. He didn't really embody the snooty aura he gave off—at least not all the time. She needed to remember he was also the man who'd danced with one of her goats. Even if the memory was fuzzy, and it was 100 percent the fault of alcohol, there had to be some semblance of a human being beneath the surface that reminded her all too much of the world she'd left behind.

But that surface was also a part of him, and she had to be careful about how much she let it influence her, how much she bent to it. So she forced her tone to be kind, even though she was refusing him. "I can feed myself, but I appreciate the offer." She swallowed. "Do you remember how to get here?"

There was an odd silence, one that made her nerves jump at the idea of him being back here. Sober. Just the two of them. Doing the opposite of what they'd been doing last time they were here.

No goat dancing. No drinking. And 100 percent no sex.

"Yes, I remember."

There was something about his voice, something she didn't particularly notice when she was actually in his presence and he looked like he'd just gotten off a golf cart with her dad. A kind of steadiness, a surety. It was confidence, but not used as a weapon. Her parents' surety in their decisions and their lives and their place in the world was usually wielded like brass knuckles. No, that was too undignified. One of those ancient but giant swords that could cut you in two with one well-practiced down-the-nose look.

Charlie's confidence *was* different. Besides, he really hadn't looked like Mr. Put-Together today, had he? He'd grown a beard that looked less like he was trying to fit in with the urban hipsters and more like he just couldn't be bothered to shave. He'd looked… She couldn't put her finger on it. It was oddly familiar, the expression, the different way he'd carried himself, and yet she couldn't label it.

"So, seven o'clock would be all right?"

She found her voice, though it wasn't nearly as casually steady as his. "Yes, that'll be fine."

"All right. I'll see you then, then."

She thought she heard him groan away from the speaker, and it made her smile, though she could also just be hoping against hope there was someone human—a little lost underneath his all-too-familiar facade.

She could hope. She could look for the good in him rather than the ways he reminded her of a life that had never fit or been any good for her. Because she wasn't a little girl anymore, confused and ill-fitting. A problem. He couldn't make her into that.

She looked around the shed where she dried and processed her herbs. It was tiny. A long table and a few benches barely fit into the little square. The weakening sunlight fell in patches across the concrete slab of floor. Plants hung from every available rafter and hook.

She'd found her place. She'd found herself. Unexpected turns in life didn't take this away. Because this was the anchor.

So she could handle Charlie Wainwright. She could find a way to parent with him. He could come with his perfectly styled jeans and coiffed hair and charming smiles and *action plans*, and it wouldn't change this thing.

This thing she'd built. This place that had become her heart, her soul, her savior.

If she reminded herself of that every day— every single morning—she couldn't fail.

# *CHAPTER NINE*

CHARLIE TURNED ONTO the gravel drive that would lead him off the highway and toward Meg's little goat compound. He had no other words for the conglomeration of buildings that made up her operation.

He hadn't given them much of a look last month. He'd been too busy freaking out at his total and utter spiral into irresponsible behavior. As he winced at the gravel pinging against the exterior of his car, he could see that it was, well, as weird as the term *goat compound*.

Her house was small, what he'd probably call a cottage if he was being kind. It was old, a little run-down and yet somehow cheerful. As if a little old lady who would offer you tea and cookies lived there.

Meg was definitely not a little old lady, and any cookies and tea had been figurative.

"Christ," he muttered, pulling to the end of the gravel drive. There was a little stone fence of sorts at the top, one he could easily step over but he assumed kept people from driving farther.

On each stone there was some iteration of a goat or flower painted in bright colors. Charlie stepped out of his car and merely stared.

The woman he'd accidentally knocked up was really obsessed with goats. The image was everywhere, even inked onto her skin, and in just the few hours he'd spent in her company, he'd drunkenly danced with a goat and soberly watched her milk goats.

She was carrying his child. He'd proposed marriage to her.

Somehow it wasn't a dream or some hallucination. This, right here, beside a row of rocks painted with goats, was his real life.

He blew out a breath and looked over the well-kept yard between him and the cottage. Flowers and bushes and bright green plants grew in beds along the tree line by one side of the house. Nearby, he could hear the goats bleating.

The door to the barn was open and Meg stepped out. For a brief second the whole goat thing didn't seem weird. She had her blond hair pulled back into a sloppy ponytail, wispy curls hanging around her face. She was wearing shorts, exposing a twirl of color he couldn't make out across the yard on the side of her calf.

In the plan of his life, Meg didn't fit at all. He never would've considered a partner with tattoos and a goat farm, and a business that depended on the strength of farmers' markets and people's willingness to buy foolish things.

He couldn't believe she thought she was solvent when this was her life. But she had a smile that made him forget all that, and even a little bit why he was here. She looked purely, 100 percent *content*. Like she knew without any shadow of a doubt where she was, who she was and that it was all meant to be.

Until she lifted her gaze to him. Her mouth remained curved, but her expression tightened. It wasn't relaxed. She wasn't content anymore.

He wished he could disappear so she could go back to that, but he couldn't. So he stepped forward. "If you're still finishing up work, I can wait."

She waved him off, pushing the heavy barn door closed before he rushed to help.

She eyed him as he placed a hand directly above hers and pushed it the rest of the way shut.

"You're going to be weird about me doing work while I'm pregnant, aren't you?"

He withdrew his hand and shoved it into his pocket. Something about her made him feel more off-kilter than he'd ever felt, even in the fog of being jobless and aimless. Meg was the thing, even prepregnancy bomb, that left him feeling the most uncertain of himself.

"Well, as I hear from my sister-in-law, growing a baby is hard work."

"Yes, and did she refrain from closing barn doors or whatever it is she does on a daily basis while she was growing a baby?"

Charlie thought back to when Mia had been pregnant with Lainey. Refrained? No, she hadn't refrained from much, especially in the beginning.

"That's what I thought," Meg said before he could form a response. "Let me assure you that growing this baby is very important to me, and I'll be taking care of both myself and it. And, even if it's coming from a good place, people telling me what to do has never been something I swallow very easy."

"All right, that's fair."

She nodded, seemingly satisfied with his response as she began walking toward the house, but he wasn't done.

"But you'll have to accept that telling people what to do has always been something I've done naturally. And I assure you, it does come from a good place. I can't just turn it off."

She stopped and turned to face him, that irritated line in her forehead he'd seen a lot during their short meeting at Moonrise.

"I'm used to being in charge. To leading people. My job was completely dedicated to me being able to convince people that my product and my way of getting it to them was the absolute best thing for their company."

"This baby isn't a product. And I'm certainly not a *company*. We're people. All of us."

He opened his mouth to argue further, but the words didn't come. It was oddly on point with his ex Emily's parting words to him when he'd said he wasn't ready to marry her. It had been four years ago, that last serious relationship, and he'd thought he'd *eventually* marry her, but he'd had things to accomplish first and Emily hadn't understood that.

*I am not a timetable or a sales report.*

He remembered that vividly. Because he'd known she didn't understand and maybe that was for the best, but...had she been right?

Did he treat people like business objects? It would explain why the past few weeks had been so odd and uncomfortable. He should have been able to relax and enjoy some time off while weighing his options, but he just...

"Hit a little close to home?"

He blinked at Meg, who was staring at him. Not quite accusingly, though. There was a certain softness to her expression that he thought might actually be concern.

"Maybe."

Her mouth curved at that, and it was such an odd feeling to admit a little bit of a failing, or something hitting "close to home," and having the response be an easy, accepting smile.

"You seem to be the type who needs schedules and plans and all that…"

"And you seem to be the type who doesn't want that."

She inclined her head toward the house and started walking again. "Actually a lot of my life is based on a very precise schedule. Goats like routine and consistency, and if I'm going to produce enough soap to be solvent each week, I have to keep a very close eye on what I produce."

She stepped onto the porch and pushed her door open. He bit back the urge to tell her she should keep it locked while she was in the barn. He'd bring up the subject eventually, but he sensed now was not a good time.

"But this—" she gestured toward her stomach, and then laid her palm there, her eyebrows drawing together "—this is something else entirely." She stood inside the cottage, him still on the porch on the other side of the threshold.

It felt a little heavy, a little weighty, that separation. Because he might have fathered that child, but he was separate from her. She was not his partner or his spouse. They were not in this together. Not really.

She was standing there, and he was standing here, and all they could do was talk about possibilities. And the ways they were different. All they could do was dance around each other awkwardly.

He could not turn her into a timetable, or a product to sell or buy. He could not package this in a way that would make it more attractive to his life, this woman with a rainbow of swirls on her calf, a sunny day tattooed on her forearm that ended in a goat at the end of her sleeve.

"Come inside, Charlie," she said gently.

Right. Inside. They had to talk. They had to *plan*, in whatever way they could agree to do that. This wasn't business, but it was still a challenge to meet.

She wasn't a timetable. She wasn't a product. But that didn't mean there was no end goal. The end goal was family. A child, and the way he wanted to raise that child. That was why he was here. To erase this line between them.

So he needed to stop psychoanalyzing himself, or letting her psychoanalyze him, and focus on that. On what he wanted. Because this wasn't a job that could be taken from him. This thing, a child, was something he could earn that would always be his.

CHARLIE FINALLY STEPPED over the threshold and Meg was surprised that relief swamped her. She couldn't get over the idea it'd be easier if he just went away, and for a moment she thought maybe he'd been considering it.

But he stepped forward and she gestured to the living room on the other side of the kitchen. He walked into it, too tall, too confident. He'd pulled himself together and cloaked himself with some kind of purpose.

The man on the porch she'd felt sorry for. She'd wanted to soothe him, or maybe share her fears with him. He'd seemed so *human* and lost for a few seconds, and she thought *that* man was a man she'd like to get to know.

Then she'd told him to come inside, and his expression had changed. *Hardened* wasn't the right word, but something akin to that. His expression had become focused and sure. And that man she didn't trust at all.

But that was a good thing. She owed it to herself and to her child to protect a certain piece of herself. She owed it to herself not to be so desperate for partnership or friendship or understanding that she fell apart.

On a deep breath she followed him into the living room. Self-preservation did not mean antagonizing. It simply meant being careful. She would be careful and calm.

He glanced around the room, and whatever he saw, whatever judgment he made, was completely hidden behind that focused intent of his expression. It was more like a general taking stock of a battlefield than a parent walking in and finding everything less.

She *really* had to get over her parental issues if she was going to be one.

"Have a seat," she managed, forcing herself to sit, as well. She wanted to pace. She wanted to wring her hands. She wanted to move and fidget and flail.

The fact she was going to sit on her overstuffed armchair and be completely still reminded her of being a kid. Interminable dinners dressed in too-itchy dresses where people expected her to be a little doll. A perfect Carmichael.

She closed her eyes against the wave of over-whelming fear and sadness. She could make a hundred decisions, but this wasn't ever going to be easy. Every conversation, every choice, every moment with him would be complicated and hard, and remind her far too much of a childhood that still hurt.

"How are you feeling?"

She blinked over at him. He'd taken a seat on the edge of the worn sofa. It wasn't the question she'd expected. Charlie was not someone she could seem to get a full grasp on. "I'm feeling fine."

"No…symptoms?" he asked, a dogged earnestness in his voice and his expression.

No, she couldn't get a grasp on him at all. "Uh,

well, um." She wasn't exactly going to tell Charlie her bras already didn't fit, but that was about the only sign something was up with her body. "Nothing much yet. It's still just a little—" she held up her thumb and forefinger "—speck."

And then, completely out of the blue, completely inexplicably in every way, she burst into tears. Just like she'd done when Elsie opened the door earlier in the week.

"Okay," she squeaked, dropping her hands into her lap. "Maybe I do have a few symptoms, because I don't usually cry for no reason."

A warm hand covered one of hers, his thumb gently dragging across her knuckles. If she wasn't in the middle of sobbing, she might have jolted at such a tender gesture from him. But she was too far gone. The tears kept pouring, this clutching panic in her chest kept swirling.

The baby was only a speck and she didn't know how to take care of it. She'd had to outline her drug use to the doctor and listen to how it might have affected her, her baby. She was starting behind already.

How would she do when it was an actual baby-size baby? A he or she? A person with a name and needs and…

Charlie took her other hand, so that he was crouching in front of her, both of her hands in his. He trailed his thumbs back and forth against both sets of knuckles, a steady, calming gesture while she tried to calm herself. To breathe.

He held her hands so she couldn't clean herself up. She could only sit there wet-faced and scared and sad and... Oh, she was going to start crying all over again.

"We don't know each other very well," Charlie said in a low, soothing voice. His thumbs never stopped moving over her knuckles, and she started to concentrate on that. How nice it was for someone to offer comfort, even when the reason for needing comfort was irrational and probably hormone related.

He hadn't asked her a question—how could it be a question when it was the simple truth? But she shook her head anyway. "No, we don't."

"So, maybe that's where we start. It's a big thing. This. Maybe before we try to navigate *this*." With his index finger he pointed at her stomach. "We try to navigate each other. Our interpersonal communication is going to be an important part of, well, that." Again, he pointed.

"Interpersonal—you're such a *businessman*."

"There's nothing wrong with that. I've worked hard to be one."

She didn't say anything. She hadn't known very many *businessmen* who didn't take their careers too seriously, who didn't turn it into their world, their life. But she also knew only a small sliver of people, all like her parents, and she couldn't believe that every person in business was like that.

Charlie didn't come from that world. He might look like he fit in it, but it wasn't the same. There could be good and bad parts to him. Just like there were good and bad parts to her.

"What if *it* wants to be a businessman?" he asked evenly. "Or businesswoman?"

She didn't want to broach that topic. She wasn't even past the *growing a stranger's child in my womb* topic. "We should call *it* something other than *it* and *that*. I feel like I'm growing a hamster."

His eyes met hers and he actually smiled. "I'm surprised you didn't say goat."

"Ooh!"

His smile died, but not in a way that made her feel bad. It was the kind of look you gave a friend when she was being crazy, and it made her think they *could* be friends. They could do this thing. They just had to, like he said, get to know each other.

"No, we are not calling— No goats."

"But they're *wonderful* creatures," she said, testing how far his bounds of humor went. "Or Capra. And we can call me Capra Carrier and—"

"No," he said firmly, but there was a note of baffled humor in that no-nonsense response and she had to hold on to the possibility there was more of that humor under the rational, focused exterior.

"Okay, what about something more literal?" she asked, realizing she was now holding on to his hands. It wasn't just comfort anymore, or at least not him giving it. They were holding on to each other.

Maybe they could learn to do that too.

"Fetus?"

She snorted. "Not *that* literal. Like Seed or Bean or something. Oh, that's kind of vomit-inducing cutesy, but it's better than Fetus."

"Seedling."

She blinked at him, because he said it in a way that made it seem…real. Big. A baby. Like even with a cutesy name, it was a life. She swallowed, afraid the tears would return.

This was so up and down and all over the place, but if she could bottle that tone of voice, the way he looked a little taken aback, a little afraid and a little determined, she could believe they'd find a place to navigate this together.

"Yes, it's the Seedling. I like that."

He cleared his throat, and his gaze dropped from hers down to their hands. He was still holding them.

"All right," he said in a raspy voice, before he slowly withdrew his hands from hers.

He got to his feet and turned away from her,

walking carefully back to the couch. She watched him, fascinated at the way he held himself together. There was a sense that maybe deep down, deep, deep, deep, *deep* down, he was as shaky and uncertain as her, but he took those careful measured steps, slowly lowered himself onto the couch, met her gaze again—this time from across the room—and there wasn't a flicker of uncertainty in his.

But she hadn't imagined it. It had been there.

"We should get to know each other. Like I said. So, let's start. Where did you go to school?"

She wanted to talk about what he was feeling, and what maybe scared him about the Seedling. She wanted to talk about how he imagined himself as a father and what he thought having a baby would be like.

And he was asking her about *school*.

Which was an easy enough question, so maybe starting there made all the sense in the world.

# CHAPTER TEN

IN THE END, Charlie conned her into eating. It was simple enough to do. He just kept asking question after question about her childhood and her life until she'd offered him something to drink—nonalcoholic, of course. With the offer for a drink came the offer for a snack, and now they sat at her tiny circle of a kitchen table eating cheese and crackers while she talked about her parents not allowing her to have pets when she was growing up.

She popped a bite of cracker into her mouth, then narrowed her eyes at him. "You keep steering the conversation back to me."

"You're fascinating."

"Oh, don't flirt like that."

"I…" Flustered, he straightened in his chair. "Just *how* was I flirting?"

"Like the preppy frat boys who think all they have to say is you're *fascinating* and *beautiful* and your top will just fall off."

He blinked, trying very hard not to let his gaze drift down to her top. Supposedly he'd seen her topless at some point, but he couldn't remember it. He'd tried. A lot. But that was *not* the topic at hand. "You actually think that was flirting—and not just flirting, but the best that I can do?"

She cocked her head, a playful curve to her lips. That had been what lured him into staying as much as his desire to make sure she was taking care of herself—and as much as wanting to get certain information out of her.

She was nothing like the women he'd dated, let alone slept with. She had a quirky sense of humor, a deep bitterness about her childhood that still didn't make sense to him and a sloppy kind of laissez-faire approach to everything from housework to fashion—the only exception being her business.

So, there was the element of being different. Of being not what he would have picked, but there was this odd thread to their conversations he couldn't analyze. It wasn't jealousy or envy, because he didn't want her life. But it was similar to that feeling he got when he watched his brother happily play husband and father and successful farmer.

Something like…admiration?

The word made him uncomfortable, so he focused on Meg. On Meg Carmichael with the goats and tattoos who was carrying his baby. That was why he was here. To understand her, so he could convince her to marry him. Because he was certain if they got married, even if this wasn't exactly how he'd planned it, he could still get the rest of those things he'd planned on.

Maybe it wouldn't be some great movieworthy love, but it could be a solid, comfortable partnership that raised their son or daughter well.

Which meant he had to like her. Of course, if they were going to raise a child together, they should like each other. No matter how different they were.

"I think that was perhaps subconscious flirting, but flirting nonetheless. I imagine a guy like you never had to try too hard to flirt."

"You have a lot of opinions about the type of guy you think I am," he returned. In this instance, he didn't care so much about her assumptions. Her thoughts on his flirting abilities didn't carry much weight; it wasn't something he was insecure about.

Why be insecure when his *actual* flirting always went over quite well?

"I do. And I haven't been wrong, have I?"

With an attempt to appear breezy, casual, he leaned forward onto his elbow on the table. "You were wrong at the bar. Silver spoon, private school, et cetera. Here I am, a farm boy with humble beginnings." He grinned.

She rolled her eyes. "Okay, one brief miscalculation. The rest is on point. *Including* the piss-poor flirting, though I'll give you points for the smile. You're not half bad at that."

"I assume you're now flirting with me? I would expect a little more originality from you."

She wrinkled her nose. "*Should* we even be flirting in the first place?"

He certainly didn't mind. At least not much. They'd have to be careful about it. In his experience, relationships tended to end in a fiery ball of "screw you, Charlie" when he wouldn't stop checking his email at dinner or the like.

He couldn't exactly build the kind of false expectations that might have her walking away like that. So he had to be careful.

But a little flirting couldn't hurt. *A little nakedness couldn't hurt.* Actually that could. He had to keep his brain off that path. Especially when they were here. Alone. With nothing stopping them from…

Yeah, he couldn't let his brain wander down the path that would give him *actual* memories. Not now.

But if he couldn't entertain a little harmless flirting with the woman he'd accidentally impregnated, then who could he flirt with right now?

He stretched his arm across the table, lightly touched his index finger to the back of her hand. Because people who thought *words* were flirting didn't get the concept. So he drew the tip of his finger down the length of hers, and he met her gaze, letting his smile spread slowly, knowingly— ignoring the odd dip his stomach did, or the way something about touching her the way he'd touched other women didn't feel the same at all.

The fair skin of her cheeks turned a telling shade of pink, even as she narrowed her eyes and looked at him skeptically. "I take it *that's* your idea of flirting?"

"I am more than adept at flirting. I wasn't doing it *before*. I was being honest. I'm interested in you. I *do* find you fascinating." And he did. That was the nice thing about his end goal. He *was* fascinated by her, so he didn't have to lie to find out what he wanted to find out. "But real flirting is a lot more than a compliment."

"Hmm," she said, pretending to consider, but he didn't miss the way she pulled her hand off the table and dropped it into her lap.

They might not be anything alike, but there'd been a basic attraction that had started this. That had led them here. If he let himself dwell on that, he'd lose sight of the point of what he was doing. Sex would not distract him from maneuvering her into a plan.

He had to act as fast as he could to get them where he wanted them to be, and then… Maybe then they could contemplate attraction.

Maybe it would even work out that well. They

could build a reasonable, rational partnership with the child's interest firmly in their minds, and then attraction…if it remained.

Maybe it could *end* in a real relationship, even a real marriage, but Charlie knew it had to start somewhere…sensible first. To make sure the foundation was solid, and would last.

"So, what about your tattoos?" He still didn't know what covered her shoulder aside from, he assumed, the rest of the sun that peeked out from the end of her T-shirt sleeve.

She pressed her lips together and studied him before responding. "What *about* my tattoos?"

There was an edge to her voice when she didn't want him to press, and he'd probably be smart to back off. To leave this as progress and call it a night. But something about the way their simple touch still echoed like vibrations in his fingers made him overrule *smart*.

"When did you get them? Why? It doesn't jibe with the image you've painted so far of your upbringing."

"You owe me about ten things about *you* before I talk any more about me."

Charlie leaned back in his chair. He didn't mind sharing about himself. It was just there wasn't much to tell. It didn't help his cause to say he studied hard, worked hard and now had nothing to show for either.

Yeah, he definitely wasn't going to share that. "So, what do you want to know?"

"What do you do for fun?"

He opened his mouth, but no sound came out. Fun. Fun? What did he do for fun?

She gave an almost imperceptible shake of her head. "You can't say anything that involves work. What have you been doing the past month without a job?"

He frowned. It wasn't an insinuation, but it scraped along his irritability like one. Still, he tried to keep his tone even. "Actually I kept working for a few weeks to ensure that the transition was smooth."

Her eyes widened and she gaped at him. "You kept working there? Even after they fired you?"

"I wasn't *fired*. I was laid off. It wasn't personal."

"You're unemployed. I'd consider that personal."

"I'll get another job," he returned through gritted teeth.

She cocked her head. "When? Doing what?"

"When I find one that suits my talents, experience and pay grade. One that will allow me to stay in St. Louis, so I can be near my family *and*…" He gestured at her stomach. *The Seedling*. They'd agreed to call it that, but he was having a hard time verbalizing it now.

It was so real. So heavy. He'd much rather view it as a situation he needed to conquer. Maneuver

Meg into marrying him so their child could have the same things he'd had growing up.

Stability. Support. The chance to become bigger than he was. They wouldn't be able to provide that while apart. At least, he wouldn't. He was too selfish to give up his share of this child's life. His child's life. A child who would have the best he could offer.

He realized he'd been silent too long, that she wasn't saying anything either. But when he looked at her, she had that soft, considering look on her face, and he wished he could wipe it off. He didn't want her consideration. He didn't want her softness.

*He* was not the one who needed sympathy here. He wasn't the screwed-up one, or the one who needed to be embarrassed by his past. Meg with her childhood bitterness, this business that probably had a five-year shelf life at best...*he* should feel sorry for her.

So, why did he feel like the fool? "I should probably go," he muttered. He was losing sight of things. Getting too overwhelmed by feelings and unimportant things. He needed to go, regroup and—

"Don't go," she said gently. Gently enough he wanted to growl. But then she hit him where it hurt.

She smiled, that easy, content smile that somehow warmed him even when he wanted to be completely irritated with her.

"Tell me about your family," she said, less gentle, more demanding.

He couldn't quite say no to that.

FOR A SECOND she thought he was going to leave anyway. For a second she had wanted him to. But it was the way he said *family—near my family*, it had finally given her a glimpse. A teeny, tiny one, but a glimpse nonetheless, that he might be more than the position he'd been *laid off* from, and had still worked at after.

"Well, my parents still live in the farmhouse I grew up in, but they sold half the farm to Dell, my brother, and the other half to a neighbor. My dad works part-time at a mechanic shop, and Mom works in the cafeteria at the middle school."

"You said your dad didn't like the farm, right? That's why they sold it off?"

He lifted a shoulder. "Yes. I thought maybe they'd move, but Dad isn't much for change. Since Dell and his wife live on the property, it keeps them close to the grandkid."

"Girl or boy?"

"Girl. Lainey. She just turned two."

Meg wondered if he had any idea the way his face changed. The way his muscles, which had been so tense and ready to bolt, relaxed as he spoke his niece's name.

"She can't say Charlie, so I'm Uncle Chawie." He took a breath, focused that gaze on hers, the kind that made her heart flutter because it was so *intense.*

She had to remind herself that this wasn't about *her.* He was looking at her like that because she was now connected to his life, but it had nothing to do with who she was or actual, real feelings or anything.

It was simply a mistake that had created a miracle, and now they both had to live with it.

He leaned forward, and she didn't trust the way part of her wanted to lean with him. Lean into each other and pretend it was as simple as that, but she had enough self-preservation to lean back, to know better.

"You know, if we got married, we would be in it—wholly—together. I know it wouldn't be true love or anything, but isn't the good of our child bigger than that?"

She swallowed; she knew he had a sliver of a point. But she also knew she couldn't give her entire self up for this child, and allowing him this would be doing just that. She deserved to survive this intact, as much as her child deserved the best she could offer it.

"I think a lot of people raise children separately

and they're just fine. In fact, better off sometimes."
Would her parents be as vicious to her if they'd
separated? Because sometimes she couldn't help
feeling like some weird pawn in their relationship
game. Or maybe their disappointment in her was
the one thing they could agree on.

"Do you really think a child is better off always
trying to navigate two separate lives?"

She closed her eyes, swamped with exhaustion. She didn't want to have this conversation,
this argument. She just wanted to sleep and have
things be simple.

But they weren't. "I think it depends. And I
think, in this situation…" *Two separate lives.* It
sounded exhausting. For her, for the Seedling, for
everything.

But she couldn't *marry* him.

"I think it's important to give our child the
truth. Honesty. Navigating two lives will be a
challenge, yes, but can you imagine if she grew
up to think she was at fault for the way we treated
each other? We can't pretend away the fact that
we don't love each other."

"We could *try* to love each other. Eventually,
once we have the important things sorted out."

In all the volleys he'd thrown her way, that
one stuck the hardest. Because those who'd tried
had only failed. The only love she'd ever known

had been Grandma's. Effortless, constant, unconditional.

It was hard to speak, but she focused on the very important words. "I don't think that's how it works."

"We could decide that's how it works. For us."

"Charlie…" She sighed, trying to find the words, or the energy for the words.

"No, you're right." He pushed his chair back from the table and stood. "It's not that easy. I like easy solutions, but there isn't one."

"No, there isn't."

"I imagine with the goats you have an early morning?"

She nodded, something about the way he was acting not sitting right. She couldn't put her finger on it, almost like there was something calculated in his retreat.

Or she was being 100 percent paranoid, which was more than a little likely.

"Then you should get some rest." He smiled ruefully. "I'll work on fighting the urge to tell you what to do."

"Thank you," she said, getting to her feet. Of course, she couldn't fight the yawn. Only nine o'clock and she was exhausted. But six thirty would come early enough.

"I'd like to come back tomorrow. I do think we need to keep getting to know each other. Like…

Seedling…we're going to have to navigate two lives too. We should find a way to understand each other, don't you think?"

Something about the way he said it, the way he kept her gaze, that focused intent in his dark eyes… Something didn't sit right. At all. But how could she refuse? How could she say no to this?

He was right. They needed to understand each other, and they needed to learn how to compromise with each other if this was going to work once *Seedling* was born.

So she forced herself to nod and smile. "Seven again?"

He nodded. "I'll bring a snack. My sister-in-law's sister makes the pie you ordered at Moonrise. I can get you one for free. *Not* to get you to eat, simply as a friendly gesture."

"Your sister-in-law's sister is Cara of Cara's Local Pies?"

"Yes."

"Bring me two?"

He chuckled. "I'll see what I can do." He held out a hand, a formal, businessman gesture. Shake hands, business done.

"How about this?" Instead of taking his outstretched hand, she placed her palms on his shoulders, moved up to her tiptoes and brushed her mouth across his cheek. Realizing far too late it was a gesture that wasn't simply easy and friendly, it was weighted.

Weighted with sex she didn't remember and a child they'd created. Weighted by the attraction that buzzed between them even when she was expressly ignoring it.

Impossible to ignore now, though she'd taken her lips off the stubbled cheekbone, her palms still balanced on his shoulders, she was still standing on her toes, so they were eye level with each other.

Mouth level.

She swallowed, her heart hammering in her chest. She could lean in and kiss him. She could test the attraction. She could do more than just *get to know him*. Hell, she could agree to marry him.

It was that reminder that had her stepping back and managing a wobbly smile. "Better than a handshake," she said, realizing she'd taken him so by surprise that he still had his arm outstretched.

"I suppose it is," he said, his voice low, maybe a little rusty.

One hundred percent lethal. Heat pooled in her belly. *The belly in which you are growing his child because you fell off the wagon* that *hard*.

Right. Priorities. Focus.

"Good night, Charlie," she managed, sounding only slightly strangled.

"Good night, Meg," he returned. For a second he still stood there, though he'd finally lowered his arm. Then he simply turned and opened her front door. So stealthily she almost didn't notice, he flipped the inside lock of the door before stepping outside and pulling it closed behind him.

He'd locked the door for her. *Because he thinks you aren't capable of locking your own door.*

She scowled at the cynical voice inside her head. She'd need to learn to mute that a little bit.

Right after she dealt with the whole bad-idea lust issue. Because between his all too effective flirting and that little moment with her lips on his skin, *damn it*, that was an *issue*.

## CHAPTER ELEVEN

CHARLIE WAS UP at the crack of dawn. As an adult, he'd slowly and consciously rid himself of the ingrained habit of waking with the sun.

But whenever he spent the night at his parents', he couldn't fight the native conditioning. While most days it caused him to be sweary and irritable until he'd had his coffee, today he got right out of bed.

Because he had things to do today. He had a plan, and he had no doubt that on the other side of New Benton, Meg was already up and milking goats.

He needed to get a better handle on her day. On why the goats. A better handle on her and her life. She'd offered pieces of herself last night, but it had all felt superficial. All the little pieces of herself she'd shared paled in comparison to the moment when she'd leaned over and kissed his cheek. The heat, the light, the shimmer. The way it lodged inside of him like something big and important, when it was merely a friendly goodbye.

He somehow had to manufacture more of that,

well, more without the uncomfortable lust under it. Lust could wait. It could come later. When things were more steady under their feet.

Sex would be something of a distraction from the point—the point being he needed to build a relationship that could sensibly move to marriage, ideally before the baby was born.

Then his life could shift back onto the plan he'd always followed, and things could make sense again.

Yes, he liked this idea so much better than wallowing and feeling like he didn't know himself.

Humming all the while, he showered and got dressed. Quick breakfast, and then he could head out to Meg's without seeming too eager. But when he stepped into the kitchen, Dell and his little family were crowded in there with Mom and Dad.

"Didn't know there was a family breakfast."

"Chawie!" Lainey darted over to him, lifting her arms with the utmost certainty he'd catch her and lift her up.

So he did exactly that, something in his chest going tight. Soon enough, he'd have this.

His own.

He braced himself for the slap of her pudgy hands as he settled her on his hip. He couldn't help smiling when they landed on his cheeks with an audible *whack*.

"Hey, Sugar Snap."

"Lainey, you have to stop hitting people in the face," Mia said warily. She sat at the kitchen table, looking pale and miserable, Dell standing behind her rubbing at the tension in her shoulders.

Charlie had to wonder if Meg would start feeling that bad. He didn't remember Mia being this unwell when she'd been pregnant with Lainey, but Meg would certainly need some help if she could barely get out of bed in the morning.

He wondered if she'd considered hiring anyone. She'd need help in the upcoming months. Maybe he could gently suggest—

"Earth to Charlie."

Charlie blinked to attention and realized just about everyone was staring at him with concern in their eyes.

They thought he was losing his marbles, and he could hardly blame them. But he couldn't explain everything that was going on. Not yet. Not until he had a better handle on Meg and the future.

"Mia and I were hoping we could talk to you for a bit." Dell glanced at the clock on the wall. "You've got time before you start your job hunting, yeah?"

Since that wasn't exactly what he'd planned on doing with his day, he hesitated, but when everyone looked expectantly at him, he could only smile and nod. "Sure."

"I'll take this one," Mom said, expertly taking

Lainey off his hands. "Maybe after they're done with you, you should take a nap or something before you head back into the city. You don't look rested."

Charlie managed to smile at his mother. "I actually might stay out here for a few days. If you don't mind."

"Oh." Mom blinked at him, a fake as anything smile on her face. "Of course not."

Charlie tried not to take it personally. He knew it was worry. Usually she was busy *trying* to get him to stay. But they all seemed to think this job situation had sent him off the deep end.

*Had it?*

Charlie ignored that voice in his head and watched as Dell helped Mia to her feet. She grimaced and tried to wave him away, but Dell held tight, even as she began to walk out of the kitchen.

"I'm on this antinausea medication," Mia explained as they walked through the house and outside. "It helps me eat, but it makes me dizzy." She smiled thinly. "Luckily I've got a personal walker over here," she said, sounding anything but grateful.

"The doctor said if—"

"Charlie doesn't want to hear about what the doctor said," Mia snapped. She plastered a smile on her face again. "I don't mean that in a snippy way. I just don't think you care about all the inner workings of growing a baby."

"Ah, well, you know. It's interesting, actually. This pregnancy has gone a lot differently than the first, hasn't it?" He took the stairs two at a time up to Mia and Dell's cabin and swung the door open so Dell could help Mia inside.

They both raised their eyebrows as they passed.

Charlie shrugged. "Just trying to be supportive."

"Yeah, well, try not to be weird," Dell returned, helping Mia to the couch.

Mia sank onto the cushions and then rested her head on a throw pillow. She stretched out. "I know this looks silly, but hear me out while I lie here like a lump. I feel so much better when I'm prone."

"You know, if you guys need help…" He didn't love farmwork, but he'd do what he could. All the while thinking that Meg was definitely going to need some help with her goats the further along she got. Had she thought of that yet? Should he bring it up?

"That's actually what we wanted to talk to you about," Dell said, sliding onto the edge of the couch and lifting Mia's feet so they rested on his lap and he could pull her boots off.

"We hope you don't find this offer a little… insulting."

"Not the way to start, sugar," Dell muttered.

Mia glared at her husband. "It's just…we thought

maybe you could help us out while you're waiting for the right job."

"Right. Well, whatever you need. I know I'm not much up on *how* to grow things, but I can follow directions."

"Actually we're talking about more business-oriented stuff. Anna and Wes have been helping Dell with the harvesting and planting I can't do."

"With a second one coming along, we're looking to expand some more. Not necessarily in land, but in business."

"And we've both done as much as we can without putting a lot more time and effort into learning about the business and sales sides of things. We could take a class, or read more, or whatever, but we're both kind of at the end of our ropes, timewise."

"So you want my help with…what?" Charlie didn't understand what they were asking. Not because it didn't make sense, but because ever since Dell had taken over the farm portion of things, he acted like Charlie's lack of farming knowledge made him completely useless to his farm business.

"Expansion ideas. I know farming isn't your expertise, but sales is."

Even though Mia said it, Charlie couldn't help looking at Dell. "You want my sales help?"

"I know this is the kind of stuff you offered years ago and I was kind of a dick about it."

"Kind of."

Dell scowled. "Point is, I *was* being a dick, and I felt like I had to do it on my own. Well, I learned my lesson on that score, and Mia and I've talked a lot about this. If you're willing, we hope you'd consider offering your perspective. And we'd pay you for it."

"You don't have to—"

"Yes, we do," Mia said firmly. "It's only right. And if you don't hate it, Cara and Wes could use help too. It's all different things. Wes wants to expand online sales of his dog treats. Cara's looking into having her own pie shop." Mia's sister and brother-in-law both had their own businesses, Wes selling organic dog treats at farmers' markets and online, Cara baking and selling pies at restaurants.

Both businesses were similar to Meg's, with the same kind of instability, but Charlie already had a few ideas on how to stabilize things—Cara's business especially.

"We know that's not exactly your expertise," Mia was continuing. "But if you've got some extra time, we *could* pay you for your services. Kind of like a business consultant thing."

"Stop babbling," Dell admonished easily.

"Oh, be quiet," Mia snapped, giving Dell a light kick. "The thing is, we know we're just a bunch of small businesses, and it's nothing that would take the place of a career. We just thought it might be something that might be mutually beneficial. You could give us some help, we could pay you, and then you wouldn't have to hurry to take a job you don't like. Dell said you wanted to stay in St. Louis, and it might take a while to find the right position."

"You couldn't possibly pay me what I was making. Even for consulting on three different businesses."

"It's not about replacing your old job, Charlie. Think of it like a stopgap. And allowing all of us to bring in someone we trust to help us grow our businesses."

He wanted to do it. He was surprised to find *how* much he wanted to do it. But he'd offered this before and had been told in no uncertain terms by his little brother that his help was *not needed*.

Dell had changed a lot in the past four years, but Charlie hadn't moved beyond how easily his multiple offers for business advice had been rebuffed. And none too kindly. Not that he'd ever let on that it hurt.

That wasn't how Wainwrights dealt with things like that. No, they bottled them up and kept going. "Look, guys, you've done fine without me."

"Now we'd like to do better *with* you." Mia placed a palm on her slightly rounded stomach.

All Charlie could think about for one blinding second was that he was going to have a kid. He was going to be a father. Either he could stand here arguing old hurts and stupid pride—or he could help the family he loved. Which one did he want for his future? His *child's* future?

He cleared his throat, because he felt off-kilter again. Off course, off center, *off.* But he also knew what his answer had to be, and hey, at least this would be something like a job.

"All right. Consider me hired."

Both Mia and Dell grinned, and Charlie had to smile back, because it was kind of exciting, really. Sure, farming had never been his passion, but ever since Dell had started his own farm, Charlie had had opinions about it.

Now his opinions were being solicited. His opinions might actually matter. His family, who usually rolled their eyes at him, *typical Charlie*, actually wanted his help. Wanted *him*. Yeah, that was something to smile about.

MEG WAS DRAGGING. She wanted to blame the lack of energy on pregnancy, she would have loved to blame it on the goats, but the bottom line was she hadn't slept.

Again, there were a whole host of things she'd love to blame *that* on, but really it was Charlie. Or rather, her body's reaction to Charlie.

Which irritated her and confused her because she wasn't even certain she *liked* Charlie. Oh, he was hot. No doubt. Sometimes he'd let an inch of his guard down, and that man…she thought maybe she could like that man.

But it was tiny glimpses of a man who otherwise didn't show much more than the mask he wore. The facade. And the problem was, she knew plenty of people who had become the mask they put on every day. They weren't carefree twentysomethings anymore—whatever had made him put protective walls up was deeply rooted in his past.

That was disconcerting on every level.

But she was still attracted to him, and that was annoying on every level because acting on it now would be messy in just about every possible way.

The goat she was milking bleated and kicked at the enclosure. She'd zoned out or dozed off or something and it was not pleased.

"Sorry, Starstruck," Meg murmured, refilling her feed and finishing up the milking. She forced herself to focus on Calliope, grateful she was the last one for the morning.

Trying to absorb some strength from the soothing routine, Meg went through all the sterilization and milk storage steps. She hummed an upbeat song to herself, trying to infuse energy into her movements.

Someone cleared his throat and she jumped,

whirling around with every intention of using her three-legged stool as a weapon.

"Charlie," she said in a whoosh of breath.

"Sorry. I tried to knock." He gestured at the barn door. "I called your name. You were just kind of..."

She rolled her eyes. At herself. At this weirdness between them. "I was out of it."

"Appeared to be."

"Sorry, I..." She almost let it slip she hadn't slept, but after all his flirting stuff that wasn't flirting but wasn't *not* flirting, she didn't want to give him the idea she'd been up thinking about him. He was cocky enough. So she gestured toward her stomach, because as long as Seedling was growing in there, she could blame it for stuff if she needed to.

Seedling would never know the difference.

He smiled gently. The smile that she didn't like because there wasn't any *light* in the expression, no sweetness, no joy. It was practiced. It was a businessman's smile.

She held the stool in front of her stomach, feeling oddly protective of her little Seedling in the face of Charlie's polish.

"I brought you lunch. I tried to call, but you didn't answer."

She swallowed and patted her pockets, realizing she'd done what she almost never did—forgotten her cell inside. "Sorry. I was reading my pregnancy book and it talked about pregnancy brain and I think I got immediately infected. I left my phone inside."

He opened his mouth to say something but then shut it again. Probably biting back a scolding, if she had to guess.

Well, at least he had the sense to bite it back, even if she wished he could have the sense not to scold her, period.

"Have you thought about hiring some help?" he asked instead.

She was too tired to be irritated by the question. "Well, sure. But I'd have to find someone I trusted with the goats. Then figure out how much I could afford to pay them, and look into employee tax stuff, and it seems a bit much when I'm getting by all right."

"But you could expand, if you wanted to."

Meg shrugged. "I guess. I kind of like the way things are. I mean, if I found the right person, it'd be nice to have help. But it's a lot to trust someone with my life, my heart, my soul. That's what this place is to me, Charlie. So, unless you're offering *yourself* for help, it's not in the cards."

"Um."

She saw him look around the barn. Most of the goats had gone out the little door and were outside, but a few pranced inside, butting each other, hopping into the haystacks. His face remained carefully blank, but she knew he was recoiling inwardly. She just knew it.

Then those dark eyes met hers and he nodded, as if that was that. "Actually yes. I'd like to help out."

She laughed. When his eyes narrowed, she knew she should stop, but she couldn't help herself. "I'm sorry," she said between giggles. "I can't picture it. I just…can't."

"I told you I grew up on a farm."

"Yes, and that you didn't like it. Look at you." She pointed to his dark-wash jeans, the preppy tennis shoes that wouldn't last a day in goat poop and mud. He wore a T-shirt today, and based on how crisp it was, she wouldn't be surprised if he'd ironed it.

He looked down at his outfit. "I'll admit, I'm not dressed for working. But I didn't come here intending to work. It doesn't mean I'm incapable."

As Meg saw it, she had two options. Continue to laugh at him, or let him do it. Let him see what helping out at a goat farm, making goat milk soap, would be like. Let him try and get it out of his system.

She'd be shocked if he lasted a day.

"So you want me to hire you," she said, being very careful to say the words in a way that didn't hint at the fact that she was eagerly awaiting the first time he shoveled poop out of the stall.

Poor Charlie might have grown up on a farm, but that didn't mean he had any idea what he was getting himself into.

"Well, I was thinking more volunteer work."

"Oh no, if you're going to work for me, you're going to be my employee." She smiled at him. "I'd love the chance to order you around."

"That can probably be arranged without payments or goats."

Oh, crap, flirting alert. Her heart was getting all jittery at that sly smile of his, the way it slowly curved on one side of his mouth and then the other. Damn him.

"Well," he continued, that amused smile suddenly focused, "I've already taken on what basically amounts to three consulting jobs for my brother and sister-in-law, and *her* sister and sister's husband, so why not a little part-time goat farmwork? You can pay me minimum wage, and I'll work until I get a real job."

"A part-time job with me *would* be a real job, Charlie."

He waved it away. "You know what I mean."

"So, when you go on an interview for some big-shot corner office sales job of the century, and they ask what you've been doing while unemployed, you'll say you worked at a goat farm?"

"No, I'll say I spent some time consulting small businesses on expanding their sales reach, goat farming and farming of any kind not mentioned unless applicable. Who knows, maybe my future boss will have a goat obsession like you do."

She wrinkled her nose at him. "It's not an obsession."

He crossed to her then, and it was only pride that kept her from stepping back. Because the closer he got, the more the air seemed to electrify. Those self-preservation instincts she'd carefully honed over the past few years were telling her to run.

But she wouldn't run from the father of her child, or from the challenge of that surety he exuded having some effect on her lady parts. So she stood where she was, ignoring the way his eyes held hers so confidently, the way his body moved like it knew exactly what it was about.

Mostly she ignored that she wanted to touch him, or smell him, or figure out how he affected her so deeply, with just a look. Just proximity.

He stopped in front of her and took the stool she was still holding like a shield. He pried it from her fingers, which she held clutched for no reason that made any kind of sense.

Once he'd loosed it from her grasp and set it down, he took her tattooed arm in his hands, trailing a finger over the space just above her wrist, where the goat was tattooed.

"This," he said, his voice suddenly sounding hushed, intimate, "is an obsession."

She wished she had the wherewithal to argue, but she was afraid if she tried to speak it would just come out a sigh, because his finger kept tracing her goat, and there was something so ridiculously sensual about it she kind of wanted to die.

Or jump him.

# *CHAPTER TWELVE*

CHARLIE DIDN'T KNOW what had changed, or what he'd planned on doing when he'd taken her arm. He probably could have pointed out the goat tattoo without touching it.

But here he was, tracing his fingers over the lines. Mesmerized by the way her skin goosebumped and how there could be all this blue and white ink on her, but she felt smooth and soft.

She would feel like that everywhere. He should *know* that, not imagine it. He'd *impregnated* her; he should be able to know more than just the few snatches of memory his brain decided to hold on to.

*Not the plan, Wainwright.* And yet he couldn't seem to listen to that voice that had ruled him for...well, for a long-ass time. All those plans, all those rules, all that focus, and he couldn't remember anyone who had ever made that voice sound like an annoying gnat rather than a life-guiding deity.

"Charlie." Her voice sounded strangled and he was probably supposed to stop touching her, stop looking at the goat, stop wondering what the rest of her felt like. Under the loose T-shirt she was wearing, under those tight stretchy pants he wasn't sure qualified as pants.

"I think we need to make a decision."

Funny, she kept talking and he wasn't at all sure she was saying words that made sense.

"A decision?" He'd been making a lot of decisions today. Well, taking offers, really. But still, moving forward, making progress.

Wait. What kind of decision was she talking about?

"To or not to. Like, if we're putting that on the table, but I think it needs to be clear."

"To...?" Or not to. Finally he forced his gaze to leave her tattoo, her arm under his finger, and meet those wide blue eyes. There had been a reason he'd come here. He couldn't for the life of him remember it.

Because she was most assuredly talking about sex. Doing it or not doing it, which had been a debate in his head. Repeatedly. But he hadn't planned on *broaching* it quite so...head-on.

He must have loosened his grip, because her arm slid away, and he felt that break in physical connection like something akin to a blow.

So he hedged, because of course he *wanted* it to be on the table, but even though she short-circuited his entire being, he still wasn't used to *doing* what he wanted. There were responsibilities to weigh, plans to think of. "Do you *want* it to be on the table?"

She blinked at him, that beautiful shade of pink flushing up her neck and cheeks. It was only years of denying his more impulsive…impulses that kept him from stepping forward, cupping those cheeks, touching…

God, he wanted to touch her again.

What was she *doing* to him?

She whirled away, which didn't help, because her ass in those ridiculous legging nonpants was something of a very major distraction.

"I don't know," she muttered, shoving her fingers through her unruly blond hair. "I don't *know.*"

She whirled back to face him, poking an index finger in his direction. "You're obviously Mr. Responsible. You tell me what the right thing to do here is."

"Well…" Responsible. She wanted him to tell her the right thing to do. That was very much his usual wheelhouse. He knew, of course, the responsible thing to do was to say no. Sex should not be on the table. Not yet. But…

"You've probably never made a decision with your dick," she muttered in disgust.

"Um, well, we're in a situation that might claim otherwise."

Her lips twitched, but she didn't laugh. He found it odd he wanted to.

"Okay, your drunk penis is irresponsible, but your sober one is not. Sober Charlie's penis is one of the most responsible penises I've ever met."

"Please tell me what the hell we're talking about, because I've completely lost track."

She blew out a breath in a mix between humor and frustration. "Look, I think we're attracted to each other or, even wasted, we probably wouldn't have ended up doing the horizontal polka."

"You didn't just say polka—horizontal or otherwise. Please tell me you didn't."

This time she did laugh, and he laughed too, because he liked the way it infiltrated the air. Even with the smell of hay and animal poop—the hallmark of his childhood—her laugh made him feel like he was somewhere bright and fresh.

"Maybe we should have a no-touching, no-innuendo, no-flirting rule."

"We could do that…"

"Why do you not sound convinced? You're supposed to be a stick-in-the-mud who agrees with all stick-in-the-mud plans!"

He raised an eyebrow. "Responsible does not necessarily equal stick-in-the-mud. It certainly doesn't mean no sex."

"Charlie, that is *not* the point."

"Well, it's *my* point."

"We can't have sex. That's the important thing. It would complicate…everything."

"True, but—"

"How is there a but?"

"As you said, we're attracted to each other, all polkaing aside. Just setting a sex moratorium might lead to what got us here in the first place."

"Uh, no. No more the Shack for me. No more drinking." She gestured at her flat stomach. "No more bad decisions. All my decisions are for the good of Seedling."

"Yes, mine too. But I'm not sure what sex has to do with Seedling."

"Charlie!" She stomped her foot and he had to work very hard not to smile with how exasperated she was with him. "You are being far too difficult about this. You're being… You're being…"

"A guy?"

She narrowed her eyes and he couldn't seem to keep his mouth in a straight line. He liked the way energy and emotion sparked off her, in her expression, in her movements. She was so…open. He'd always dated contained, careful women. Always thought that was his type, that was what he wanted.

But he liked her spark, her flash. A lot.

"Hear me out here. It's like…" He struggled for an analogy that would make sense considering their very unique situation. "Like when you work with someone you're attracted to. Every day you walk into the office and they're *there*. You have to walk by them, and see them, and it makes the air heavy. It makes your skin feel too tight. Day after day, they're *there*, in your space, being that thing you're trying to resist." He wasn't quite sure when his voice had gone low, kind of raspy, or when they'd taken steps toward each other.

Close. They were close. They shouldn't be close, but he couldn't resist. He'd never *not* been able to resist and it was fascinating, all in all, free-falling the way he did around her.

*Which led to getting her pregnant and you not even remembering it.*

But reason's voice was just a whisper when she was near, the sharp intake of her breath and the faint blush on her cheeks serving only to spur him on. "So, every day you pretend. And you pretend. And you probably get a little more desperate every day until…"

He snapped his fingers and she jumped. He got no small amount of satisfaction from that. This wasn't just *him*. It wasn't some break with reality caused by upheaval. Whatever existed between them echoed in both of them. Maybe attraction was all it was, but it was mutual.

It was potent.

And, once again, he'd forgotten the point of being here.

MEG FELT LIKE she was *vibrating*. All those things he'd described—the heavier air, the skin being tight—added an unnatural heat and unabashed longing that should most definitely abash her. She felt like she was vibrating from the inside out.

She knew what it was to want, to long, to be desperate for something. She'd beaten that need. Time and time again, she'd crushed the desire to have something she knew was bad for her, despite the appealing sense of freedom and goodness it would briefly give her.

Charlie wasn't a drug, or a drink, but he surely would be bad for her. Well, potentially. It would complicate things, no matter how yummy that complication might be...

It wasn't just them. It wasn't just her. She had to consider Seedling and the fact that Charlie wanted to be a part of that. So she had to stop being a hormonal, desperate mess ready to jump him at the slightest touch—and the smoothest, hottest explanation of attraction she'd ever heard.

She cleared her throat, waving a hand in the air. "You slept with people you worked with? That's kinda sleazy."

"No," he said evenly. "It was just an example."

"It sounded real," she said, realizing too late her voice wasn't infused with disbelief. It sounded a heck of a lot closer to jealousy. *Oh, ew. No.*

"The point is, you do something like swear it off, and the next thing you know, you're doing just that."

"But you said yourself, you're a guy with plans

and all that stuff. How can you say you wouldn't be able to stick to a plan?"

"Sticking to a plan is all about being reasonable and realistic enough to know when a plan won't work."

"I'm not going to have sex with you just because I'm attracted to you."

His mouth curved, a lazy, self-satisfied move that she should have hated. It should have made him seem smug or unattractive, but all she could do was smile back.

"Okay, I'm not going to sleep with you *again*, just because I'm attracted to you."

"Which is wise. Though I think we need to be careful about ultimatums and the like. We should do our best to navigate our attraction in a reasonable, adult manner, with what's best for Seedling always in the forefront of our minds."

She had to work hard not to grimace. But he was right. It was the mature, rational thing to do. "Absolutely," she forced herself to say with far more conviction than she felt.

"After this."

And then Charlie Wainwright shocked her for the second time in their brief, if intimate, acquaintance. The first had been him even *being* at the Shack in the first place, and now the second was his hand—surprisingly strong and a little rough—

curling around the back of her neck, pulling her forward.

Pausing only a second before he lowered his mouth to hers in a swift, easy, *swoonworthy* move. Any memories of their previous kisses were fuzzy at best, far-off things hazed by alcohol. This kiss felt hazed by *fire*. The way his hand moved up her neck to cup the back of her head, the way his mouth angled so his tongue could enter. She had to be aflame; it was the only possibility.

There was a tinge of frustration to his mouth, the inescapable heat of whatever attraction thrummed between them. Curiosity. Exploration, as his tongue met hers.

She melted into it. Inevitable. Yes, acting on this was some kind of inevitability. She lifted to her toes and twined her arms around his neck so she could press her body to his. So she could feel all the things she couldn't quite remember about the night she'd been naked with him, had sex with him, made a *baby* with him.

Suddenly seconds, maybe minutes, after denying the prudence of the action, all she wanted to do was take him to bed. Or to the ground. Wherever would work. She wanted to know what it felt like to have him inside her. She wanted, desperately, to be reminded of what Charlie Wainwright looked and felt like naked.

She wanted to know where his hands would

touch, where his lips would taste. She wanted to touch and taste herself. She wanted... She wanted...

He ended the kiss, pulling away slightly and keeping his grip on the back of her head so she couldn't follow where his mouth went.

It took seconds to manage the wherewithal to open her eyes, to meet his gaze. *God.* She couldn't catch her breath. Couldn't quell the riotous response of her body. Maybe it was pregnancy hormones, because a *kiss* couldn't light her on fire. Not like that. It couldn't make her yearn with the fervor she'd once felt for addictive substances.

"I just needed to remember what it was like," he said in that gravelly whisper that skated along all the most sensitive parts of her. "Because I couldn't remember what you felt like, what you tasted like. It's been driving me crazy."

"And now you know," she choked out. "So it won't. Anymore."

"And now I know. And wish I didn't because I think it might haunt me." He blew out a breath, his big hand still cupping the back of her head, fingers tangled in her hair. She didn't want him to remove it. Not now, not soon. She wanted that warm weight there, feeling like some kind of anchor to the whirlwind of sensation in the rest of her body.

"Who *are* you, Meg Carmichael?" he muttered, his gaze burning into her.

She didn't have a clue. Because every time she thought she figured it out, something flipped. Something broke. Something unexpected lit her up from the inside out.

"Probably a mistake," she thought, except she realized too late it hadn't just been a thought. She'd said it aloud. To him.

She closed her eyes, embarrassment washing over her, and she tried to step away. Escape the way his gaze had softened.

He didn't need to see her soft, insecure underbelly. She needed to protect that, to hide it. She'd tried to eradicate it to no avail, so she'd learned to bury it under confidence she'd mostly felt, easy smiles and quirky jokes.

Goats.

"Meg."

That soft, slightly confused pity in his voice scraped. Hell, it downright cut. "I need you to let me go, all right?" she said, her breathing still uneven, her eyes still shut tight.

His grip loosened and fell away, and she nearly swayed from being on her own two feet. Wasn't that dangerous? To forget that was where she always had to be.

She forced herself to open her eyes, to look at him, to keep her chin up and her shoulders back.

*Fake it, baby, fake it.*

"If you really want to help out around here, you're going to have to learn some new skills."

She refused to slouch at the concerned way his eyebrows drew together, refused to look away from the way his eyes studied her, trying to figure her out.

*Good luck, buddy.*

She'd done a lot to get where she was, but that didn't mean she had any clue why the warped pieces inside her didn't fit together like everyone else's did.

"I've got all the time in the world," he said at last.

And that was a scary prospect.

# CHAPTER THIRTEEN

CHARLIE FOLLOWED MEG around for the rest of the day, learning the ins and outs of goat farming. It was surprisingly precise, though that shouldn't be a shock. He'd watched Dell and his father farm, and raising things to sell—animals or plants—was nothing if not *precise*.

It was the outcome that never was. Which, aside from his father pointing him away from farming, had been the sticking point for Charlie. He liked results. He liked goals that could be met, ones that couldn't be swept away by bad weather or animal sickness.

Or your company being bought out.

Neither he nor Meg talked about the kiss as they worked. They pretended it had never happened. As though it hadn't crawled inside him and flipped everything upside down.

Because he hadn't been lying about wishing he hadn't. Not remembering was actually much better than *remembering*. Like wishing he'd never known her name. Because now that he knew—knew that it felt like no kiss had *ever* felt before—the last thing he wanted to do was stop or be reasonable.

But she seemed to need it. There'd been a crack in her usual affable armor. He'd seen maybe a glimpse of it at the bar that night, but he'd been drowning in his own problems, and a metric ton of alcohol.

Since then, she'd been nothing but strong and determined, and even in the moments of confusion and argument, she had been cool. Collected.

But then she'd called herself a mistake. She'd all but begged him to let her go when he hadn't exactly been holding her against her will and, well, now he didn't know what to do. Except tread carefully and do as she asked. Try to remember his *plan*. A plan would make everything better.

If the goal was to get her to marry him in the next eight months, which wasn't *that* crazy as he seemed to like her more and more, and he was definitely attracted to her, which was important, he had to be careful. Pushing would screw it up and so would losing his head.

He *was* the responsible one. No rebellious past, though she still hadn't shared the full details there. He might not have a job, but his prospects were far more solid and dependable than hers.

Meg was locking the barn up, the sun setting off to the west making her hair glow. She really was beautiful. It had been the first thing he'd thought when he laid eyes on her at the market. This woman babbling about goat milk soap was quite possibly the most beautiful woman who'd ever smiled at him.

"You hold up pretty well, Wainwright," she said, trying to hide a yawn with the back of her arm. "It's like you grew up on a farm or something."

"Funny how the shit and the hay never really leave you."

"Don't forget about the bone-deep satisfaction."

"Yeah, I never got that part." Of course, he'd never been allowed to try. Not that it bothered him. He'd never felt it the way Dell had. Maybe if he had… He wasn't sure how to finish that sentence, actually.

"How about I buy you dinner at Moonrise?" he asked.

"You know, people are going to start talking," Meg returned as they walked, her face turned away from him so he couldn't see her expression or decipher the out-of-place note in her voice.

"Well, they'll talk a lot more when it becomes obvious you're pregnant."

"It won't bother you that the New Benton gossip mill will be whispering 'Goat Girl is pregnant and she's been spending an awful lot of time with that upstanding Wainwright boy'?"

He stopped midstride because he hadn't really thought about that. That was exactly what the women at his parents' church would whisper to each other, and certainly purposefully loud enough for his parents to overhear. Because Mom had bragged endlessly about his success, and Dad had probably been worse.

Yeah, he really hadn't thought of that.

"Wow, you went a little pale. Sorry. Figured you already assumed."

"No, I hadn't. In fact, I only just came to the realization that I have to tell my family."

It was her turn to grow pale, and she looked at him with those lost, wide eyes that he thought truly might end up haunting him someday.

"Family," she whispered solemnly, as though he'd chanted some ancient curse that would send them all to purgatory.

"Well, that's what we'll do," he said resolutely, making the decision quickly. He wouldn't spring it on his family yet, but it was time they at least got acquainted with the idea of Meg.

"Wait—what?"

"We'll go have dinner at my family's house."

She took a big step away from him. "Oh no. No."

"We won't tell them about the baby yet. Even married couples tend to wait until the first trimester is over. But this way they can meet you, and…"

"And you can give them the impression this wasn't a drunk hookup with Goat Girl?"

He frowned. That wasn't what he'd been thinking. Not exactly. "Don't you think it's better to meet each other's family and at least get somewhat acquainted before we say, 'Hey, guess what, your next grandchild is on the way and parented by this random stranger!'"

Meg blew out a breath. "No. No. A million times no. You're not meeting my family."

She said it with such finality his jaw dropped. "Ever?" She was...what? Embarrassed of *him*? "You think they won't like me?"

She laughed, a very sharp kind of laugh with bitter edges. "They'd love you. God, they'd love every last inch of you." She sobered, and her eyes were suspiciously shiny, and Charlie had to wonder if hormones were at play, because this made no sense to him.

She cleared her throat. "I don't have much interaction with them. They wouldn't let me into my grandmother's funeral. We're not close. I'm not even sure I'll tell them."

"You won't tell them you're having a kid? Their grandchild?"

She hugged herself then and turned her back to him, beginning to take long, quick strides toward the house. "I...don't know," she said, every syllable of each word wrapped in pain.

He felt it like his own. Which was new. He tended to be able to look at other people's problems fairly rationally and unemotionally. He was a fixer, and sure, he did want to fix this, this pain, this hurt. But he also wanted to protect her from the people who'd hurt her, to find them and hurt them back. This feeling must have to do with the fact that she was carrying his child. A protective-ness-by-proxy type of thing.

She stepped into the house and he followed, wanting to soothe the tension wrapped around her shoulders, visible in the way she still hugged herself tight.

He wanted to be the one doing the hugging.

Very, very out of the ordinary, and if things weren't *so* out of the ordinary that he was secretly waging a campaign for marriage and stability, he would have ignored it. But a partner, a husband, a coparent was someone who would act on that obvious need for comfort.

Which was very confusing, all in all. Wanting to, but not wanting to, but thinking it was the right thing to do.

He felt scrambled, and he wasn't used to that either. So it seemed like a good plan of action to reach out and touch her shoulders, to gently guide her into the circle of his arms and patiently, pla-tonically, hug her.

She was still stiff, but incrementally she fell against him. She softened. She leaned. A warmth he'd never experienced before bloomed at the center of his chest. Because for as much as Charlie led and made the right choices, people didn't…lean on him. People didn't accept comfort *from* him. No one had ever looked to him for that.

He was often viewed as too hard, too contained, too condescending for *comfort*—the giving or receiving of it. He'd always thought that was a good way to be. So no one ever looked at him and thought of him as *weak* or *wrong*.

But if he'd missed out on this, this warmth and comfort and *goodness*, well, he really had been missing out.

She sighed against his chest, and he rubbed his palm up and down her back.

"I hadn't really thought about it either," she said at long length. "Telling my family. They're not a part of my life." One of her hands slid between them, resting over her stomach, her knuckles brushing right above the fly of his jeans.

Which took warm comfort to a different place in his head, and he had to concentrate very hard on her words and not on the proximity of her hand to his crotch.

"I don't think I want Seedling to know them."

"Are they really that awful?"

She tipped her head back, searching his face for something, and if he knew what she was searching for, he'd find a way to offer it. Which was also an odd feeling, because very rarely did he offer things purely for the sake of the other person.

"Maybe you wouldn't think so," she said in a quiet voice, so incongruous to the woman with the bright smiles and easy, joking manner. "But they made a practice out of making me feel unworthy, like I was nobody. I will protect my child from that with everything I am."

He pressed his palm to her cheek, wishing he knew more, understood more. Wishing they had gone about this the *right* way instead of the drunken one-night stand, to pregnancy, to finally getting to know each other way.

"Then of course I think they're terrible."

"Even if you would've agreed with them, that I'm unworthy? That there's something wrong with me? I broke all their rules, I acted out, I covered my body in tattoos, as brightly as I possibly could, in defiance, all so they'd forever have to look at me and be reminded of the *bad choices* I'd made."

He rubbed a palm down the length of her arm, her sky, her sun, the little birds in the distance of this big picture of…peace, he realized. She'd been searching for peace. And sunshine. Light. She'd put it on her skin, where she could keep it forever.

"How old were you?"

"Old?"

"Age. It matters. How old were you when you

did all this stuff? Defied your parents. Acted out. Were you a dumb teenager? Or was it last year?"

She pressed her lips together, but they curved as though trying to push away a smile.

"Charlie, I need you to do something."

"Anything." And that was true.

"I need you to forget everything we said this morning about ignoring the attraction, about doing what's best for Seedling, and I need—let me repeat that—I *need* you to kiss me."

There was some glimmer of rational Charlie, somewhere deep, deep down, telling him not to. He heard it dimly, beneath the steady pounding of his heart, beneath the sea of *want* her words— her need—unleashed in him.

Then her mouth was on his and that voice was thoroughly silenced.

HER FAMILY HAD always made her feel reckless. Reckless and edgy and needy. They turned her into a mess of a girl, even far away, even as an adult.

She'd send them a thank-you note if Charlie kept kissing her like she was the air he needed to breathe, touching her like everything about her was *necessary*.

The opposite of wrong and unworthy. Definitely not a nobody. She felt *right*, she felt endlessly *deserving* of his attention, and oh, he made her feel like a somebody. Yes, his kiss reached in, did all of those things, and she wanted more.

She *needed* more. Like a drug, like a drink. She was already living with the consequences of one unprotected, drunken hookup; she might as well have a sober, fill-her-up-with-light-and-worth hookup.

She could feel him pulling away, probably coming to his senses, but she wasn't ready for that. So she dipped her hands under his shirt, grazed her fingertips around the waistband of his pants. Skin to skin, the reminder or knowledge that despite being very *businesslike*, his body was hard. *Honed.*

No matter how she tried, she couldn't remember what it had been like. To touch him, to kiss him, to be with him. "What do you remember about that night?" she asked, trailing her fingers up his chest, the warmth of his body heat enveloping her arms in the cocoon of his shirt.

"I think I remember you had a birthmark." His eyebrows puzzled together, like he wasn't certain of the memory at first. But then his gaze homed onto her chest, exactly where the small brown splotch hid beneath her shirt.

He dipped his index finger under the hem of her shirt and dragged the material upward, trailing the point of his finger up the center of her stomach, then chest.

"Right…there," he said when it was finally visible.

One fingertip, a gentle graze, and she thought she might vibrate until she fell apart. She understood what he meant now, after the kiss this morning. Because wanting to remember had been driving her crazy, but she was beginning to think knowing might actually be worse.

In the best possible way.

"I guess that's something," she said.

"And," he continued, his voice low and smooth, "I remember that you smelled like your soap. The owl one."

"That's lemon verbena."

His mouth curved, and she thought that could be her new addiction. To watch his lips take that slow, meaningful upward curve. Never a flash, never a grin, just an easy slide into a smile.

"Right. Lemon verbena." His finger was still holding her shirt up, the tip of it pressed against the small birthmark.

Everything centered there. Her heartbeat, the shivering feeling under her skin, the heat. All of it pulsing where his one fingertip pressed, and she could hardly get in a decent breath, or let out one. Because everything had shrunk down to this.

One by one, the rest of his fingertips touched down just below her breast, and he used both hands to pull the shirt over her head. He slid his fingertips down her arms, then up her sides, and his eyes drank her in as if every inch of her mattered.

Something inside her shook at that, but she ignored it and stepped closer to him, taking his shirt off exactly the same way he'd removed hers—letting her fingertips graze as much of his skin as she could, taking her time over the dips and ridges of muscle. Slow. Deliberate.

When she managed to drag her gaze from his deliciously *honed* upper body, those dark eyes met hers with a fierceness and intensity that made her think of something exploding. A small blaze cracking at once into engulfing inferno.

Before she'd realized what was happening, their mouths were fused. Desperately. The kiss was fierce, like it was everything they were capable of together. Holding on to each other, drowning in each other. His fingers tangled in her hair, hers pressed into his shoulders, each hanging on tighter than they had any right to.

They had *no* rights to each other, but she couldn't help feeling as though Charlie were *hers*. *Mine*. Brought to her by some magic of fortune—a fortune she'd spent most of her life certain had overlooked her.

Until goats. Until this baby. Until Charlie.

Gratitude and fear and hope and absolute desperation swamped her so hard she had to break the kiss simply to breathe, but he pressed his forehead to hers, his hands bracketing her cheeks, his fingers still tangled in her hair, that dark gaze overwhelmingly *sure*.

Half of her was desperate to stop, to bolt, but half of her thought it would kill her to step away. His gaze held hers, a considering, thoughtful, slow and weighted study.

Like if he looked hard enough, he could unwind every piece of her. See into everything.

That word—*everything*—landed heavy in her gut. So hard, so out of the blue she had to hold on to him to keep upright.

She could never let him see everything. She knew where that would lead. No matter how many sweet words he gave her *now*, when he actually knew…

He couldn't know. Ever. She didn't share her past with people, because those first few times before she'd been clean for good—for *good*—she saw the way people's estimation of her changed. Even nice people. Even people she'd thought were safe.

She'd never planned to tell Charlie *all* the details of her past, but it was clear she couldn't tell him anything. Not really. He could never know the things she'd done, the mistakes she'd made. How many times it had taken her to get it right.

It would change everything. He wouldn't look at her like this. He wouldn't ever step back when she needed him to. He wouldn't look at her like she was a wonder, because he would certainly know she wasn't.

She was screwed up. Broken. *No, not anymore.* She was here, wasn't she? She was here. And she had to keep not being screwed up, for their child.

Oh *God.* No, he couldn't know. It would forever condemn her to being less in his eyes, not just as a person, but as a parent, and she couldn't do it. No matter what they did *here*, he was a part of her life. Her child's life. Not someone she could cast off as she'd tried to cast off her family.

He would always be there. The father of her child.

She couldn't possibly survive knowing he would look at her like her family looked at her. That he might not trust her, that he might always *wonder* if she was truly strong enough to be a mother.

"Did you change your mind?" he asked gently. Too gently. Like she was fragile, and worthy of not being broken. Like he cared, like he would fix whatever was wrong. Like he *could* fix anything.

But she didn't want a fixer. Or anyone who thought she needed fixing. She wanted that moment when he'd touched her like she was *everything.* She would rise to that everything. She would mold herself into the woman she'd need to be.

"No." She wanted this. She wanted *him.* She

wanted that feeling he gave her, and she was beginning to realize she'd hide a lot of things, agree to a lot of things, if it allowed those feelings to grow. "Consider this our finger snap," she said, brushing her lips across his jaw.

"Finger...?"

She snapped her fingers, like he had when he was talking about interoffice attraction, and he huffed out a laugh. "Ah."

But then he lowered his mouth to hers, pulled her closer, until they were skin to skin, until nothing existed except whatever it was that leaped between them.

## *CHAPTER FOURTEEN*

THERE WERE PROBABLY better ways to go about doing this. Better options, better roads to take at this particular juncture.

But Charlie couldn't think of any of them. All he could think of was the soft press of her skin against him, under his palms. Everywhere he touched, she was soft and smooth and warm and inviting, and half covered in inky colorful swirls.

It didn't detract from her beauty in the least. The tattoos seemed to be part of her, entities she'd been born with. The sun that shone from her shoulder across the bright blue sky and birds and vibrant white of clouds below. The rainbow of curling lines on her leg. Bursts of color and beauty. Surely this woman who made the reasonable, rational part of his brain roll over and die was a mythical creature.

She smelled like no woman had ever smelled, felt like no woman had ever felt, and where was reason when he was drowning in something bigger than himself? Why would he *want* to find it?

She pulled away, just a fraction, but it wasn't

like a few minutes ago when she'd stilled and looked at him with a kind of frantic worry, before her gaze had held his and she'd calmed. Relaxed.

As if he was the answer to something she'd been searching for. "Come with me," she said, taking one of his hands and interlocking their fingers. She pulled him deeper into the cottage, to a heavy old door that looked original to the aging house around him.

She stepped into the room, smaller than even the bedroom in his apartment, filled almost entirely by a large bed—unmade, mismatched sheets and quilts, a few random items of clothing littering the surface.

It could have been littered with porcupines and it would have looked inviting. As long as she was the one leading him onto it.

She'd slipped out of her shoes in the kitchen, and he toed off his while she shoved half the blankets off the bed and onto the floor. He didn't even cringe at the careless, sloppy move.

She must have cast some kind of spell on him. One he would willingly be swayed by—over and over again. Because he'd never felt this restless kind of want. Never been buoyed by feeling or emotion or needing something this badly. It was new and so bright and vibrant he wanted to follow wherever it would lead.

It felt imperative to get on that bed, to have her

beneath him or over him, just near him—touching as much of him that could be touched. She must have had the same thought, because they scrambled onto the bed together, reaching for each other's pants and working to get them off, laughing when their limbs got tangled in the effort.

"Okay, you get your pants off, I'll get mine," she said, her voice as breathless as her laugh, her smile as beautiful as anything he'd ever seen.

And so he did as she instructed and divested himself of his jeans and boxers as quickly as humanly possible, turning to her just as she was kicking off her pants.

She rolled to him, mouth curved into that smile that spoke of some joy he'd never found—in all his life—but then there it was. As if it was something he'd been searching for.

As if she was.

He ran his fingers through her tangled mess of blond hair. "*How* are you so perfect?" Every place the sun had marked her skin, every place she was pale, every place that featured swirled color and pictures. Every part of her—perfect.

She stilled for a moment, and he thought he'd done something wrong, but then she all but melted into him. Her body, her mouth, and there were no answers for such an abstract question, but it didn't matter.

Because she was, and she was in the circle of

his arms, moving against him, until he rolled her over onto her back, leveraging himself above her. She arched against him, and everything centered to where they would meet. Where he would lose himself in her. He'd never been one for losing, but this would be a lot like winning too.

He traced the curve of her shoulders, the gentle weight of her breasts, trying to memorize every inch of her, torturing himself by resisting the way she arched against him, resisting the inevitable until it would become irresistible.

He wanted to stretch these moments out until they felt like hours, days, forever. He didn't know who this idiotic voice in his head was, but he kind of liked it. He liked not feeling like Upstanding Charlie Wainwright, Former Vice President of National Accounts, for once in his life. He was just a guy, totally, stupidly enamored of this woman.

He smiled as his hands trailed over her body, he couldn't help it. Who knew it could be possible, let alone feel *amazing*, to do something so completely out of character. Of course, sex was involved, so probably a lot of people knew that particular change. And she was smiling up at him, and that was as intoxicating as the smoothness of her skin, the warmth of her below him, moving against him, trying to egg him on.

He kept touching her, because she was infinitely

touchable, her scent—that *lemon verbena*—everywhere, and he wanted it to always be everywhere.

His hands reached her stomach and they stilled there, because the reason they were even together just then was what grew inside there. He rested his palm on her belly, surprised by all the different ways and places this could fell him all over again.

A child. His.

She rested her hand on top of his, the warmth of it spreading through him differently than her nakedness underneath him did.

*Their child.*

Their eyes locked, and he lifted her hand from where it covered his to his mouth, turning it over and pressing a kiss to her palm—hoping the kiss vibrated through her the way it did him. Then he kissed her belly, and up. To her shoulder, her neck, her jaw, and then to the soft sigh of her mouth.

Slowly, with more patience and presence than he'd ever wanted, let alone had, he slid inside the heat of her, drowning in how right it felt to be joined just this way.

What had started in a blast of heat softened into something else entirely. Slow. Deliberate. Something like a promise, though he didn't have a clue what it held.

So he just moved with her, letting the pressure and those feelings he couldn't name build.

Letting everything that didn't make an inch of sense *happen*, because nothing about him and Meg made much sense, but it was happening.

It was the best thing to happen to him in a very long time. It was that thought he held on to as they fell over the edge together.

MEG HAD CRIED after sex before, but it had always been regret crying. *Why did I do that?* crying. The tears currently burning her eyes as she attempted to blink them back had nothing to do with those feelings.

She wasn't even *sad*. She was awed. That something could feel good and important and big, and at the same time be scary as all get-out. But when it was over, she didn't want to run. She wanted to wallow in it for a very long time.

His arm, which was curled around her shoulders, pulled her closer, and she leaned her forehead into the crook of his neck, slowing her breathing until it was in time with his.

She wasn't exactly sure what had happened— or why. Or rather, if it had happened only because the life they'd created carried so much weight between them, but sex had never been like that for her before. Not sweet and slow, not drowning kisses and reverent touches. Not a slow build to amazing release.

What had just happened with Charlie was a

*revelation*, and she wasn't even bothered that talking about her parents and how they made her feel had started it. She didn't feel destructive or defeated, because it had been *beautiful*.

For the first time, she allowed herself to hope. To hope that she and Charlie could create something beautiful between them. She allowed herself to hope that things happened for a reason, and they'd come together as much to create a life as to build one together.

*Way to get ahead of yourself, Meg.*

Yeah, she really needed to tone that down. It wasn't out of the question; she just needed to rein herself in. They needed to build a really solid foundation. So that nothing could crumble and fall apart. If she was going to build something with Charlie, it was imperative that things last for as long as it was the best thing for Seedling.

Which meant she also needed to make sure she eradicated any pieces of her life that might allow Charlie to find out who she'd been, and what she'd done, and how many times she'd failed.

She'd done that mostly already. Moving out here into the country, building a whole new life with whole new people. She'd have to make sure there were no loose ends. She could do that.

Charlie's hand came to rest on her stomach, and she wasn't sure if that should bother her or not, on an intellectual level or even a vain one, but mostly it made her feel mushy and wonderful, and that he had so much potential to be a good father.

That, above all—except maybe her being a good mother—was what she wanted for the baby they'd created. Parents who would care. Who would put the child's needs first. Who would never, ever use a life as a pawn.

"When's your next doctor's appointment?" he asked, his voice low and sleepy.

"Oh, end of the month. I'll be ten weeks and they do a viability ultrasound thing." She hated that word. *Viability.* Everything about this baby was *viable*, thank you very much.

"Viability? That sounds terrifying."

Meg smiled and snuggled closer, every part of her vibrating with this hope thing. It seemed no matter how different they were on the surface, they were very much alike where it counted.

"I know. But we'll be able to see Seedling. An actual picture."

His arms tightened around her, and it didn't even occur to her that she'd used the word *we* until he pressed a meaningful kiss to her temple.

"I have the date and time written down on a card on the fridge. It's not until eleven that day, which means I'll be insufferable with nerves and angst all morning."

"Hmm." His finger trailed up her leg, from knee to hip, until she shivered. "Well, I'll just have to distract you."

"I could probably deal with that," she said, grinning at him. She rested her palm against his short beard. "So, is this a fashion statement or some kind of unemployed protest?"

"I'm not unemployed," he replied with enough of an indignant tone to make it funny instead of defensive.

"We should probably talk hours. Payment. I'm your boss now, after all."

In an easy move, he had her pinned again, looming over her. She liked that. A lot.

"I am your *peon*, Ms. Carmichael."

She grinned at him, at the flash of humor, at this side of Charlie she never would have guessed if she'd been forced to decide based on her first impression. That he could be funny and sweet and genuine.

"You could stay," she whispered, feeling the weight of it. She was asking him for something, and a rejection would…

Oh, crap, it would really hurt. She thought she'd been chasing those feelings of importance, of being valuable, worthy, but maybe she'd been setting herself up for failure.

*No.* No. Because failure wasn't allowed anymore.

"I'll stay," he murmured, dropping a kiss to her forehead.

Tears welled up again, but she blinked them back with a smile on her face.

## CHAPTER FIFTEEN

THERE WAS A GOAT standing on Meg's head. It was such a bizarre thing Charlie didn't even know what to say in greeting.

"Now, Ziti, you'll get your turn for treats. Being a little butt isn't going to change that."

"You…talk to your goats?"

Her head whipped around to face him, and the goat neighed irritably. But it did not remove its paws or hooves or whatever from the top of Meg's head. "Charlie! Jeez. You scared me. I thought you were still asleep."

"Sorry," he said, hesitantly stepping toward the goat. "Can I help? Are you stuck?"

She smiled indulgently, which gave him the oddest feeling of being out of his element. Something he pretty much never was. Except here. With her.

"I'm fine. Ziti is mad I didn't let her go first. She ate my bracelet, so she's in trouble."

"So, you talk to *and* punish your goats."

"I do," she said primly, reaching behind her to give the goat a gentle nudge so its hooves fell to the ground, and she stood up from the stool she'd been sitting on. "It's how you keep a goat herd healthy and happy, Charlie."

"Right. Of course." In crazy-ville. He'd never thought he'd be a willing participant in crazy-ville, but here he was…spending more nights with her than not over the past week. Helping out on a goat farm in the mornings and evenings, spending his afternoons consulting with Cara and Wes, Mia and Dell, studying up on small businesses and agriculture and farmers' markets.

Of all damn things.

Every morning he woke up with the strangest feeling in his chest. Something akin to joy. He was only a little worried about himself.

"I've actually been thinking about adding to the herd so I could expand, offer goat milk cheese at the market. I've been testing how to make it." She touched her stomach lightly as the goat she called Ziti butted her gently in the thigh. "Although I guess I should wait on any of that."

"I've spent the past week researching small business things. More for Cara, because I do have some grocery contacts. I could help if you want to start some kind of foundation, a plan for after."

"Grocery," she repeated dully, seemingly going pale in front of his eyes.

"What's wro—"

"Who's Cara?" she demanded before he could

ask, before he could step toward her and soothe away that odd break. She was sitting back on her stool, moving the goat that had been on top of her into the little contraption she used to hold them still while she milked.

"Who's…? She's my sister-in-law's sister. Cara's Pies. Remember?"

"Oh. Right. Yeah."

It was an odd question, but it made him think it might be good for Meg to meet Cara and Mia. She didn't seem to have any friends, and she'd straight-up said she wouldn't tell her family. She needed someone, and as much as he wanted to be that someone, the pregnancy stuff, some of that might be better with someone who'd actually been through it.

"You know, they're both pregnant. And Mia, my sister-in-law, this is her second. The three of you actually have a lot in common. We should all have dinner or something. Yes, we should do that."

"Oh. Well."

"Cara even has a tattoo," he teased. "You're like two peas in a pod."

"Where, exactly?"

"Pardon?"

She turned her head, though she kept working with her hands on the goat. "Where is *Cara's* tattoo?" she asked, enunciating each word with more force than necessary.

It suddenly dawned on him what these strange questions meant. It pleased him too, though maybe it shouldn't. "Are you jealous?"

"Of course not!" She whipped her head back to the goat.

Because he was so irrationally pleased, he felt like soothing her rather than teasing further. "Cara is completely not my type. She was kind of a permanent screwup growing up, more interested in partying than being responsible."

Her shoulders tensed, and even though she didn't turn to face him this time, he had an idea of the kind of hurt or maybe even pissed expression he'd see in those blue eyes. Because that had come out all wrong. It also made it clear how little he knew about what she'd done growing up, aside from feel alienated from her family and, of course, the tattoos.

"But she's a brunette. Never been attracted to brunettes," he offered, hoping to break the tension with a joke. Why, he had no idea. He was terrible at *jokes*.

She stood, taking a pail of milk over to the counter. Her lips kind of quirked, though that hint of hurt didn't leave her eyes. He wanted to soothe it away, but he didn't know how.

"I'm a natural brunette," she intoned, working to consolidate the morning's milk production.

He stood, immobilized over how badly he'd botched this, until she looked at him and laughed.

"Charlie, I'm *joking*."

Maybe about the hair, he thought, but there was something under this entire interaction that wasn't a joke. It wasn't even jealousy. But he didn't know *what* it was, and that was irritating.

"Listen, I have plans in town this morning," she said. "I can't show you the ropes until ten."

"What plans?"

She busied herself with the milk. "Personal plans."

Something burned through him, something he didn't particularly want to address or name, but since he'd done both when she'd been jealous, he couldn't ignore it.

He was jealous too. He wanted to know what she was doing. He wanted to know her *personal* plans and all her plans, and it had as little to do with his desire to maneuver her into marriage as sleeping with her did.

Once she was done with the milk, she turned and looked at him, everything about her closed off and… He didn't know the right word. She just seemed *off*, and he didn't know what to do about it. He really hated not knowing what to do.

But all his brain could think was she had *personal* plans she wasn't going to tell him about.

"I suppose I don't have any right to know your plans."

She cocked her head, eyes narrowing a fraction. "No, you don't have any *right*." Then she let out a gusty sigh. "Do you know Elsie Riley?"

He thought through his mental list of names, before it clicked. "Dan's wife."

"Yes."

"Dan, who you're friends with?" He remembered those moments in the cab, when Dan had been *nice* to Meg, and kind of a dick to him. Charlie couldn't even be irritated by it now. He was glad for it. That there was someone who would stand up for her.

"Yes."

"You know, she used to waitress at Moonrise. She never failed to berate my tipping—and I'm a *very* generous tipper, Meg."

Her smile spread across her face like sunrise. "Hmm. I don't know if I believe that," she said as playfully as she'd spoken all morning. "Anyway, I have breakfast with her on Tuesdays. I bring her soap and food and we talk."

"So she's your friend."

"Yes."

"Good. I was worried you didn't have any."

She raised her eyebrow, but he refused to feel bad about it. "You never mention anyone," he continued. "You're isolated out here. I'm simply glad you have someone to talk to."

"So you don't need to introduce me to your sister-in-law and her sister. I do have friends."

She didn't say it like a question, but it felt like one. It felt like hurt, and he didn't know how he was stepping in it this morning, over and over. "I'd still like to introduce you to them, to my family. For a variety of reasons."

She looked away from him, crossing her arms over her chest. She looked teary and confused and hurt and he couldn't figure out what he'd done, what he possibly could have done to hurt her.

"What kind of grocery contacts do you have?" she asked in a whispery voice, her gaze on the side of the barn opposite him.

He cocked his head. Man, she was *confusing* this morning. "I sold food containers. I supplied pretty much every grocery store in the St. Louis area with the containers they use for salad bars, delis, et cetera. Why?"

She swallowed and closed her eyes.

"What is bothering you, Meg? Tell me."

"I just feel weird today." She shook her head, finally bringing her gaze back to his with a rueful smile. "I don't know what's wrong with me." She shrugged, then forced a smile that had none of the same light as before, but she stepped toward him and brushed a kiss over his mouth. "I need to go clean up before I head over to Elsie's. Why don't we skip today, and you can come back tonight?" She grinned slyly, brushing her mouth against the corner of his mouth, once, twice.

He bit back a groan and tried to focus on the here and now. He had to clear his throat to speak. "I can clean up here."

"But…"

"You've been teaching me how, haven't you?"

"Yes, but you don't have to do that. You've put in far more hours than I'm going to be paying you for."

"I'm not worried about the money. I just want to help."

She swallowed, audibly, visibly. He brushed his fingertips over the unruly hair at her temple. "What's wrong, sweetheart?"

It struck him that he'd never used endearments like that, even with the woman he'd figured he'd marry eventually. Endearments didn't roll off his tongue.

But with Meg they did. Of course they did.

"I feel like crying and raging for no good reason," she said emphatically, those tears still shimmering in her eyes. "And if this isn't hormones, then I'm possibly losing my mind."

"We'll go with hormones, then."

"Yes, let's." She kissed him again, lingering this time, and he was more than happy to linger in that.

"Thank you for being a…good guy."

He'd been given a lot of labels in his life. Responsible. Serious. Rule follower. Hard. Cold. But he wasn't sure he'd ever been called *good* in this sense, and it warmed something in him. He wanted to be good like she thought. So he would be.

"WELL, WHAT'S WRONG with you?"

Meg was beginning to think she would never again walk over the threshold of the Riley house without bursting into tears. She couldn't seem to keep any reserves intact when Elsie *looked* at her and *knew*.

She was a mess. Every time she thought she'd stitched the remains of her tattered self together, Elsie stripped them down.

"Come on now. Sit on the couch and tell me what's wrong." Elsie's hand, stronger with every passing week, curled over Meg's arm and led her to the couch. She took the food and fussed over it, letting Meg sob her guts out.

"I should be doing that," Meg said through sniffles once she found the strength to speak.

"Nonsense. The doctor gave me a clean bill yesterday. I can putter about again. Even said I could go for walks, long as I was with somebody and we kept 'em short. My strength is coming back. So, you sit down and tell me what's the matter."

Her mother used to demand the same thing. "Tell me what's the matter…" Except it would always end with "with you."

Elsie's demand never ended that way.

Meg took a steadying breath. She hadn't been lying to Charlie earlier when she said this was hormones. This felt so much bigger, so much more frantic than she'd felt in years.

"Charlie…"

"That boy hurting you?" Elsie's shoulders went back, and Meg could believe the doctor said she was regaining strength. She looked like she'd bowl over anyone in her path. "I will tan his hide. I'll send Dan over there with his baseball bat and—"

"He's *wonderful*, Elsie. It hurts how wonderful."

"Well, now." Elsie straightened her shirt, then took a seat next to Meg on the couch, opening the tray of muffins Meg had brought over from Moonrise. "That's a whole other thing, isn't it?"

"He wants me to meet his family. He wants to introduce me to all these people." And she wanted to keep him all to herself. Keep them all to themselves too. She knew what happened when you got families involved. Even if his was lovely, they'd have things to say about her.

*Grocery contacts.* He had *grocery* contacts. He'd sold supplies to *grocery* stores, and it had been like every piece of joy she'd been feeling over the past week of being with him, of thinking they had some weird possible future, had burned to ash when she'd heard he had that kind of connection to her father's business.

"And you're…upset by this?" Elsie asked carefully, not so subtly pushing a muffin toward Meg. Funny, really, always pushing food at each other, always comforting each other.

She was awed by these people who could take her in and take care of her and think it was just the way it should be. Did she hide the screwed-up pieces of herself *that* well? Or was she not as screwed up as she'd thought?

*Of course you're as screwed up as you think.* "I'm sure he means well, but he doesn't understand."

"Understand what?"

"How can he introduce me to these nice, lovely people who raised someone like *him*? So they can look at *me* with my tattoos and my…getting knocked up and…" She was going to cry again. How were there so many tears and emotions still buried in there? Hadn't she expelled them all yet?

"I know the Pruitts and the Wainwrights, Meg. They're good people. Whatever you're dredging up, it isn't fair to put it on their shoulders."

"You don't understand."

Elsie really didn't. She didn't see it—see that deep down she was screwed up and flawed and always one step away from failure. Elsie didn't know all the times she'd fallen.

"If you think you aren't as good as those people, you need to take a good hard look at yourself, young lady."

"Elsie, I—"

"No, ma'am. You will see here. It takes a goodness to come have breakfast with me every Tuesday morning. It has lit up my *life*, and I have worried less about my inevitable end, and Dan has worried less, and I am healing, baby, and it is because you have given me hope and companionship."

Meg didn't have anything to say to that. How could she have *anything* to say?

"You know the best thing you can give that child of yours?"

"The knowledge I'll do whatever it takes to keep him safe and happy?"

"It's the mistake we make, thinking parenthood is all about the kids. All about giving them what we didn't have. I think when we do that, when we bend over and over doing that, we twist something in them. I only had one, I guess I don't know, but I've spent a whole lot of time thinking about where I went wrong."

"Elsie—"

"Don't interrupt my wisdom, child. The best thing you can do as a mother is to believe you are doing your best. The belief that *you* are worthy of being considered a good parent. You're as good as anybody. Nobody gets to tell you you're not, sweetheart. And you shouldn't be the one telling yourself that either. You tell yourself that, you try to be perfect *for* that child, you're hurting both of you."

*Sweetheart.* Charlie had said that to her this morning. *What's wrong, sweetheart?* She hadn't had the words for how hearing the word *grocery* come off his lips had shattered everything inside her.

It was truly amazing how certain words could turn to poison.

"He knows my father," she whispered, because wasn't that really what this was all about? She could transfer those feelings into nerves over meeting people who were important to him, but the real thing, the heart of the matter and the freak-out was that.

"Charlie knows your father?"

Meg nodded and swallowed, the panic from this morning building again. "He worked with him. Maybe not directly. But close. He said he sold to grocery stores and…"

The silence that grew had Meg closing her eyes, bracing for the impact. She knew what came next.

"Oh, sweet Lord, girl. You're *that* Carmichael?"

How often had someone asked her that? It was a common enough name, but the stores were everywhere. Everyone who lived in the St. Louis area had been to a Carmichael Grocery. It was a tradition, an institution, and so was her family. People were always asking or wondering. *Are you* that *Carmichael?*

"No offense, Meg, but you don't dress like a woman with that kind of money."

"I don't have *that* kind of money. My parents do. And they made sure they kept me from just about all of it when I started my...rebellious phase."

"You know, I used to wonder if Dan and I made more, had more, if we could have kept Hannah clean."

"That, Elsie, I can almost guarantee you, isn't true. My parents paid for a few fancy treatment places, but it never mattered. You know why?"

Elsie shook her head, eyes shiny with tears.

"Because they didn't love me and they made sure I knew it. Because I knew even if I got clean, I'd never be more than a failure in their eyes. Every mistake I ever made they took as a personal insult, and I took that as a slap. A bruise. Which isn't even their fault. They were...just raised that way, to see only what was on the outside. So, whatever is keeping your daughter on that path, it isn't you and it isn't money. It's something in her, and until she sees it..."

"What got you to see it?" Elsie asked, her voice

almost a whisper, and it was like they'd traded places, wisdom for wisdom.

"I guess I realized—no, accepted—they weren't ever going to love me. But my grandma did, and I was hurting her by doing this to myself. She wanted more for me. She loved me even when I made mistakes, even when I looked strange or said the wrong thing. No matter what, she held my hand and pulled me through. She got me out of it, away from it—which did have to do with money, I'll grant you—but she helped me get somewhere I could really get my head on straight and heal."

There was a long, weighted silence.

"But then she died," Meg whispered, knowing there was some lesson she needed to learn here, but not being able to see it. Not yet. "And I fell off the wagon a little. So…maybe I wasn't healed."

Which meant there was still a lot of healing to go.

# CHAPTER SIXTEEN

"MEG? ARE YOU READY? I told Mom we'd be there at six." Charlie paced the kitchen, Meg's tendency for not being ready when they had to leave wasn't so much annoying as it was... Okay, it was annoying.

Instead of snapping or making snide comments, as he might have in the past, and probably would've now if she wasn't carrying his child, he tried to find ways to *manage* his irritation.

It wasn't working tonight, probably because he'd rather feel irritated than nervous. Nerves were not something he dealt with well. Because this was all outside his control.

He really didn't like that.

She finally stepped out of her room, smoothing her palms down the front of her shirt. "How do I look?" she asked, nervousness emanating from every last inch of her.

"Beautiful, always, but I think you're going to be awfully hot in that. We're going to be outside barbecuing."

She fiddled with the cuff of her long-sleeved

shirt. "I just thought I probably shouldn't show off my tattoos."

He raised an eyebrow, because not once in the past few weeks had she been self-conscious about her appearance. He wasn't sure what reaction his parents would have to her, though his siblings would be *endlessly* amused she was who he'd brought home. Tattoos and goats and farmers' markets.

"Let's just go, huh?" she said, gesturing toward the door.

"You'll boil to death. I don't think that's good for the baby."

"But otherwise you *would* encourage me to cover up my tattoos?"

He took a deep breath in, let it out, tried to remember how he'd dealt with frustrating customers. "You can stop *picking* at me anytime, Meg."

"I told you I didn't want to do this. But you set it up anyway."

"You never *expressly* told me that."

"You could have asked. Or, here's a shocking thought, respected my choice. Trusted my judgment."

He didn't yell. He wouldn't yell. He was a composed, rational person, and she was pregnant. So he *had* to be the composed, rational one.

"You should meet them. You should meet them now. And more important," he started, evenly, calmly—or not at all calmly—digging his fingers into his palms with the effort of it, "I think you will find a group of people who could be something of an extended support network for you. Which I would think you'd want."

"Why would I want…?" She shook her head, whatever she was going to say lost in an expression of misery. "This feels like a lot of pressure and I'm not particularly great in the face of social pressure, specifically."

The hint of vulnerability snuck under his defenses and he crossed to her, resting his hands on her shoulders and giving her a gentle squeeze. "Don't be nervous, they'll love you. The only ones who might not say much to you are Wes and Mia's father, and that isn't personal. They're just quiet. My sister is probably going to *descend* upon you."

"I just…" She blinked up at him. "I wouldn't want you to regret introducing us. Or feel strange. I know I probably don't look anything like anyone you might've taken home in the past. And that doesn't matter to me, but it might matter to them."

"I think that's crap."

"Huh?"

"I think it obviously matters to you or you wouldn't be acting like this meek version of yourself. You aren't meek, and you have nothing to be ashamed of."

She blew out a breath, and it clutched something hard in his chest to see that underneath all those irritating questions, she just looked terrified.

He didn't want that. He didn't want his choices to *scare* anyone. He wanted to move forward, to put things into motion, to make *sense* of what the future held.

She pushed a palm to her stomach. "What if someone notices?"

"Meg, no one can tell simply by looking at you."

"What if pregnant people can recognize each other?"

"I highly doubt it."

"You're not planning on telling anyone, right? Actually I've changed my mind. Go ahead without me. I'm staying with my goats and never leaving again." She tried to bolt, but his hands clamped harder on her shoulders.

"Are you always this dramatic?"

"When facing something I don't want to do? More often than not."

"That can't possibly be true."

"There's so much…" Again she didn't finish, she merely blew out a breath and looked miserable.

"You know, you might feel better if you actually talked to me. Whatever it is that's been bothering you lately. I don't think it's just hormones."

"I don't make good first impressions," she mumbled, looking away. "I'm forever saying the wrong thing, making the wrong joke. Especially when the people are important. When I know I need to impress someone, it's always the last thing I do."

"You don't need to impress anyone, Meg."

She rolled her eyes. "Your parents' families must have gotten along."

"Well, I suppose they did."

"It's something else entirely when they hate each other—most especially when one of the grandparents hates the mother of the child. It's like poison."

"My mother would never hate you. I don't think my mother hates *anyone*, but she certainly wouldn't hate you. There's nothing to hate."

"Aside from being the one-night stand you knocked up. And from looking like this. And… and…"

He wasn't sure he'd ever wanted to rip out his hair more, and he'd dealt with a lot of frustrating people in his life. But he focused on the fact that she *was* the woman he'd "knocked up" irresponsibly, then forced himself—over and over again—to not lose his cool.

"I'm thirty-five," he said, trying to sound calm, affable. There was no way he pulled affable off, considering he had to grit the words out between clenched teeth. "Beyond the very fact that I'm an adult and have been handling my life for well over a decade, my parents are reasonable, sensible people. Like me. We don't judge by appearance alone, Meg."

She didn't say anything to that, just stood there looking at the floor, and he wanted to shake her until she saw some sense. Instead he did the last thing he wanted to do, but the thing that seemed imperative to do.

He told her the bone-deep, soul-illuminating truth. "My family is very important to me. I will very much want them to be a part of our child's life. I promise that isn't a threat to you, as my family will treat you with nothing but respect. But even if you don't believe that promise, the only way you're ever going to find out for sure is if you come and meet them."

"I don't know a whole lot of families who aren't dysfunctional."

"I never claimed we're not a little dysfunctional. Families are littered with their own problems and issues. We're not perfect—at all, but we love each other." He loosened his grip on her shoulder and moved a hand to her abdomen.

That never failed to fill him with awe, with pride, with fear. It was the combination of feelings that had his daily search for a permanent job relegated to some dim corner of his brain.

"More important," he said, somehow feeling both freed by the feelings he was sharing with her and scared to death of how easy it was to tell her things, "they will love this baby. No matter what. Which means they would never treat you poorly, because no child deserves to see his mother treated poorly."

She stood motionless for a few ticking seconds, her blue eyes searching his as if she was hoping the truth was somewhere in their depths. Finally she placed her hand over his.

"All right. I'm sorry." She rubbed her hand over his over her stomach. "Families are hard for me."

"We're going to have to sit down at some point and discuss that in detail. You know that, right?"

Her smile was fake. "Yeah, sure."

For the first time he wondered—even if he enacted every plan, maneuvered her into marriage, even love—would he ever really know or understand the mother of his child?

He had a sinking feeling the answer was not if she could help it.

MEG COULD HAVE SWORN she was in a movie. Or a sitcom. Yes, this was an elaborate ruse and she was really in the middle of a family sitcom taping.

It wasn't that the Wainwrights and the Pruitts were perfect. There were arguments, frustrations, a two-year-old's temper tantrum when she was told she couldn't ride one of the eight dogs that ran around outside in the expanse of the Wainwright yard. No one looked perfectly coiffed—in fact, everyone was invariably mussed from some aspect of their day or another.

It was just that everything Charlie had said was true. She was treated with nothing but respect— even with his family not knowing she was pregnant. Kenzie, the little sister, was a little overzealous in her, as Charlie called it, interrogation.

But all the teasing, all the yelling, all the *things* were what she'd started to believe was a fairy tale when it came to families. Love. She'd come to the conclusion that love, aside from small doses like Grandma's, didn't exist.

Not for her.

Great. Now she was teary again. Seriously there was something wrong with her. She couldn't grasp or untangle all these emotions. They swept up and over her like a wave—which only made her feel pathetic, which only made the emotions worse.

*Ugh.*

Charlie was in some deep, involved conversation with his brother about baseball, so Meg snuck away. The food was starting to make her a little queasy anyway, and she could certainly stand a trip to the restroom.

Just for some silence. Just to get her head back on straight. Just to breathe through the fact that her child was going to have this.

*This.*

Damn it, she really was going to cry.

She hurried into the Wainwright farmhouse, which was thankfully empty. Charlie's mother had kindly shown her where everything was earlier, and complimented her on her soaps.

There had been nothing to be nervous about. The Wainwrights were exceedingly pleasant and kind.

She didn't belong.

She closed the bathroom door and leaned her head against it. They were nothing but lovely and she was *still* having an emotional breakdown.

Maybe it was just she couldn't fight the insecurities as well as she usually did because so much of her body's energy was taken up with growing a child. If her body was doing that, giving all that energy to Seedling, then she would deal with seven more months of tears and freak-outs. She just *would*.

Determined, Meg washed herself up and left the bathroom, hands on her stomach. She would be strong because this wasn't sad or scary; this was wonderful. Her baby was going to have a real, supportive family.

"Are you feeling all right?"

She should have known Charlie would notice her absence immediately. Would he ever give her the space to shore up all her insecurities and fears before he bulldozed his way in to make sure she was all right?

She knew she should be comforted or pleased by it, but she needed those defenses. She needed him to stay far away from the truth of her past. That she'd always be an insecure addict underneath it all.

*God, Meg, really. Get it together. You're clean. You're going to be a mother. You can't let yourself believe that you haven't gotten better.*

"Meg?"

She blinked at Charlie, and she so desperately wanted to tell him. To lay all the fears, all her mistakes and failures at his feet. She wanted to reveal every inch of herself, so he could reject it and she could go back to being alone.

She had no doubt he'd reject who she really was. Not after seeing this—this family and love. He would never understand the way she'd punished herself. The way she'd reached for drugs again and again because it was better than the bitter disapproval of her parents.

How would he ever be able to understand that?

His fingers brushed her cheek. "Meg, sweetheart, you have to tell me what's wrong."

That was exactly what she could never do. Not and give Seedling everything he or she deserved. "I'm just overwhelmed," she forced herself to say.

"By what?" he asked gently, an arm going around her shoulders, pulling her next to him.

She relaxed into that gesture, tried to gather

some strength from his. "They're all so wonderful. It's very disorienting."

Charlie kissed her temple, an easy, casual touch he'd probably never understand how much it meant to her. Casual, caring gestures had never been a part of her life, and he offered them without thinking.

"Do you believe me now, that they'd never judge you?"

She didn't. She understood what Charlie meant, that they didn't judge by appearances, but she also knew that if they knew everything she'd done, they'd disdain her as much as her parents did. People not knowing she'd been an addict was how she'd built this new life for herself. The more she met good, kind people like the Wainwrights and Pruitts, the more she understood that she needed people like this in her life.

And she very much needed them not to know that underneath it all, she was nothing but a conglomeration of mistakes.

But she couldn't explain that to Charlie. Not in a way he'd ever understand. They were too different. It was best to act as though her life had begun with the knowledge she was pregnant. Everything that came before was…dark. Nothing.

That would be what was best for everyone.

"I see now what you mean," she said carefully. As much as she was trying to hide her former addiction, she didn't want to *lie* to him. Not when they could be building a future.

"We should tell them," he said, giving her shoulder a squeeze. "I don't like pretending this isn't happening, and I think it'd be a good time."

She tried to back away, but he grasped both her shoulders. "No. No, I'm not ready, Charlie."

"I'm not sure you'll ever be ready, Meg." He started leading her toward the door. "But it's here, and I think we have to tell them. I promise, it'll be fine. Whatever you're worried about, it isn't important."

She was so horrified how easily he said that comment, she didn't even realize he was propelling her out the door.

"My worries *are* important," she forced herself to say, even if it came out as little more than a whisper.

He was *still* pulling her along, onto the porch, down the stairs. "Of course they are. That's not what I meant. I just mean this will be fine. I promise. Trust me. I think you need this as much as I do. Hiding it does no one in this situation any favors."

"No. No, I... No, Charlie. We can't do this. Not now."

"Give me one reason to wait. One reason why it shouldn't be right now."

She tried to think of something—anything that might sway him—but her brain went blank.

"See? It's for the best." He gave a little wave to the crowd outside. "Hey, guys, we have something to announce."

Meg closed her eyes against the wave of embarrassment. "Please don't do this, Charlie. I'm begging you."

"It'll be fine. It's the best thing to do, for both of us. You're going to see, I promise." He motioned to his family to come closer and gave them all that charming businessman smile. "Meg and I are going to have a baby."

There was a little pause of silence, then a bustle of bodies and voices. Congratulations and people touching her, surrounding them.

She tried to smile, to accept the offered congratulations, but the press of bodies and voices was too much. It was too hot in the evening sun; everything was too much.

"I...I... Excuse me. I'm not..." The jostling roll of nausea waved through her and she forced herself to weave through the group. She hurried back into the house, where there'd be cool air and space and silence and...

How could he have just *told* them, after she'd begged him not to? He'd steamrolled her.

Arms wound around her as she reached the porch, soothing words being whispered into her ear, but not Charlie's masculine voice. Feminine ones, somehow certain and reassuring, as she was led into the house.

Once inside, she was gently seated on a couch. "Get her some water. And maybe a cool washcloth."

Meg looked up at Mia, the short woman with sharp green eyes and a no-nonsense kind of surety.

"Do you need to go to the bathroom?" she asked gently.

The cool air had helped the nausea subside and Meg shook her head miserably.

Another woman, Cara, appeared with a glass of water and handed it to Meg. "Probably over-heated, poor thing. Your face is all red."

Meg tried to breathe, tried to find some thread of sanity. "I didn't want him to tell," she found herself whispering to this pair of women she didn't know. "Please tell me you're emotional messes too. That this isn't me having a nervous breakdown. It's a pregnancy thing. Please tell me it's a pregnancy thing." Because she felt like she'd had a final break with sanity.

Meg felt the couch depress on either side of her as she clutched the cool glass of water.

"Are you kidding me?" Cara said, patting her back soothingly. "My husband is permanently traumatized. It's all tears and hysterical laughter."

"I've been too busy hugging the toilet to be

emotional," Mia offered gently. "But when I was pregnant with Lainey, I was irrationally angry *all* the time."

"She really was. She almost threw a glass of water at me at my own wedding."

"I wasn't going to throw it!"

The sisters laughed and Meg managed to slowly get ahold of her tears, her crazy breathing. "I feel like a crazy person."

"That's pregnancy for you," Mia said, patting Meg's hand reassuringly. "I can almost promise you, you're not having a mental breakdown. You're just growing a human being inside you. It's a big thing. Now take a drink."

Meg obeyed. "Thank you. I'm so sorry." She shook her head. Oh, how embarrassing. "I don't know what came over me."

"You're overwhelmed, and apparently Charlie wasn't listening to you—"

"Surprise, surprise," Cara muttered.

Mia sent her a silencing look before returning her gaze to Meg. "Trust us, everything is fine." She smiled kindly, and somehow Meg did feel comforted. "Perfectly normal."

"You're lucky Mia isn't related to you," Cara muttered, still rubbing calming circles on Meg's back. "All she's done since I told her I was pregnant is tell me horror stories."

"Hush," Mia said. "It's not exactly...beautiful.

But being a mother is. You'll get through the hormones and the mood swings and the vomiting and the horrible, horrible heartburn and…" She trailed off and then smiled guiltily. "Okay, I'll stop now."

"Thank you," Meg managed. "For stopping *and* for reassuring me." She couldn't fathom why they'd done it. Why they were being so nice. "I don't know…" She almost said it, and she thought she almost said she didn't know how to do this, or anything, but she only trailed off.

"I don't know" seemed to sum it all up.

"It's a *lot* of I don't know," Cara offered. "The first time, it's so…" She placed a hand over her stomach. "I've been more scared than joyful, I think. But the thing that helps? Talking. Especially to someone who's done it before. Mia's talked me down more times in the past four months than our entire lives, and that's saying something."

"Here." Mia hopped up and walked into the kitchen. When she returned, she was writing something onto a little Post-it. She handed it to Meg. "Our phone numbers. If you ever need to talk. It can feel lonely, and I think that makes it worse. Charlie can be sweet, when he wants to be, but the guys…they don't get it. They can comfort and pat your back, they might hold your hair or give you a foot rub, but you look at them and they've got that deer-in-headlights horror thing going on when it isn't anything you can explain sensibly."

Meg took the offered piece of paper and blinked at it. She was too shocked to cry. Too surprised at their sheer openness and niceness and acceptance.

"Anytime. Really. Charlie brought you here, and I don't think he would have done that if he didn't really care about you."

Meg swallowed. Was that it? This thing they were building. *Care?* She was a little startled to realize how much she wanted that—as much as she wanted a good father for her child. But he'd just paraded her out there and...

"Why didn't he *listen* to me?"

"Because he's Charlie," Cara returned.

Mia let out a sigh. "He's a Wainwright. They have very..." She seemed to think it over. "They're stubborn. The whole lot of them, and it takes a lot for them to realize they're wrong."

Meg closed her eyes. The last thing she wanted was to have fight after fight with someone who couldn't admit he was wrong. She didn't want to be steamrolled like she just had been.

"He's a good man, but I don't think he's had much practice worrying about what other people want," Mia said carefully.

Meg thought about that but then found herself rejecting Mia's interpretation. She thought Charlie spent quite a bit of time wondering what people wanted, but much like her, he had trouble figuring out what it actually was.

"But, you know, love is a great teacher," Mia added cheerfully.

Meg's stomach clenched. Love. She wanted to reject that too, wholly. But she didn't know how.

"Can I come in now?" Charlie's voice asked from the opening that led to the entryway.

Mia and Cara glanced at her as if asking what she wanted. These two women she barely knew had given her shoulders to cry on, immeasurable reassurance and the promise for more.

"It's all right."

The women stood, and though Meg felt some trepidation at facing Charlie, she also felt strangely stronger. As if Cara was right about *talking*, that it could make things better.

*Some things anyway.*

Mia gave Charlie what looked to be a reassuring arm pat as she passed.

"Don't be an ass" was Cara's parting shot.

Charlie frowned after Cara, but when his gaze returned to Meg, it was all…contrition. "I'm sorry," he said simply.

"Why did you push?"

"Because you weren't going to get there on your own. Because I wanted them to know and…" He shoved his fingers through his hair. "I needed you to see that it would be different than you thought."

Meg took a deep breath. Yes, it was stubbornness; he was a stubborn man. But it wasn't just to get his way, or because he didn't worry about what she wanted; it was because he'd needed their acceptance. Even knowing he'd get it, he'd been driven by a need for, well, what Cara and Mia had offered her.

Comfort. Company.

"Your family loves you, but they don't...*get* you, do they?"

His gaze flicked to hers, a startled surprise etched across his face. He opened his mouth, but no sound came out. Slowly he slid onto the couch next to her. He opened his mouth again, and then something in his posture slumped. "No," he agreed hoarsely.

She reached out to touch his face, the rough edge of his beard. "Are you going to let me?" she whispered.

His dark eyes met hers, something a little tortured she thought she recognized in the dark chocolate of his gaze. "I think I have to get me first."

She leaned her head against his shoulder, because that—more than any of today—*that* she understood.

# CHAPTER SEVENTEEN

CHARLIE LED MEG back outside, her hand in his. They hadn't said much else, and it seemed that his apology had smoothed over any ruffled feathers.

She was quiet, but her hand squeezed his, and her words kept echoing around in his head. *Your family loves you, but they don't...get you.*

She had put feelings into words, words he'd never quite been able to piece together. He'd been close lately, but she cut to the center of it.

Would this year ever stop changing everything inside him? It wasn't bad exactly, but it was exhausting.

When they went back into the yard, the family was still there, still ready to offer congratulations and hugs.

He'd known without a shadow of a doubt she needed this. To feel a part of a family, or at least a group of people who would support them.

As much as he loved his family, as important as they were to him, he'd never realized just how big a gift that was. He'd never spent much time considering there were people out there who didn't have parents who loved them unconditionally even when things weren't perfect or even happy.

"We're so happy, Meg," Mom offered, pulling Meg into a warm hug. Meg looked back at Charlie, something like bewildered, but she let go of his hand and hugged his mother back.

And then the rest of the congratulations rolled in. Kenzie hugged him and Meg, and Mom hugged him and then Meg again, lingered with her, saying reassuring, happy things and talking about how they needed to get to know each other better.

It was a blur, really, of well-wishes and handshakes and hugs and backslaps and he didn't know why he felt so separate from it.

Because this wasn't the plan? It wasn't how it was supposed to go. He'd lost sight of so much of that the past few weeks in his perfect, happy little world that he knew was simply a figment of his imagination.

"When are you due?"

"March. March twentieth," Meg said, her voice unsteady, though her smile wasn't. Her smile was big and bright and it brought him back to the moment a little bit. Her smile, her hand slipping back into his.

"Two new grandchildren next year, then, unless Mia goes early." Mom placed a hand over her heart. "This is such wonderful news. Oh, we have so many things to discuss. Not all at once, but there is something I need to show you right this very instant." Mom grabbed Meg's free hand.

"What thing?" Charlie asked, his grip on Meg's other hand going tighter. He knew his mother well enough to know that gleam in her eye, and that she was planning to do her level best to embarrass him.

"Oh, let her go, Charlie. I'm just going to show her your baby pictures. She has a right to be warned."

"Warned?" Meg asked, eyes wide.

"That's highly unnecessary," Charlie said through gritted teeth. "She's exaggerating. She's trying to embarrass me."

"Nonsense!" Mom said, barely containing her glee as she gave Meg's arm another tug. "Meg should know that if the baby inherits those monstrous eyes, she or he will still be able to grow into a fine-looking young man or woman."

"Mother."

"Downright terrifying," Mom was saying to Meg, only half joking. "Just the biggest eyes anyone had ever seen. People never could tell me I had a cute baby. They had to say those hideously patronizing things like 'won't he be handsome?' and 'look at you, you had a *baby*.'" Mom tsked as she dragged Meg along toward the house.

Which in turn dragged Charlie, until Meg turned to him, that pleased smile even brighter on her face, laughter on her lips. Delighted and happy, and he couldn't do anything but let her hand go. Let Mom show off his embarrassing baby pictures.

Whatever would keep that look on Meg's face, he was on board.

As Mom and Meg disappeared inside, Dell appeared behind him and clapped him on the shoulder. "Warned you it was catching."

"Yeah, yeah," Charlie muttered, still watching where Meg had gone.

"She's colorful," Kenzie added, coming up on his other side. "Very *colorful*." At the murderous gaze he sent her way, she held up her hands. "Don't *hurt* me, I was only commenting." Then she grinned at Dell. "Oh, he *likes* her."

"I think he very much does," Dell said, sporting an entirely too-smug grin of his own.

"Meg and Charlie sitting in a tree," Kenzie sang. "Getting ready to have a ba-ay-bee."

"You're hilarious."

"And you're going to be a daddy." Kenzie wrapped her arms around him. "I can't wait to be the most annoying aunt ever to *three* little ones."

Charlie could hardly stay annoyed when his perpetually condescending baby sister had her arms around him. So he wound his arm around her shoulders and stood there with his sister and his brother, not sure what this moment meant, only that it meant *something*. And he'd remember it. For a very long time.

"Keep in mind, Kenzie, every obnoxious toy you give to our kids, we'll repay you. Tenfold," Dell warned, ruffling Kenzie's hair despite her growl of rage.

*Our kids.* He was suddenly aware of his *age* and the passage of *time* and how it was down-right cruel. He'd been a child on this very ground, tormenting these very people, and they were still tormenting each other, but they were adults, pro-creating all over the place.

It was kind of wonderful and horrible all at the same time, but Meg came out the front door with Mom, family photo albums clutched to her chest. Most of the terrible faded away to possibility.

"YOU REALLY DID have the most terrifyingly large eyes. How did you grow into them?" Meg clutched the picture Mrs. Wainwright had allowed her to keep. Baby Charlie. Handsome, self-assured Charlie had been a truly ugly baby.

She couldn't stop giggling over it. "I'm going to put it on my mantel. No, my nightstand."

"Your endless delight is so much fun," he said dryly, pulling his car onto the gravel drive that led to her little cottage. The world had gone dark except for the bright half-moon guiding them home.

Her home anyway. It was odd to want to share it. It was *odd* to have fallen into this thing, and yet when she wasn't overthinking every angle of how screwed up she was, it felt so right.

She held the baby picture to her chest as Charlie bumped up the driveway. The moonlight illuminated the goat shed and the old cottage, and her heart felt so full.

But she wasn't going to cry about it, because good God, she'd done enough crying for fifty pregnant women.

Cara had been right, because *talking* to people, being around people…it had eased some of that pressure, some of that fear. She hadn't made a bad impression; she'd been accepted.

Elsie had given her that—Elsie *and* Dan, and this had reminded her that they too would be part of Seedling's family. She got to build the best community for her child, and that was what was important.

Far more important than Meg's insecurities running rampant. More important than her past. It didn't matter who she'd been. All that mattered was who she could be.

Charlie stopped the car, but he didn't move to turn off the ignition or get out.

"Are you coming inside?" she asked, wondering the last time he'd been back to his apartment in the city. He'd been spending so many of his days and nights in New Benton. Maybe he wanted to head back.

She wouldn't let her heart sink at that. This

was still all very new, which meant they still had separate lives. Even if it was nice to have help *and* nightly company, that didn't mean it was imperative.

It would be dangerous to think of it as imperative. She had learned, over and over again, to count only on herself for happiness. Herself and her goats. She could enjoy Charlie, she could build something with him and ingratiate herself into his family, but that didn't get rid of the simple truth.

She was the center of her life. She was the thing she had to depend on. She was an island. With visitors.

"Are you *inviting* me inside?" He said it while his mouth did that slow curve into a smile, and she *melted*, even though he seemed to know exactly how charming he was. And he *definitely* knew what her answer would be.

Warmth and happiness bloomed in her chest. Gratitude too. Gratitude that her falling off the wagon, that Grandma's death, they could mean something. The beginning of a new phase in her life. A good one.

She'd hold on to that. Bad things could beget good ones. Hadn't her life been a study in that? Self-sufficiency could still have relationships. Standing on her own two feet could include holding someone's hand.

She reached across the console and rested her palm against his jaw. "Thank you for this. Especially after my major drama-fest beforehand. You were right. They're…everything. I'm so glad Seedling gets to be a part of your family."

He moved his head so his whiskers scraped against her palm. "We should talk about yours, Meg," he said seriously. Too seriously.

She didn't want that. She *couldn't* show him that. Her family was tied up in all her failures, her addiction, all those pieces of herself she was determined to forget.

"Let's leave today as the day you were right and I met your lovely family. Some other day can be the day we dissect mine."

"I'm right most days."

She laughed, light infusing the spot of darkness the mention of her family created. "You are very, very certain of that, aren't you?"

"Why wouldn't I be?" He let out a little sigh. "Aside from being unemployed, of course."

"You're not unemployed. You're my very handsome goat assistant."

"Goat. Assistant. Perhaps I should put that on my résumé. What's the classiest term for 'shoveler of poop'?"

"I think that's when you use the term *waste management*."

His dark eyes flashed with humor, and it was the closest Meg had come to pure joy with someone else in a very, very, very long time.

*Maybe ever.*

"I like you." It was the barest truth she knew how to tell without coming unglued. Without relinquishing the control that kept her moving most days. She liked him, and he should know it.

"I like you too," he replied, his voice suitably raspy as if he understood how *important* that was, how much it took for her to say something like that.

It meant a lot that he would say it back, because she somehow knew Charlie wouldn't lie to be conversational. He wouldn't be here, right here, if that weren't true.

So she kissed him. Because she could, because she wanted to. She wanted to build something with this man. He wasn't anything like what she'd initially feared. No, he was good. He was real. And she could be worthy of that goodness, that realness, as long as he never saw what had come before.

## CHAPTER EIGHTEEN

CHARLIE COULDN'T THINK of a time where he'd ever been this nervous. No job interview, no test, no big presentation to the entire company. Never had his lunch threatened to revolt at the sheer enormity of what lay before him.

He forced himself to look at Meg, who was as white as the waiting room walls around them. She had her hands clasped together so tight they seemed drained of all color too.

He wanted to offer her a smile, a reassuring one. He wanted to offer her something, to commiserate at just how *awful* this wait was, and the word *viable* flashing over his head.

But he didn't know how to move—no smiles, no gentle hand touches. He had no words. Because if he moved, if he offered any, he wasn't sure what reserves would be left. And he thought he desperately needed those reserves.

For whatever came next.

When Meg's name was called, they both jerked as if a grenade had been lobbed at them. Charlie forced himself to stand, but Meg remained sitting.

Way too pale, her hands still clasped together like she didn't know how to let them go.

"Meg."

Slowly her gaze met his, wide and blue and *terrified. You have to do something. You have to reach out.* Stiffly, afraid of all that it would cost him, he held out his hand.

Just as slowly and stiffly, she unclasped her hands and reached out, sliding one into his outstretched hand. He helped her to her feet, and they walked toward the nurse, hand in hand.

When she slipped her hand in his, he could breathe easier. Easier than when they'd been waiting. Easier than possibly he had all day. She linked her fingers with his and they walked into the room cramped full of equipment and a computer and a bed-type thing.

The nurse offered directions, and Meg remained frozen. Until he squeezed her hand. He'd tell himself that was what had snapped her out of it. Because it would make every gesture like it come infinitely easier. If she needed it. If she needed him.

She disappeared into the little bathroom off to the side, and Charlie arranged himself uncomfortably on the chair in the corner that would allow him to watch the proceedings while the ultrasound technician situated herself.

"There's nothing to be nervous about," the

woman said kindly, doing who knew what with the computer and machines until Meg stepped out in the hospital gown.

"All right, have a lie-down up here," the tech said, patting the paper-covered exam table.

She got Meg situated, doing all sorts of horrible-looking things with all sorts of horrible-looking instruments. But she talked Meg through it, and in the end it wasn't like Charlie had a choice. Except to close his eyes.

But he wasn't a coward.

The woman was silent as she worked, one hand and what it was doing with one of the horrible-looking tools hidden under Meg's exam gown, the other typing away on the computer.

Charlie inclined his head to look at the screen that was pointed toward Meg. There were splotches, and a lot of black static. Occasionally the screen would flash, or the tech typed letters or numbers that appeared on the screen, but Charlie didn't know what any of it meant.

"See that flash there?" the tech finally said, pointing to a dot where something flashed over and over.

He nodded wordlessly, transfixed on the steady blinking. "That's the baby's heartbeat. One-seventy-one beats per minute. Which is perfectly healthy. In fact, everything looks right on target."

"So, everything's okay? Everything's...viable?" Meg asked in a tremulous voice.

The technician offered a broad smile. "One hundred percent, honey. That baby of yours looks exactly like it should."

She pulled her hand out from under Meg's paper gown and pulled the gloves off her hands. "Now, Meg, if you want to change back into your clothes, I'll print out some pictures you can take with you."

Meg slid off the table and disappeared into the little bathroom, and after a few more button pushes on her varied machines, the technician handed him a strip of printouts.

Black-and-white, the words *BABY CARMI-CHAEL* in type across the top. The last name would be something they'd need to discuss, but not now. Not when he could see his *viable* baby as a real, living thing. It looked like a gummy bear, all in all, but it was clear. A body, little arm and leg buds, a head. A heartbeat.

He hadn't realized Meg had returned until he felt her little gasp of pleasure next to him. "Oh" was all she said, but it spoke volumes.

They stood shoulder to shoulder, staring down at the picture. Like time had ceased to exist, and everything centered on this picture.

"That's our baby," she whispered, tracing the outline.

"Our baby," he repeated, felled, again. Over and over again. In the most wonderful way he'd ever been knocked off his feet.

"I know it's a big day, guys, but you're going to have to leave so I can get ready for the next appointment. Feel free to sit in the waiting room as long as you need to."

"Right. Of course." Charlie didn't manage to take his gaze off the picture they held together, but he at least got his brain engaged enough to move them toward the door, then out and down the hall.

"I can't stop looking at it."

"You don't have to." He squeezed her shoulder and gave her full ownership of the picture. He led her toward the door out of the hospital complex. "Look all you want. And I'll drive us to Moonrise for lunch."

"No," she said, shaking her head, though her eyes never left the picture she clutched in her hands. "Take us somewhere we won't know anybody. Then we can keep it out and look at it together."

"Even better." He planted a kiss on her head and led her to the car. Things couldn't be better.

IT WAS THE most beautiful thing she'd ever seen. She wanted to blow it up and frame it. She wanted to wallpaper her house with it. She wanted to never look at anything else because this was a *baby*. Her baby. Hers.

Even though it was so big and scary and over-whelming, there was a *baby* on that picture.

"I should have taken you to McDonald's. The food and ambience will be lost on you com-pletely," Charlie teased. But it was teasing because he hadn't cracked his menu either. All they'd done since they sat down at the restaurant was stare dopily at the picture in front of them.

Meg had barely even noticed that it was a nice place. The kind of place her parents would have taken her to for interminable lunches where they'd pick at her manners and her posture and…

She sat up a little straighter as if out of reflex, finally breaking her gaze from the picture. *Oh no.*

"The pasta is good here. So's the pork chop."

"Yeah." She looked back at the menu. She'd never been *here*, per se, but it could have been right out of her childhood. It could have been right out of that life that had crushed her into bits.

She'd been so blindsided by the perfection of a picture that she'd entered here willingly and stupidly.

*It's fine.* Charlie was tracing the picture of *their* baby with his fingertip—over and over. The same awe and reverence in his expression as she felt. So this was fine. He wasn't going to complain about her table manners, or the appropriateness of her smile or clothes.

He was *Charlie*. Not her parents.

"M-maybe we should just go to McDonald's. G-go home." She was stuttering. She hadn't stuttered since second grade. She took a deep breath and tried to breathe, tried to be calm.

She was fine.

"Hey, what's wrong?" He reached out across the table, as if to take her hand, but she lifted it in a wave. Wave it off. Pretend she was fine. The last thing she was going to do was rehash the ways she'd always failed her parents and this life.

Not today, when everything was magic. "Just feeling a little sick all of a sudden."

"You need to eat something," he said with a self-assured nod. "I was reading it can help with any nausea to make sure you're eating a little bit throughout the day—not just three decent meals."

She felt some of the panic fade at that, too blanketed in the warmth that he would care—not just to read up on how the baby was developing, or what she should be doing to help grow the baby best as she could, but to read about what might help *her*.

Yeah, she was a little more than *fine*. "Well, I guess I should look at the menu, then. Do you think they can bring up some bread and butter or something?" Because suddenly she was hungry. Hungry and happy and… She touched her index finger to the picture again.

"This is the most amazing thing that's ever

happened to me," she whispered, because the emotions were bubbling out of her, and though it wasn't easy or in her nature, *sharing* what she was feeling did really help offset the crying breakdowns she'd been prone to lately.

It was hard to open herself up like that. So often she could see the end result being ridicule, but with baby stuff…it was easier. Because Charlie would have to be cruel to hurt her with that, and she didn't believe he was cruel.

"Me too," he said, his voice gruff, his finger touching hers—all centered on that little miracle of a picture.

They soaked up that silence, fingers gently touching. Meg could have lived in this moment, and she vowed that no matter what happened with them, no matter what missteps she took when it came to a *relationship* with him—she would remember this moment. This joy.

They'd figure it out. They'd always choose to make something work, because for both of them this was the most amazing thing—and so she could be assured they would always work together to make sure it was their priority.

*Unless…*

So many unlesses, and she didn't want to think about them. Didn't want to give them credence, but they lived in her like organs. Those whispers, those beliefs, those chinks in her armor.

She could only hope her child would never feel this. Would never constantly struggle to believe in his or her worth.

*I won't let you.*

"If you want to order a bunch of things, we can always take leftovers home."

*We. Home.*

Maybe she should tell him. Maybe she should *share*. It worked for the pregnancy things, for the baby things. To tell people what she was feeling. It lightened the load. It made the anxiety and fear far less potent.

But how did she tell him something that would give him the ammunition to ruin her? To sweep everything away from her? How did she give him all those feelings and insecurities when it would most surely make him wonder if she could do this?

She couldn't have him worrying she'd relapse. Someone had to believe in her. She had to prove someone right instead of wrong.

"Where do you go?" Charlie asked, leaning forward across the table. "Where is your head when you look so damn terrified?"

She blinked at him. Where did she go? Oh, just to all the dark, ugly recesses of her soul. She forced herself to smile. "Pregnancy is terrifying, Charlie."

She didn't think he bought it, based on the grim

line of his mouth, but the waitress appeared and took their lunch orders.

She didn't want him to ponder her terror or where her mind went. She didn't want him worrying or trying to figure her out, because anything he found out would only lead to him looking at her differently. He would see her as an addict, someone not to be trusted.

It would be him telling his family against her wishes, only worse—with everything. Every decision boiling down to him being the *actual* responsible one. The one who knew best, because he certainly hadn't spent his twenties failing at sobriety and a clean life. He'd been climbing his way up the company ladder.

She couldn't allow her future to become her past, and so Charlie could never know the extent of her instability. No matter how kind and sweet and caring he was, she couldn't allow someone to take the reins and find her lacking, her decision-making suspect, her failure at sobriety inevitable.

"Have you thought about names at all?" she asked. "I haven't wanted to dwell on it until the whole viability thing was over, but I do have some pretty specific ideas for a girl."

He stared at her for a moment, and she had to hold her breath. Charlie's will was a thing of iron. Sometimes she thought he might be able to unravel her simply by willing it so.

"I haven't thought much about names. I won't be picky. As long as it isn't goat-related."

She managed to smile, to exhale, to feel some semblance of normal. "No goats. Just…if it's a girl, I'd want to name her after my grandmother."

"I'd *never* argue with that."

"Do you have any family names for if it's a boy?"

"Well…"

He said something, but she didn't quite hear it because another woman's voice seemed to jump out of the hum of the crowd around them. "Margaret."

The word rang dimly in the back of her head, like something she should remember, but she didn't want to think about whatever that was. Not when they were talking about names. Names for their baby.

"Margaret."

The sharp command finally broke through, memory flooding over her. Placement. She sat straighter, and she was sure she paled, because she could all but feel the blood draining out of her.

Mom's world-weary sigh. "Fine," she muttered, finally coming into view from behind. "Meg. What are you doing here?"

Meg blinked up at her mother, and then—even more shocking—her father not far behind. Out to lunch. On a weekday. *Together.*

She couldn't speak, because she realized way

too belatedly that the picture was laid out on the table between her and Charlie. A long row of evidence. If Mom looked down, she would see it. She would know.

*She'll ruin everything.*

So Meg swallowed, her hand shaking as she casually placed it on top of the table. She kept her mother's gaze as she inched her hand, slowly, carefully, as inconspicuously as possible, toward the picture.

"Is there something I can help you with?" Meg asked, trying not to sound too acidic or anywhere near panicked. Distant politeness. Like what Mom always employed.

"A friend of mine called me up and told me she thought she saw you here, and we were just so surprised after all the times you told us places we frequented were beneath you."

"I never said that," Meg returned, feeling cold all over.

Mom pursed her lips together, and then Meg made a fatal mistake. She flicked her glance to the picture on the table because her fingers were *so* close. One more inch and she could casually lean her arm over them and obscure—

"What's this?" Mom snatched the picture up right before Meg could place her arm over it.

"Baby…?"

It was Mom's turn to pale, and Meg wished

she could get some satisfaction from it, but all she felt was sick.

"It says Baby Carmichael, Jeffrey," Mom intoned dully, tipping the picture so Dad could see.

The nausea waved through Meg, hard and uncompromising. "I... Excuse me." She pushed out of the booth and hurried to the bathroom, making it into the fancy stall just in time to heave the contents of her stomach.

Tears burned and fell. Her stomach heaved again. Her parents knew. They knew.

And she'd left them alone with Charlie.

## CHAPTER NINETEEN

CHARLIE STOOD TO RUN after Meg, but two middle-aged people stood firmly in his way.

"If you'll excuse me," he said through gritted teeth. "I need to make sure she's all right."

"Don't be silly," the woman said with a dismissive wave. "You can't go into the women's bathroom. *I* will check on her."

"Why would I let you do that when the sight of you sent her running?"

The woman pursed her lips and gave him a dismissive once-over. "And just who are you?"

He came up a little short at that, because he knew Meg wouldn't want this woman to have that information. It didn't take a rocket scientist to put together these people were her parents. Partially because of the way they'd acted, but also because he knew the name of the man standing there.

Jeffrey Carmichael.

Charlie had golfed with him once, was all he could think. Some customer outing with Carmichael Grocery and he'd been put on the CEO's team.

These were the parents who'd treated Meg so poorly.

Directly tied to a business he hadn't been trying too hard to get back into because he'd been so wrapped up in this weird new world.

He didn't know how to tell them to go to hell, considering Jeffrey Carmichael likely knew exactly who he was.

And Charlie knew exactly what the head of Carmichael Grocery could do.

"Let's sit, son," the man said, genially enough. "Lisa will go check on Meg, as it *is* a women's bathroom, and regardless of what Meg might have told you about us, we aren't *evil*."

Charlie swallowed down the retort. Partially because…hell, it was natural. This man could make it so he never got a job in the St. Louis area in anything related to food ever again. But also because he didn't want to make a scene.

He would be reasonable and rational and careful, because he knew so very little. When Meg reappeared from the bathroom, he would do whatever it was she wanted. He would whisk her away, he would spit on these people, he would do whatever she needed him to do in order to take that terrified look off her face.

"Sit, son, sit." Jeffrey slid into the seat Meg had vacated, and the absolute *last* thing Charlie wanted to do was sit. Sit with this man. A man who likely knew far more about what put that scared, faraway look on Meg's face time and time again than Charlie did.

"You look familiar. You're with Lordon, aren't you?"

"I was," Charlie returned dully. It felt like a betrayal to be sitting here with this man, but he didn't know how to avoid it. What he should do instead.

"Ah, you got booted in the buyout, then."

*Booted.* It sounded a little less pleasant than *laid off.* But he couldn't deny the fact that he had indeed been *booted.* "Yes."

"So what are you doing now?"

Charlie didn't know where to look. At this shrewd man obviously assessing him in some way, or the hallway that led to the bathrooms. Perhaps he should be barging in there, women's room or no women's room.

But he didn't know how Meg wanted him to handle these people, because she'd kept avoiding the subject. Changing the conversation whenever he brought it up. She didn't seem to want him to know anything, and so he didn't know what to *do.*

Which pissed him the hell off. "I've been doing some consulting," he said, purposefully vague, purposefully giving as little as possible.

"I see." There was a harsh gleam in the man's eye that nearly made Charlie's blood run cold.

Charlie had met the man before, but he'd never developed an opinion about him. A golf outing, and seeing each other in passing rarely. He was the head of a customer company, and therefore Charlie hadn't formed any judgment.

The idea was to sell, not make friends.

But he had some judgments now, and they weren't all based on what little tidbits Meg had told him. It was the way the man held himself, the way he surveyed Charlie as though he were a *thing* rather than a person, let alone the father of his grandchild.

This man would be his child's grandfather. It was deeply unsettling.

"I don't blame you for being uncomfortable." Jeffrey lounged in the booth Meg had vacated with a simple kind of ownership. A sense of rightness about his sitting there.

Charlie had to fight not to sneer.

"I'm sure Meg's filled your head with all kinds of stories. Her childhood was most definitely not an easy one, and she's found that the best target of blame for much of what she brought upon herself is…well, us." There was such a calculated way he looked across the table, as if he was trying to size up just what Charlie knew, what he felt.

It was uncomfortably familiar to the life he'd been leading not that long ago. Sales was about reading people, finding their weaknesses, using them against them. He'd never put it in quite those words before, and Mr. Carmichael wasn't a salesman, but...

It felt the same. It felt grossly the same.

"It's difficult to watch your child struggle the way Meg struggled."

Charlie wanted to believe it was a genuine statement, but he couldn't get past the way this felt like chess. Like a game. If his parents had talked about one of their children's struggles...his mother would have been visibly emotive—not casual. His father would have been tight-lipped and hard, but not...assessing.

Whatever Mr. Carmichael was getting at, it was to get a response, an answer, something.

There was one positive to Charlie having been like this man, even if only a little bit. He knew how to play the game. He knew how to give away nothing.

"I'm sure it is," he said. The best play was always to say as little as possible, to force the other party into the moves. Because the more they moved, the more you could dodge.

The old tactics came back so easily, and yet he didn't feel good about it. He felt a little sleazy. He'd been a good salesman, and he hadn't bent the rules or played dirty. He'd never compromised his morals.

But that didn't mean some of the tactics he'd

employed weren't problematic when you used them in real life. Actual life with actual people.

He could see how he'd always done that, without meaning to, without purposefully thinking to. It had just…been easy.

"You see, we poured a lot of money into—"

Mrs. Carmichael huffed back to the table, slapping her purse onto the smooth top, making the silverware rattle.

"She said she's fine and she'll come out in a moment." Mrs. Carmichael scowled at Mr. Carmichael. "She literally *tore* the picture from my hands." She gave an injured sniff before turning her cold blue gaze to Charlie.

She looked like Meg, but she was different too. Something cold and hard ran underneath this woman, and even when Meg was closed off or changing the subject, she was never cold. She was never hard.

It was the thing that drew him to her the most. Her warmth. Her light. Even when she was struggling, she was like…home. Something comforting and where you were supposed to be.

He knew he couldn't sit here anymore. He couldn't take this. He had to get to Meg.

WHEN MEG MANAGED to step out of the bathroom, Mom and Dad were sitting in the seat she'd vacated. Sitting at her table. With Charlie.

She nearly doubled over and wretched again, but Charlie was too quick. Before he'd even looked up to see her step out of the bathroom, he'd been out of the booth and on his way to her, quickly taking her by the arm as she approached.

"Tell me what I need to do."

"Just get me out of here." *Far, far, far away.* "Home. Please take me home."

"Are you hurt? Are you okay? Should we go to the doctor?"

She felt like she'd been physically assaulted even though Mom hadn't deigned to walk into the stall. That was Mom's specialty. To peck away until Meg felt like she'd been stabbed, over and over again.

*You really think you're capable of raising a child? You really think he'll let you keep that child if he knows you're nothing but a drug addict? When he knows, because I can assure you, Meg, no grandchild of mine will be raised by you. This baby is a Carmichael.*

She was too numb to cry. Once upon a time she would have numbed her pain with alcohol or drugs, bad decisions certainly, but she had Charlie supporting her and moving her toward the door, the ultrasound picture tucked securely in her pocket.

Meg straightened as they passed where Mom and Dad were now standing, arguing with a waitress.

She was going to be a better parent. She was going to give her child everything, *everything*. She'd never believed in the surface world her parents worshipped like a religion, and she never would value anything over her child like that.

They'd be dead sorry if they ever tried to take Seedling from her.

Dead sorry.

Though Mom's words had crawled into her, were likely doing damage even as she walked into the sunny summer afternoon, arm tucked into Charlie's, she felt…*strong*. She felt sure.

She would fight anyone and anything to keep her child safe. Healthy and safe and *loved*.

Charlie led her to the car, but by the time they'd reached it she could walk fine on her own. The initial shock might have cut her off at the knees, but grabbing the ultrasound picture back from Mom while Mom had gone through a veritable list of why she wasn't capable of being a mother…

But she *was* a mother. She slid into the passenger seat, resting her palms over her stomach. She couldn't help wishing she could feel something. The picture helped—to know something really was in there, living, moving, *heart beating*.

But still, she'd love a little comfort, a little surety. Something she could feel.

Charlie climbed into the driver's seat. He was silent, and she was glad. There was so much going on in her own head, her own heart, she didn't know how she'd answer any questions he might have.

He started the engine, pulled out of the parking lot, not uttering a word until they were on the highway, on the way home. Home. Home, where all the poison couldn't touch her.

*You'd like to think that, wouldn't you?*

Charlie flicked her a glance, and she couldn't read the expression on his face. "You're all right, then?"

Meg looked down at her stomach. All right? Probably not, but… "I didn't cry in front of her, isn't that something?" She laughed, the sound escaping her mouth. Part giddy, part probably insane. "I mean, I cried, don't get me wrong, but once I heard her voice, I didn't cry. I didn't cower. Because I wanted to protect Seedling more than I wanted to…" She couldn't finish that sentence. It gave her away.

Maybe she wasn't that strong at all, because Mom's words had penetrated. They'd left their mark. Things she'd already thought—*do you think he'll let you keep that child if he knows you're a drug addict?*

*You are.* She'd wanted to tell Mom she *had been*, not currently *was*.

Suddenly she knew what she had to do. "Do you still want to get married?" Because that would offer a certain blanket of security. If they got married, and he found out about the drug addiction…maybe that would make it okay. He could trust her if they built a marriage.

Charlie's already tight grip on the steering wheel tightened. "I don't think this is the time to talk about it."

"It's the perfect time to talk about it." Panic beat through her, determined panic. Her parents couldn't—and even more maybe wouldn't—touch her if she was *married* to *Charlie*. "They'll leave me alone if they think I'm married to the likes of you," she said, more to herself than Charlie. More because the plan was *brilliant* and she couldn't keep that inside.

This would solve all their problems. Maybe not permanently, but she couldn't think about the big picture when her mother's words were echoing in her head. It was just important to get this sorted now. To protect herself and Seedling *now*.

"The likes of me," he echoed.

"You talked to my father." She didn't mean it to sound so accusing, but he seemed hurt by how she'd phrased things and that wasn't fair. He'd been sitting there *talking* to her parents.

She didn't want to ask. She didn't want to know what they might have talked about, what might have been said. She didn't want to know what

Mom might have offered in the seconds she'd been with them.

She didn't want to know anything about what they might have told him, or what Charlie might have told her parents. She wanted to pretend that had never happened. That these separate worlds had not collided.

They could do that. They could—

"I know your father."

Her skin went cold, that numb feeling spreading farther, deeper. He *knew* her father. So he had worked with him. *Grocery contacts* rang in her head, over and over again.

"He recognized me," he continued, each word pushing that cold deeper and deeper into her chest. "Maybe not enough to put a name to a face, but he recognized who I was."

"Because you know him," she echoed stupidly.

"I golfed with him once. I let him win, of course. He was the customer. The customer is always right."

The silence that followed was heavy and dark. The kind of silences Meg remembered from her childhood, when everyone was hurting and broken, and silent with it. Drowning in it.

"You don't want to marry the *likes of me*, Meg," Charlie said at length, such contempt dripping off those last words. "We'll get you home to your goats and you'll realize it soon enough."

She stared at him, the way he held his jaw so tight it must hurt. He must be grinding his teeth to dust. Handsome and hard, and so many sides to him. So much depth and strength to him, and she wasn't so certain she didn't want to marry him—at least in part—because of him. Because of who he was, because of what he gave her.

"A few weeks ago it didn't matter what I wanted," she said in a voice that was little more than a whisper. Little more than pleading. "You thought it was a plausible solution for the both of us. I like you, Charlie. I've grown to…" She struggled with the words, the feelings, how they all mishmashed in her head. So many doubts undercutting so many feelings. "It isn't the same as a few weeks ago."

"Isn't it? I know your father, Meg. I golfed with him. The fact of the matter is, I don't know you at all."

Which shouldn't hurt, but it did. Because he knew all about her life *now*, the life that mattered. They'd been in each other's pockets for weeks—how could he not *know her at all*?

She pressed her forehead to the cool of the window and closed her eyes.

Her parents hadn't even *tried* that hard and they'd still ruined something.

## CHAPTER TWENTY

WHY WAS HE BALKING? Charlie didn't have a clue. His marriage proposal all those weeks ago in Moonrise hadn't been made out of any foolish thoughts like love. It had been made because he thought it would offer them the best environment in which to raise the child they'd created.

He'd only ever suggested it because it was a solid plan, a route from A to B, and the one he'd always assumed he'd follow.

Now she was seeing it for what it was, and agreeing. And he didn't know why he suddenly wanted nothing to do with it, why he could only wish she'd never uttered those words.

He should be agreeing. They should be driving to the license office right now. They could be married within the week.

But all he could think was *not to the likes of you*, and no matter how he tried to reason and rationalize himself out of the hurt—it pounded and echoed through him.

So he didn't say anything. He left it at not knowing who the hell she was, because it hit him

hard—how little he knew. It hit him hard that he
wanted something she wouldn't offer. It hit him
hard that he wanted more than he'd thought he did.

He knew nothing about who she'd been or what
made her parents her own personal demons. He
only knew he'd been going along happily thinking that marriage of any kind was the end result
he was going for, and finding...

Damn. Damn, damn, damn.

The person he knew—the parts she was willing
to show him—he liked that person. More than he
could remember liking much of anyone. He liked
her laugh and the way she never made him feel
like a robot.

She brought something out in him he'd always
known was there, but had struggled to show. Always. To everyone. Even his own family. He joked
with her and he laughed with her and he comforted her and she...

Let him. Wanted him. Accepted him.

He didn't want her marrying the likes of *him*.
*But you should. That's the whole point.*

Charlie let out a breath, slowly, carefully, trying not to draw any attention in the heavy silence
in the small space of the car. Heavy, oppressive
silence that felt like cinder blocks pressing down
on his chest and lungs.

The highway he'd driven to and fro to get to
home most of his adult life seemed more inter-

minable than it ever had, and there'd been a lot of interminable trips. But this one stretched long and painful.

When he finally crossed the limits of New Benton, it felt like the sky should be dark. Like sheer days had passed since they left, near sick with nerves and hope.

Such a stupid thing to feel defeated. To feel beat down. His child was *viable*. Perfect. Real and alive and next year he or she would be *in his arms*.

None of these other things mattered. Not really. What mattered was that child. And the fact Meg hadn't had a chance to eat.

"We should get you some food," he said, his voice rusty and forced.

"I have food at the house," she replied, her voice sounding as ill-used as his.

He nodded. What else was there to do? Agree. Take her home. Marinate in his misery *and* stupidity. So he drove and he drove, and the fifteen minutes it usually took from the edge of town to her place felt like it was about fifteen hours of silent torture.

He should say something. He should do something. He should find the words for what was going on inside him.

But he didn't want to, he found. The words were there, all the hurt, all the frustration, all the *need*, but he didn't want to give it to her. Not when she couldn't seem to give him jack shit.

He drove her home, and he didn't make a move to get out when he stopped. He stared at the steering wheel.

"Thanks. For the ride," she offered, pushing the door open and starting to step out.

"Anytime. Every time, really."

She didn't say anything and he didn't dare look at her as she closed the door. All there was left to do was drive away.

But they couldn't leave it like this. They... couldn't. Something had to be said. Some conclusion had to be drawn from the situation. So, he pushed out of the car.

And stood there, because she was looking up at him with that wide-eyed terror thing going on. Like she was afraid of him, or at least his words, and he didn't know what he'd done or what she was so afraid of.

That was the thing. The only possible reason for it was that she didn't *want* him to know, and he didn't know how to jump that hurdle.

"I should go." Because he was stupid. Clueless. And nothing made him angrier than standing here in front of her not knowing how to *reach* her, how to give part of himself so she *could* reach.

She stared at him, the watery blue of her wide-eyed gaze just *eating away* at him. But what else

could he do? What the hell was he supposed to
*do* with all this hurt?

She just stared and didn't offer a thing, and he
wanted to rage. Pound his fists against something.
But he was Charlie Wainwright, so his balled fists
stayed at his sides. Because he wasn't that kind
of man.

*What kind of man are you?*

He had no idea most of the time, and every
time he thought he might, he grabbed on to it and
something swept it away again.

But no. He knew what he was. Who he was.
Organized, responsible, dependable Charlie. He
just needed a plan. Somewhere under all the stupid emotion there had to be a reasonable, rational
course of action.

"I'll be by tomorrow. To work."

"Okay."

He rolled his eyes. At her. At himself. At the
whole damn thing, and he turned to go because
they couldn't seem to find words today, and
maybe that was all they had. Crappy words and
heavy silences.

"Charlie, I…"

She stepped forward and he held his breath. He
wasn't sure why or even what he was hoping for,
he just needed…

She pulled the ultrasound picture out of her
pocket and then took a few steps over to her

truck. She pulled out a tool from the back of it that looked like pruners or wire cutters and carefully and precisely cut the line of pictures in half so there were two sets of pictures.

She held one out to him. "Here. We should both have them."

He took his half of the pictures. *BABY CARMICHAEL* in capital letters across the top.

She'd cut it in half. As if they were two separates. If it wasn't an image of his child, he would have crumpled it. He would have done a lot of things, because this impotent anger bubbling inside him needed an outlet.

But even in picture form, he wouldn't take his anger out on his kid. Not ever.

"We'll have to talk about last names at some point," he said, because he was a dick.

"Yeah" was all she said, and she turned around and walked away. Into the house, the closing of the door a resounding *snap* amid the goat bleats and the quiet summer evening.

He was left standing in her yard, clutching a picture of his baby, not having a clue how he got here. It felt like every other breakup he'd ever had.

Except for the first time the pain was a living, breathing thing. He didn't know what to do with that, so he got in his car and tried to drive away from it. It occurred to him he could keep driving.

Out of New Benton, back to St. Louis and that apartment he'd only stepped foot in to get things.

The apartment he'd been thinking of letting his lease run out on because…

"Because you're an idiot," he muttered to himself, feeling like even more of one when muscle memory or something took over and instead of taking the highway back to the city he turned onto the road that led to the Wainwright Farm.

He didn't want to be here. Around people. He kept telling himself that, even as he parked next to Dell's cabin and walked up the walkway. He didn't want to be around people. He didn't want to talk to anyone. He wanted to be alone.

He knocked on the door.

Mia answered, more color in her cheeks than she'd had for weeks. "Hi, Charlie. Come on in. Though try to be quiet. Lainey's napping."

Charlie managed a thin smile and stepped inside.

"So, you had the appointment this morning, yes?" Mia prodded, grinning from ear to ear as she walked toward the kitchen.

"Yes. Everything looked good."

"Perfect."

He stopped in the middle of the living room. His grandparents had lived here for a time, but he always thought of it as Mia and Dell's. They'd spent the past few years building their family here, and suddenly he couldn't be here and be normal. He couldn't be around them and not feel something.

Though hell if he knew what that something was. "You know, I don't know why I came here. I…I think I should head back to my apartment."

Mia turned around to face him just as Dell entered from the kitchen. They both stared expectantly at him, and it hurt. He didn't want to think why it hurt.

*Because you want this.*

No. He didn't… He had to…

"What's wrong?" Mia asked, taking a step toward him, a mix of compassion and worry in her eyes.

He noticed that he wasn't the only one staring openmouthed at her question, Dell had the same expression on his face, but Mia just rolled her eyes.

"I may have *taken* the Wainwright name, but it doesn't mean I have to play the weird *let's pretend everything is fine when someone is hurting* game all you Wainwright *men* employ. When someone looks like they've been emotionally stabbed, you ask what's wrong."

"I have not been emotionally stabbed," he said indignantly, even though that was *exactly* what it felt like.

"Oh, of course. You're a big strong man and totally fine and it's nothing to do with the fact you and Meg had the ultrasound this morning and now you're here, alone, growling like a lion with a thorn in its paw."

"Know a lot of lions?"

Mia merely raised an eyebrow.

He didn't want to talk about this. He didn't... "We had a fight, I guess. Meg and I." *Fight* seemed the wrong word, but it tumbled out. What was he doing? He didn't unload his problems on other people. He didn't hope for *advice*.

He handled things on his own. He always had. "About what?" Mia asked gently.

Why was she asking him these things? People did not ask if he was all right.

"I couldn't even tell you. Not really. Everything was fine, and then..." He'd been firmly put back in that place she'd put him in at the diner. The condescending *likes of you*.

He could have gotten over it, he could even have accepted it as something she didn't mean, but he didn't know her any better than she seemed to know him, and at the center of that was that she wouldn't let him into this family history of hers, which made her run to the bathroom, which made the color drain from her face.

So what the hell was he supposed to do? How

was he supposed to put that in words for Mia and Dell? Without falling apart?

He fished the ultrasound picture out of his pocket. Because this was what really mattered. "You know, it isn't so important. This is the important thing."

"Can I?" Mia asked, holding out her hand.

Charlie handed it to her and she looked at it, eyes immediately going misty. "Oh, isn't it just amazing?" she asked in a watery voice.

"Why are *you* crying?" Dell asked helplessly.

"Oh, shut up," Mia muttered without any heat, wiping her eyes. A cry sounded from the hall and Mia handed the picture back to Charlie. "I'll go get her. You," she said, pointing at Dell. "Do something."

"Like what?"

"Support him, jackass." Mia disappeared down the hall.

"She seems to be feeling better," Charlie offered tonelessly.

"Yeah, the medicine really helped."

They stared at each other in silence before turning away. Charlie shoved a hand into his pocket, still holding the picture with his other hand. "I'm fine."

"Hey, let's not straight-out *lie*."

He stared at the ultrasound. "No, I really am. Because the important thing is the baby is healthy.

Anything else is…" He blew out a breath. "I've never felt like this," he muttered. Angry and hurt all over again. "I don't get her at all. I don't get *myself.*"

"By her I assume you mean Meg?"

"Yes, Meg. She's so bright and funny and she gets…" *Me. She gets me. I thought she got me.* He didn't know how to say that out loud, so he paced the small living room. "I don't know what to do with this."

"And by this I assume you mean feelings."

He stopped pacing, let out a painful breath. "Yes, I suppose that is what I mean."

"Yeah, that's the kicker." Dell sighed gustily. "Look, it's… In my experience, you're going to be stubbornly miserable until you accept that you've got to get over yourself and change a little bit."

"*I'm* not the problem."

Dell laughed then, and Charlie couldn't help bristling. *He* was usually laughing when Dell argued with *his* advice. He was the older brother, the life-together brother. *Not anymore.*

"I'll give you the possibility that Meg might *also* be the problem, but very rarely is it just one person."

"Are you saying Mia was part of the problem when you two were pushing each other away?"

"No, Mia was perfect." Dell grinned. "But she's an exception."

"You're addled."

"Likely, but listen. Love is—" Dell cleared his throat "—hard. It's complicated. It's a lot of give-and-take that is really damn uncomfortable—and that's not even just in the beginning."

"I didn't say anything about love. I barely…"

Dell merely raised an eyebrow.

"It's not about love," Charlie repeated, and it didn't escape him that he sounded desperate and panicked.

"You have my sympathy," Dell said. He glanced at the hallway, where Mia reappeared, a sleepy Lainey curled around her. "But you'll find that if you can get over yourself, nothing could possibly be more worth it."

Charlie couldn't argue with that if he wanted to, not in the presence of it. Love and family and support and appreciation.

But he didn't know how to get *over* himself. He didn't know how to deal with the word *love* echoing around in his head. "This was not the plan."

Dell's echoing laughter in response to that would stick in his head for a very long time.

# CHAPTER TWENTY-ONE

MORNING SICKNESS WAS HELL. Everything she ate sounded good one minute but then was rushing up the next. Every smell that usually soothed her turned her stomach. She could barely walk into the barn.

She wanted so badly to text Charlie this morning and tell him not to bother to come help. She didn't *need* his help. But, unfortunately, today she did.

If Elsie had been a little bit stronger, Meg would have asked her, but the woman was still recovering from chemo—for all her clean bills of health, she couldn't wrestle goats and carry heavy cans of milk.

So, no, Meg had to suck it up and let the man who didn't *know her* help, because she legitimately could not take the smell of the goats this morning. Every time she tried to step inside, each cell in her being revolted.

"So much for pregnancy being magical," she muttered, stomping around and pouting because she didn't know what to do with herself. She had herbs to process and soaps to mold and package and all she wanted to do was lie on the bathroom floor hugging the toilet miserably.

"You're worth it, Seedling," she murmured, putting her hand over her belly on the offhanded thought the baby could sense her irritation, her restlessness. "You are, don't get me wrong, but, boy, does this suck right now!"

Maybe she could move the entire milking apparatus outside. It would be a pain, and she'd have to hold her breath to make it happen, but...

The sound of a car on gravel had her head swiveling to the front. To Charlie. Her shoulders relaxed because *thank God* help was here, even as her heart tensed because, oh, what the heck was she going to do with him? Just looking at him hurt.

But she didn't know how *not* to look at him. How not to follow his every move, because he was like some kind of sun she revolved around. A force she desperately wanted to be near, next to, *with*, but something always kept her away. Something like the universe and her own stupid head.

When he approached, she steeled herself to stand there and face him and not run away crying like part of her wanted to do.

"Hello," he offered, his tone flat in a complete failure at geniality.

"Hi. I...I'm glad you're here."

"Are you?"

"I'm having some morning sickness issues and I need your help."

His eyes studied hers, that penetrating gaze that made her feel like slime. Not because *he* thought she was slime, but because he didn't. Because he could look at her and want something from her other than...bad things.

She closed her eyes.

"Meg, no matter what happens between us, I am always here to do whatever it is you need so that you can take care of the baby, yourself and your business."

"Why?" She wished she could keep her eyes closed, but she wasn't that much a coward. "Why? Why, why, why?"

His eyebrows drew together, all barely restrained frustration, and she wanted to push him for no reason she could make sense of.

"Why would I *help* you?"

"Yes. Why would you help me? Why would you want to? Why are you here?" *Why are you wonderful and gorgeous and something I want that will inevitably find out I'm not worth it?*

"It's simple."

"It isn't simple!" Oh, she was so *angry* and she didn't even know why. Because she wasn't really angry at him, except he was saying it was simple. Simple? Simple to feel so mixed-up and out of her depth and like she *used* to. When was the last time she'd felt so worthless and so insecure? It had been a long time.

So, no, this wasn't simple, and as much as she wanted to keep those thoughts to herself, they seemed to have a life of their own, needing air, needing to be voiced. "It isn't simple at all! Because I don't understand! I don't understand why you left, why you think you don't know me, why you came back. I don't understand *anything* and it isn't damn simple."

"You think I understand?"

"You just said it was simple!"

"Me helping you is simple. Me being here is simple. Feeling like I don't know you? *Wanting* to be here? Listening to you talk the way you do sometimes when there's terror in your eyes, no, *that* isn't simple and hell if I know what to do with it."

Only when he mentioned seeing her terror did she realize they'd been yelling, that things were getting all kinds of out of hand. She tried to breathe, but it was hard to do evenly, smoothly. She placed a hand over her stomach, that center of calm and sanity. "I don't know what you're talking about."

"Bull. Shit, Meg."

She blinked at him.

He took her by the shoulders, somehow both

gentle and firm at the same time. His dark eyes bored into hers, desperate and determined and all sorts of formidable words and scary feelings.

Scary because they were feelings she wanted, she recognized. Scary because she didn't know how to have those things.

"You know what I'm talking about. You know exactly what I'm talking about. Sometimes you go somewhere in your head and you look petrified and anytime I'm a little extra nice you look a little horrified before you settle into it. You know exactly what I mean when I say the blood simply *drains* from your face anytime I mention *anything* that has to do with your parents—even if *I* don't know it has to do with your parents."

His grip tightened and he didn't so much shake her as give her a little jerk. "What is it that goes through your head?"

This was even worse than yesterday. Yesterday had hurt. He didn't know her and he walked away and it hurt like hell, but she knew what to do with that. With hurt. She didn't know what to do with someone…wanting something more from her. Because he cared instead of wanted to mold her into something else entirely.

"Why are you doing this?" she whispered, because couldn't he see she didn't have the words? Couldn't he understand she didn't know *why* she felt this way, that it was only that she did?

"Because I think I'm in *love* with you and I don't know what to *do* with that!"

It was like a bomb had exploded, taking out everything around them. She couldn't hear a thing. She couldn't move. She wasn't even sure she could breathe.

Love. He'd said…love. In regards to *her*. "B-but you said you didn't even know me," she managed, her voice nothing more than a high-pitched whisper.

"I don't! I don't know the whole you because there are all these things you keep hidden, all these secrets you refuse to let me in on, and it drives me insane. But I know you remind me of sunshine when you smile, and I want to touch you always. I like being here and it should be the last place I'd ever want to be, but you're here, and you make anything and anywhere the place I want to be. I don't know how or why, I only know that is how I feel and it's *insane*."

Oh God. Oh God, oh *God*. "Charlie."

Suddenly he let her go, so suddenly she all but tripped.

"I have to go," he muttered, shoving his hands through his hair, taking determined strides back toward his car.

"What?" she nearly screeched, scurrying after him.

"I have to go figure this out. I can't do it here with you looking at me like that."

"Like what?"

He whirled on her. "Like it's possible, Meg. Like anything…" He shook his head, turning back to his car and jerking the driver's-side door open. "No."

"Charlie, you can't just drop that bomb on me and *leave*."

"Fine." Before she knew how to prepare for it, his mouth was on hers. His arms banded around her and held her so close to the uncompromising hardness of his chest she could barely breathe.

But he was kissing her, *holding* her, apparently loving her, and she didn't want to breathe. She wanted to sink, to melt. So she did. She leaned into him, pliant and willing, meeting the soft glide of his tongue, sliding her palms up his back as his fingers got lost in her hair.

She didn't know how long they stayed like that, how long they let one kiss lead to another, touch after touch. Exploring and soft, but not demanding.

Because he thought he might *love* her. *Her*.

He pulled back a fraction of an inch, his eyes blinking open in time with hers. He gave a sigh, something sad contained in it. "Meg." His fingers traced her hairline, his eyes searched hers.

"Don't stop." Stopping would mean talking, and she'd rather explore and feel and show.

She didn't have words. She didn't have a way to verbalize all the fear and insecurity inside her, but she could show something in the way she touched him, the way she gave herself to him.

A few insistent bleats filled the air and she had to sigh against the unfairness of goat schedules. "Except we have to stop. They have to be milked. I haven't been able to stomach it."

"I'll do it." His thumb grazed her jaw, back and forth, soft and sweet. "And then we'll talk, okay? Really talk?"

She knew what that meant, what he wanted, and more, she knew that if she had any hope of this really being love. *Love* love, she would have to be willing to talk. To put to words her fears, and the things that had shaped her.

She would have to give him things she'd wanted buried. It was the only option with love on the table, because as much as she didn't want to lose that, she knew if she kept this from him, she didn't have love at all.

"Okay," she said, more than a little terrified. "We can talk."

He brushed a brief, gentle kiss across her mouth before stalking to the goat barn like a man on a very unpleasant mission.

But he was milking her goats, and telling her he might love her, and she had to do something. Grab on to it. Not just for the baby, but for herself.

Which was scarier than everything else in her life put together.

WHAT WAS HE DOING? *What are you doing?* "What am I doing?" It was a constant three-part refrain as he went through the process of milking Meg's goats.

It was oddly relaxing. There was a repetitiveness to the system that gave the thoughts in his head a certain kind of lulling rhythm. *What am I doing?* Pull—squirt. *What are you doing?* Pull—squirt.

He'd kept himself distracted as he worked through the entire herd of milkable goats, and then he went through the process of sanitizing and storing the milk. But once he was done with the heavy basics of Meg's usual chores, he could no longer deny the simple truth.

He'd told her he might love her. He'd grabbed her and kissed her and been some kind of crazed version of himself and it wouldn't do. It would *not* do.

He scrubbed his hands over his face, trying to scrub some reason or sense into his brain, but it didn't work. Nothing *worked.* No amount of thinking, processing. No number of attempted plans he'd tried to work out over and over again lying in the twin bed in his old room at his parents' last night.

There were no answers, there were no plans,

there was only this bone-deep feeling of uncertainty and confusion and fear and...

Yeah, that love thing. He couldn't get over the fact that he wanted to be here, with her. That, baby aside, he liked the man he became when he was with Meg. Even this one—the one who had no idea what he was doing.

Because it was real. A lot realer than he'd ever been. It took no masks and it took no swallowing his tongue. It took no careful words. He didn't have to be perfect or responsible or the epitome of a businessman. He didn't have to impress anyone, or prove that he'd made the right choices to anyone.

Yes, anyone probably meant most especially his father, which had then become something like showing Dell. He'd lived the majority of his life trying to prove something that...well, he'd never really had to prove.

Because Dell had taken the farm even against Dad's wishes, and he'd built a life he was sickeningly happy with. So all the attempts to build the life someone else wanted of him had been wrong.

He'd been good at what he'd done, and there had been parts of it he'd enjoyed. But there had been an emptiness to it he'd ignored, because it didn't fit the *plan*.

Now he had Meg. He had his family seeking his expertise. It felt like people knew him, understood him, and that had done a lot to fill up that emptiness or tear down that armor or whatever it was.

Love. He *loved* her. There was a chance here to have a real life, without a plan, without forcing himself into a hole he didn't really fit in.

He stood in the doorway of Meg's barn. He didn't love milking goats or processing milk, and he didn't love helping Dell with farm chores. He didn't hate it, but it wasn't as though farming had become a new passion.

But there was something to be said for building something that was your own. For being outside and seeing the sky.

Maybe, just maybe, there was something to be said for moving forward without a plan. *That sounds idiotic.* Because the reasonable part of his brain hadn't simply rolled over and died, but it refused to give him a better alternative.

So he marched toward Meg's cottage having no idea what he would do when he got there, only knowing he needed to move forward. He needed to move, and if there was no set of footsteps to follow, no concrete goal to reach, well, maybe that was just a life he'd been avoiding for as long as it could be avoided.

Now it was here.

He forced himself up the stairs of the stoop. He stepped into the cottage like he might have stepped into any potentially fraught business meeting.

And then winced at the comparison. But she stood with her back to the door, carefully pulling a piece of toast from the toaster and placing it on a paper plate.

"I did everything you normally do," he offered, sounding like a robot.

"Thank you. Would you like some toast?" she asked, sounding far too polite.

"No, I wouldn't." He wanted answers and something to make sense, and maybe scariest of all, the thing he was really trying to avoid thinking about, he wanted her to have some *inkling* of return feelings for him.

But they only stood there, in uncomfortable silence, him by the door, her by the toaster. No words. No way to interrupt the droning quiet.

She stayed in the same place, staring down at the plain piece of toast she'd taken all of one bite of. She took a deep breath, let it out, and he was about ready to bail, because this wasn't how it was supposed to go and he didn't know what he was supposed to do and—

"It's just…" She poked at the bread, frowning down at it as if it had done something wrong.

"Love is a big scary thing," she said carefully and quietly, slowly rotating the piece of toast on her plate.

"Yeah, it is." A big fat scary-ass thing he'd rather do anything than deal with, but it wasn't—apparently—something he could plan away or reason away or ignore. It sat there on his chest and he needed it to stop doing that.

She turned to face him, though it took a while for her to lift her gaze to his, and so many questions and so much uncertainty reflected in her eyes he didn't know what to do with it all. Why it wasn't working the way it was supposed to, why it was more of a question and a problem than the answer every stupid movie and book made it out to be.

"Do you really think…you could love me?"

There were a lot of ways he could take that sentence, but the inflection on *me* as if it was so insane, so crazy someone could love her…

He stepped forward. "Why do you say it like that? As if it's some kind of surprise I could love *you*. Why would that be something you have a hard time believing?"

For a few painful moments she only stared at him, that wide-eyed way that never quite masked the hurt or fear. But didn't face it either. How did he get her to *face* it?

"You know you have to tell me," he said, not

sure why it felt imperative. Like it was now or never. Like they had to move, talk, *give*. They had months before the baby was born, but he didn't know how much longer he could keep trying to make sense of this and not find an answer.

She turned then, breaking that gaze, shutting herself off and away. "Tell you what?"

He could walk away. He could *force* himself to forget he'd ever uttered the words. He could move forward and keep her at arm's length. He could do that, he had to believe he could do that.

But he could see clearly, in this moment, himself. The way he'd held himself apart, kept his problems inside. Every girlfriend who had said he was closed off or cold had been right, because he'd never known how to open himself up to that. Give himself like that.

He'd never known how to share his fears or his problems in any real way, not with his family, not with his friends. Never known how to ask to be a part of anything, to be thought of differently. He could see it so clearly as she did it to him. That she hadn't opened up because of that fear, because of that certain lack of knowledge.

Unfortunately seeing it didn't make this any easier, because she was the person who'd opened him up and changed him. She had offered him a way to give all those pieces of himself he'd never given.

But he wasn't that for her.

*Why not?* He hadn't fought for much in his life, not really. Things had been easy. He'd worked his ass off, but he'd never come up against a real complex obstacle.

Until now. He didn't want to be the kind of man who backed down, over and over again, because he couldn't fight. That wasn't the kind of man or father he wanted to be.

Charlie Wainwright could damn well fight. "We can't be at this point and you still think that it doesn't matter, that you can beg me off. You have to give me this part of yourself, or nothing else will matter. What I feel, what you feel, whatever our future is going to look like. None of it will matter unless you can give me this."

"So you love me because of all that stuff you said outside, and you need me to…do what, exactly?"

"Tell me what puts that look of terror on your face. Tell me why on earth you're *surprised* I *could* love you. I get being surprised, I do, because nothing about this has been *normal*, but that isn't what you said. Your tone made it sound like you're some kind of unlovable creature. You think that. I *see* you think that, and I want to know why. Why and how you could *possibly* think it."

"I try not to," she said in a small voice.

Which was the teeny tiniest step forward, and he held his breath for the next move.

## CHAPTER TWENTY-TWO

MEG FELT UNMOORED. Unglued. Un-something. It was such an unsettling feeling to have someone see through her enough to get it—that deep, insecure part of her—but not be able to understand it.

She didn't want him to. Not at all. It was such a weakness, such an ugly thing. It was better hidden and dead.

*Except it isn't exactly dead if he can see it, is it?*

He saw it, even if he didn't understand it. He *loved* her, and no one had ever used that particular weapon against her. She didn't know how to shield herself from *love*.

"I've told you my parents weren't very nice people." Because even if it was childish, she didn't know how to start her story without beginning there.

"In very generic abstracts, and I've seen enough of that with my own eyes to know it's probably true. What I want to know is *how*. I want to know the story. A beginning and a middle and some kind of end. A cause, an effect."

"Life isn't that linear, Charlie. Some things are

messy and hard and they don't have beginnings and endings and concrete causes and effects." Some things lingered, no matter how clean you got, how much of a life you built. Some hurts never healed.

"Give it a shot," he said, teeth clenched. No, not said—demanded, and in another lifetime the demand might have pissed her off, but all she could think was he thought he could love her. Really love her. She didn't know how to do anything but be *soft* over that.

"I used to be pigeon-toed."

"O-okay."

"I don't know if they call it that anymore, but I walked with my toes pointed inward. The pediatrician told my mother I'd grow out of it. She took me to five or six different doctors, demanding they put braces on me or something that would 'fix' me, but they all told her the same thing—it wasn't a big deal. That, right there, is the metaphor for my childhood. They only ever saw me as something *wrong*, even when they were being told everything was fine. I was never what they wanted, and eventually they stopped trying to fix me. The appearance mattered more to them than anything else in the world, including me."

"Did you ever talk to someone who... Did you ever have some..." He trailed off, looking immeasurably uncomfortable, and she was irritated enough by the fact that *he'd* been the one to push this, that she answered.

"Counseling? Therapy? Oh yes. Eventually I got tired of being told how wrong I was, so I set out to prove it. I *wanted* to make them angry, because a reaction was better than criticism. Yelling was better than the laundry list of things I'd tried so *hard* to do right only to fail. So first there were school counselors, middle school and high school. Then there were the psychiatrists my mother insisted I see—who also said I was fine, by the way. *Normal teenage rebellion.*"

Until it went beyond normal, because neither doctors nor psychiatrists could make her into a girl fit to be a Carmichael. She stared hard at the mangled piece of toast on her plate, trying to keep herself in the present.

She wasn't in a psychiatrist's office while her mother berated him for being a fool, and then her for being a disappointment. Defective. A stain.

"Of course you were fine." Charlie's voice was soft but certain, and it helped anchor her where she was—years removed from the toxic life of her youth.

"I do actually know I'm not defective." She looked him straight in the eye, because it was true. She might have her insecurities, she might have a hard time trusting someone to see it, believe it. But she knew she was fine.

If he was going to demand she tell him, if she had to watch his opinion of her change, she definitely had to be certain of her own. She had to have her own foundation to stand on here. The belief that she wasn't defective. She wouldn't go back.

Oh, she might love Charlie, but he couldn't ruin her life, this life she'd built, this child she'd helped create.

She trailed her fingers across her abdomen. Love. She loved him, and Seedling. She did. Wholeheartedly. And somehow, in the oddest of ways, *that* realization made it seem far more possible to tell him everything.

"Good, because that sounds horrible. Tragically horrible, Meg, to be treated that way as a child."

She could *tell* he wanted to reach out and touch her, but everything about her stance was protective. She didn't want to be touched or soothed. She needed to tell him first. She needed to stand in that power, that truth, before she could run the risk of falling a little bit apart.

"Well, I gave it back to them tenfold, all in all," she said, doing her best to sound ambivalent. "Embarrassed them in front of their friends and business associates. Made sure I was the biggest disappointment I could be. My grandfather was sick at that time, Alzheimer's, and my grandmother was his primary caretaker. She'd always been that…soft spot to land, but I barely saw her while she took care of him. She didn't have the time or the emotional wherewithal. So things got ugly. In that house, in myself. I wasn't always good. I wasn't always right. So, while I know I'm not defective, while I know we all have our weaknesses, I just… I could see where someone like you might not see me in a positive light. Where someone good and right would have a hard time loving someone who's done such ugly things."

"Do you think I've been perfect?"

"Maybe?" She laughed, somewhere between amused and flustered. "I could see you being very, very perfect. You have that way about you. Determined to do the right thing. Always."

"I…"

"See, you can't even argue with me."

"No, I can't…not exactly." He rested his hands on her shoulders, because he must have had some sense that she was turning in on herself, turning away. It was hard to believe she wasn't a little defective in the face of his goodness. But he didn't stop talking, stop explaining, stop giving.

"I've always had a very dedicated sense of right and wrong," he continued, "and I followed that sense, yes. But you know, when I was sitting there with your father in that restaurant—"

When she tensed, he smoothed his hands up and down her arms, a slow, consistent comfort.

"—I could remember the games businessmen play. The way they treat people, look at them like objects, and I don't know that I ever did anything truly *wrong*, but I wasn't a particularly good person either. I wasn't a particularly *present* person. I was detached from myself, and it was comfortable. But that didn't make it right or good."

"It isn't the same." A little detachment, a few business tactics. *Please.*

"What horrible things did you do that you're so sure of that?"

She thrust out her tattooed arm. "Trust me, some days this was enough. A boyfriend on a motorcycle." Pills. Vodka in water bottles. Stealing.

"Where was your father in all this?"

She waved a hand, trying to find that sense of calm where past hurts couldn't touch her. "Business trips. Fancy dinners. Work. Whatever." When he was home, managing to find whatever good parts of Meg Mom hadn't squashed so he could poke at them, as well.

Every attempt Meg had made to embarrass them or hurt them had only ever backfired. "They didn't love me. Not ever, I don't think. The only person who ever did was my grandmother."

Charlie touched gentle fingers to her temple and brushed hair behind her ear. He traced her jaw with the thumb of his other hand and she'd never felt so…*seen*. He didn't stop at the surface, or look right through her, and it had been so rare. Even those friends she'd done stupid things with whom she'd thought understood her *so well*. No, it had been a figment of teenage drama and stupid substance abuse.

"*I* love you," he said carefully, his gaze never leaving hers, as if he wouldn't move, wouldn't stop, until she saw it. Believed it.

It was so big, his certainty. That determined, simple deliverance of words. She wished she could build armor against it, because it was so much. She didn't know how to accept it or give it. She wanted it, desperately, but she thought the fear of accepting it might be bigger than that want. "I don't know what to do with that. I wish I did. I wish I knew how to…be loved."

He kept touching her face, those gentle, easy caresses, and it was almost like being hypnotized. By the determination in his dark eyes, by the simple surety in those easy touches. By his voice, insisting again and again that *love* was possible.

"Our baby will love you." His voice was low, but it didn't diminish the power of that. Of his utter confidence. "Unconditionally. Not just because they won't have a choice, but because I already know you'll give them so much."

"How? How do you know that? She…" She closed her eyes against the memory of Mom telling her she wasn't fit to do this. Because she didn't want that memory, she wanted Charlie's surety.

"She what?" Those gentle fingers moved from her face, down her arms, to her hands, where he laced them with hers.

"She said I'd never be able to do it. The mom thing. And I know she's wrong." She straightened her shoulders, forced herself to be strong and look at him. "I absolutely know that, because I can't be worse than her. I can't be. I *won't* be. But how can *you* be so sure?"

"I've watched you take care of your goats."

"Oh my God. You've gone insane. You're comparing goats to babies."

He actually laughed and smiled, and she'd forgotten how easy it was to get that reaction out of him. How much she liked doing it.

"The thing is, you give your whole self to them. To Elsie. To everyone. I don't think you realize that."

She blinked at him. He had a point. He might not understand it, that it was easy to *give* to animals or people who needed something. The chance of rejection was so low, the reward so high.

But even if he didn't get why or how, she *would* give everything to their child. She was determined on that point, and slowly, painstakingly over the course of her adult life, she'd learned that if she was determined enough and worked hard enough, she could do what she set out to accomplish.

"I know you'll make a wonderful father," she said, because aside from it just being true, she couldn't take all this scrutiny of her—even if it was the positive kind. *At some point he'll see the truth.*

No. There was no truth to see. This was her truth. She wasn't perfect, but she was damn well *good enough.*

"Do you *know* that?" he asked, with just enough uncertainty she didn't hesitate to lean into him, to hold on to his hands as tightly as he was holding on to hers.

"You're so good at taking care. At stepping in and doing the right thing." That he would ever think otherwise, that *he* could have any insecurity, was baffling to her.

"Maybe the former more than the latter." He looked over her shoulder when he said it, a self-deprecating tone to his voice, as though he were trying to make a joke, and failing, because he felt it to be too true.

"You've taken such good care of me." Over and over again, he'd been here. He'd offered himself, his family. Heck, he'd offered his name. From the very beginning he had stepped up to be a part of this. She couldn't believe it wasn't just *natural.*

The corner of his mouth quirked. "I guess I'm

learning." His thumbs brushed over the insides of her wrists. "You're the first person I've ever wanted to learn for."

She had to breathe carefully, or she thought she might cry or launch herself into his arms and never let go. Something. She wanted to have the same calm acceptance he had. "That's all we can do, I think. Try and learn. Get back up again when you fail."

"And what do you do when you succeed?"

His thumbs kept moving back and forth against the skin of her wrists, making goose bumps travel up her arms. The touch was constant, and wonderful, like he couldn't just hold her, he had to touch.

"I don't know, I guess. Keep going?"

"You've built a lot. I assume your parents didn't help."

"My grandmother did. Financially, in the beginning. I'm no rags-to-riches story. More like riches to other riches. I one hundred percent couldn't have built this without her money, or her belief in me."

"Maybe not. But that doesn't take away the hard work it took to get to a place where you could support yourself and your child on a business you made and love. That's a special thing."

"I'm not fragile, you don't have to constantly be pumping my ego."

"You asked me how I could love you. You

don't get to back out when I tell you exactly how and why."

"Touché," she grumbled, burrowing her head a little farther into the crook of his neck. She liked being here. She liked…him. More than that. It really was more than that. The big thing he seemed so sure of. She wanted that. That certainty, that belief in something big and wonderful.

The only way to have that, truly, was to take it. To be brave and take it. "I love you too." She breathed in sharply. "Holy shit, that's scary to say."

He laughed, dropping her hands and wrapping his arms around her. "Well, at least we're in the holy shit scary together."

She slowly wound her arms around him, holding on tight. In it together. Yeah. "Yeah."

"And that's it?" he asked, his voice a serious whisper in her ear. "That's all the things you've hedged from telling me?"

She stilled and tensed.

"There's more," he murmured into her ear. "It won't change anything, Meg. I promise you that. I love *you*. Whatever you've done, it's resulted in this woman I love. Nothing changes that."

She wanted to believe him. Wanted those words to be stronger than years' worth of her mother's put-downs. She wanted to believe in Charlie, and he was here, wasn't he? Telling her it didn't matter.

"I...used." She swallowed, knowing a half-truth wouldn't work here. "Drugs. Alcohol. I used anything that might numb the pain, the constant sense of failure."

He shifted, something in his body changing, but he didn't push her away. He held her. She waited for him to pull away, to step back, to demand specifics.

But he held her and stroked her hair, and clearly he didn't understand what she was saying if he wasn't recoiling at least a little.

"I was an addict. For years. I've been clean for eight, well, clean of drugs. Alcohol was six, until Grandma's funeral, but only that one night. But all that time, all those years, I used. I drowned myself in pot and pills and hard liquor and—"

Finally he began to pull away and Meg couldn't begin to get a handle on the mixture of relief and fear that he finally got it.

He was going to walk away, and she knew what to do with that, even if she was afraid of what would happen in the aftermath. Someone withdrawing made so much more sense than someone sticking by her.

But he didn't step away. His hands came to her shoulders. His brown gaze held hers, and she couldn't read his expression, not beyond the terrifying realization he *wasn't* walking away.

"I can't say I know much of anything about substance abuse."

She wanted to laugh. Oh, Charlie wouldn't say something like addiction. No, he'd call it *substance abuse*.

"But I know you." His eyebrows drew together, much like when he'd been trying to work through words of love. Like he didn't quite understand his feelings, but he was working through them. Finding a truth he hadn't expected. "I know you, and I love you, and... Did you think that would change how I felt?"

"Yes."

"But you've been clean for eight years. That's... a long time, Meg. Adulthood. Why shouldn't I trust that?"

"Because you're you! Because you sneered at my tattoos when we first met. Because your family is perfect and loving. Because you've never, ever done anything wrong except manipulate a few people in a business setting."

"Maybe I didn't ever harm myself. With substances or otherwise, but in a very complex way I understand the need to...drown things. Feelings. I just did it with denial instead of alcohol."

She stared at him, realizing after a few seconds her mouth was hanging open. "This isn't what I expected."

He laughed then, trailing his fingers over her hair, her cheek. "*None* of this is what I expected."

He stepped closer so their legs were touching. He cupped her face and looked at her as though he could see inside, as if he could *pour* all those words of love inside her. "I've never done the unexpected. Not in my whole life. I never wanted to."

"Why would you want to now? With me? I'm a giant—what would you call it? Capital risk? Volatile investment?"

"You're neither of those," he said gently. "Not a mistake or a stain." His voice was like a balm, but it stripped away the last pieces of her strength.

"What am I, then?" she asked, too exhausted to care that tears had escaped.

He sighed, his thumbs dragging gently across her jaw. "I guess…that's something we both need to figure out. Who and what we are. But I'd like to do that together. How about you?"

Together. Even after he knew the worst of her. She couldn't help thinking it might be too good to be true. Together. Figuring out who they were. It was a dream. A fantasy.

But once upon a time, getting clean had been a dream. Then finding a place she belonged had been a fantasy. And now she had both. So…why shouldn't they figure it out together?

For Seedling. For themselves. For a future. "I like the sound of together," she managed, leaning into him. The fear didn't disappear, but it was muted with hope.

# CHAPTER TWENTY-THREE

"I'M TELLING YOU, I have a bump."

"Sweetheart, I have been sharing that bed with you for a month." Charlie grinned at her from where he was changing out of his goat milking clothes and into ones that could be smelled in public. "I would *know* if you had a bump."

She scowled from where she sat at the edge of the bed. They'd never really discussed it. Not specifically. It had just been, week after week, since they'd said those first terrifying I love yous, he spent more and more time exactly here.

He'd let the lease run out on his apartment. He'd sold off all his furniture and appliances and moved half of his things here, and the other half to his parents' house.

No one discussed it, and he never said out loud that he didn't have the apartment in the city anymore. It was just a thing that happened. Which was how everything in the past month had been. Things just happened. He didn't try to plan them; they didn't discuss. They just *lived*.

He couldn't remember ever feeling this happy.

There was a freedom in having no plan, a lightness in not knowing what tomorrow might look like. A comfort not to have to dissect every little choice or decision.

Or he'd gone insane, but it was a happy insane, so he wouldn't question it.

"Look!"

He glanced over at Meg, realizing he'd been lost in his own thoughts when she had a different pair of pants on. She was lying on her back on the bed, her legs hanging off the edge.

"I cannot button my pants. I have a bump." She pointed to the waistband of her jeans, unbuttoned, unzipped, so he walked over to indulge her.

He *liked* indulging her. He liked making her smile, and smiling in return. He'd never found that kind of easy belonging anywhere.

"Charlie, *look*." She demonstrated the true inability to button the pants once the zipper was up. "I have a bump!"

She seemed so utterly pleased with herself, and it was an amazing thing. They had the pictures—one on the fridge, one in a frame on her nightstand, and then they each kept one on their person—but something about a *bump* did make it feel a little bit more real.

He rested his palm on the slightest of curves of her stomach. Just enough to keep her from buttoning her pants comfortably, but a sign of the little thing growing inside.

"Amazing," he said, without an ounce of *indulging* in his tone, because it was amazing. Amazing to see, to feel. He leaned over and pressed a kiss to the center of the bump. "Amazing."

She grazed her palm over his hair, and he moved up farther to plant the same soft, reverent kiss on her mouth.

She sighed against his lips, trailing her fingers over the short growth of hair on his chin. "You have a meeting."

He grunted, because the meeting with Cara and Wes was about the last thing he wanted to do with his time at the moment.

"Don't act grumpy. I don't think you have any idea how happy you are when you get back from those."

"From what?"

"Meetings with all of them. You're always so energetic. I think you may have found your passion."

"My passion is telling other people what to do?"

"Yes, mostly," she replied deadpan, making him laugh against his will. "Although I believe you call it 'small business consulting' when you're trying to sound important."

"Hmm."

"It's true. Think about it. You might have found the answer to your perpetual unemployment, *aside* from being my goat milk boy. The farmers' market is rife with small businesses, and while they couldn't all need you or afford you, it wouldn't hurt to expand your client base."

He pushed himself off the bed. It was a weird thought. He wasn't sure it was a bad one, or even unwelcome, and he hadn't been trying at all to get another sales job. He'd been so busy helping everyone it had become a thing he'd do tomorrow or the next day or some weekend when he had time, and no time had popped up.

"You're quite the little businesswoman, aren't you?"

"Or I'm trying to keep you in my pocket."

"Lucky for you," he said, kissing the tip of her nose before returning to the closet so he could finish dressing for his meeting, "I like being in your pocket."

"Then you should think about it, a little more seriously." She fiddled with her button again. "Now, what on earth am I going to wear?"

"Those things you claim are pants that I claim are devices sent to torture me with an uninterrupted view of your ass?"

She laughed, such a light, tinkling sound. "Now, there's an idea." But she didn't move, she lay there staring at the ceiling, swinging her legs, a smile on her face as she rubbed her hand over her *bump*.

"How about I pick up dinner on my way home?" he offered. He'd been purposefully careful about that word—made sure to avoid it. *Home.* This was where he wanted his home to be, but he hadn't exactly been invited. They hadn't discussed it. So...

But she smiled, that soft, dreamy smile that made his chest tight because she seemed happy. It was rare he saw that wide-eyed somewhere-else look on her face these days. Things had changed.

They had no secrets. They had love. This life he hadn't been planning or organizing or *worrying* over was dreamlike in its perfection. Who knew mistakes could give you everything you ever needed?

"Text me right before you leave and I'll let you know what I want," Meg said from her place on the bed.

"Yes, ma'am."

She sighed. "Oh, that is my favorite."

"And you think *I* enjoy telling people what to do." He finished dressing, then crossed over to her and gave her a quick kiss—because anything more and he most definitely would be late. "I'll be back later."

Meg let her fingers trail down his arm as he stepped away. "We will be waiting. Me, Seedling, goats."

"Thank you for putting Seedling ahead of goats."

He left the cottage to the sounds of Meg laughing and said goats bleating and he couldn't stop *smiling*. He drove across town, barely paying attention to his surroundings. He didn't think he'd ever driven through New Benton feeling like he might belong here.

It was a heady feeling to think he'd found his place in the hometown he'd been sure didn't suit him. It was oddly exhilarating to think he wasn't so stiff and unrelenting that he couldn't be a part of these things. Things he'd always sneered at because...

Because he didn't know *how* to be a part of them. He'd wanted to please his father, and that had meant not even trying to love farming. But more, it had never been natural for him. Few things had been. He didn't have Dell's touch with the land, Kenzie's infinite patience with animals. He'd had a head for numbers, and the rest hadn't been easy.

So he'd shied away and convinced himself he was better. Better than farming and New Benton and his brother.

But it had been a way to cope with feeling alone, and misunderstood. And damn, that was quite the realization.

He pulled his car to a stop at Wes's cabin, barely knowing how he'd gotten there. Muscle memory and habit, he supposed. Because that sort of life and self-realization rang in his head like a gong.

He shook his head in an attempt to clarify his thinking as he walked across the expansive yard to the cabin Wes and Cara called home and business. There were a variety of animals roaming about the yard and they barely bothered to acknowledge Charlie's presence. When he knocked on the front door, a gruff voice on the other side called, "Come in."

Charlie stepped inside a large kitchen, where he'd met Cara and Wes for a lot of their business consultant meetings. Wes was hunched over his work making dog treats, his German shepherd at his feet.

"How's it going?"

"Good," Wes replied. "Cara and Mia are in the office. I'll be in when I'm done."

"Take your time. I've mostly got stuff for Cara today."

Wes nodded and Charlie walked through the kitchen back to the office. He stepped into the room to find Cara and Mia bent over a book.

"Oh, I recognize that tale of horrors," he muttered. "I hid it from Meg so she would stop obsessing about all the possible pregnancy complications, and I'm not afraid to hide it from you two, as well."

They smiled up at him, two women he wouldn't

have given the time of day to ten years ago. And now they were his *family*. Friends. They trusted his opinion when it came to their businesses, their kids would play with *his* kid and it made that heart-expanding feeling in his chest even bigger.

In his entire life, he'd never been as happy as he was on this day. Waking up with Meg, seeing the evidence of their baby growing, being a part of his family as wholly and fully as he *ever* had.

*Plus*, he had amazing news for Cara's ideas about expansion. "Well, Paul Collier and I talked for two hours yesterday." His grocery contacts had definitely come in handy for Cara's business.

Cara immediately threw the book on the other side of the couch. "And? Don't toy with me, Charlie!"

He handed her the file folder he'd put together on Collier's offer to carry Cara's Pies. She grasped it greedily and made high-pitched squeaking noises as she read through the papers.

"Oh my…" Cara trailed off as she flipped through the papers. "This is amazing." She looked up at him, her eyes suspiciously shiny. "Charlie, this is *huge*."

"It definitely has the potential to be that. If you cry, I'm taking the papers back and leaving immediately."

She rolled her eyes, giving a little sniff. "But this is such a big deal. A grocery store wants my pies. *Mine!* This is… I can't believe we conned you into doing this consulting out of pity," Cara said, shaking her head as her eyes perused the papers again. "You've just at least doubled my income."

*Pity.* The words hit him hard. *Did it out of… pity.* The word echoed in his head. *Pity. Pity. We did this out of pity.*

"Pity," he said aloud, not meaning to.

"You were moping around like a zombie, and your mom was about to lose it and get you a job at the post office, and who knew this was the answer all along." She finally raised her eyes from the papers, smiling and laughing so damn jovially.

But moping…and his mother… Hell, this meant not just Cara had *pitied* him, but Wes, Mia and Dell. They'd offered him these "consulting jobs" out of pity. Every good feeling whooshed out of him until he simply felt hollow.

He didn't belong. He hadn't finally stripped away all those hard layers inside so his family could see him, accept him. He'd been *pitied*.

He wanted to laugh. At least, he thought that was the weird feeling in his chest. A laugh. Sure. Because why the hell should he be *hurt* by that? It didn't matter. Why would it matter? He wasn't going to be *hurt* by pity from these people. How foolish they thought *he* needed to be *pitied*.

This wasn't his passion or what he'd been meant

to do, that much was shiningly, irrevocably clear. Any talk otherwise had been stupid words uttered by a besotted woman and an idiotic man.

"Charlie, please don't—"

"It doesn't matter," he said, holding up a hand to Mia, who he knew was going to try to gloss over Cara's words and placate him. *It doesn't matter.* And that was the truth of it. This work Meg thought was his passion wasn't really anything. Certainly not important or stable. It wasn't people *finally* seeing him for who he was or what he could offer. It was simply…pity.

"Look, I shoved my foot in my mouth," Cara said. "I didn't mean *pity* pity. We knew you'd do a great—"

Cara—of all people—had pitied *him.* Presumably Mia and Wes and his own brother did too. Dell, who'd done nothing but screw up and then luck into this…life.

Charlie had been insane to think this was happiness. That this past month was anything but shirking responsibilities and ignoring the realities of life. Dell and Mia, Cara and Wes, they could all play at this little small business farmers' market life, but it was *playing.* It was not a real world.

At least not one for him. When he played, people *pitied* him. When he played, he forgot everything that was important. Everything that had got him to this point where he *could* help people who *pitied* him.

It was like stepping into a familiar old piece of clothing. The cold that took over, the talking like a clipped businessman chastising his team. Finding no humor or nonchalance in the situation.

"I'd actually wanted to tell you both that I can only offer my services for the remainder of the month. Then I really do have to get serious about finding a real position."

"But tomorrow is the thirty-first," Mia replied, wide-eyed, and maybe there was even some hurt lurking in her expression.

He refused to see it. "Yes, well, like you both do, I have a child on the way, and I can't keep putting off the necessity of finding actual work." Work that might be able to flip his world upside down when he lost it, but not work that could tear his heart out.

He'd been lost when Lordon laid him off, but he hadn't been…*hurt*. His pride had been injured, he'd had a little identity crisis, but…well, he'd been stupid to think he could change his identity.

The man he wanted to be, the man he'd been the past few months, it was nothing more than a dream. A pretense. No one saw him as that, because it wasn't actually real. He was always going to be practical, upstanding Charlie Wainwright, and trying to be anything else had been an exercise in wasting time.

"You *have* been doing actual work for us, Charlie," Mia insisted.

"I have, yes, but I can't keep collecting a pittance from you all *and* provide for my child." He realized suddenly he'd never even asked Meg what her insurance situation was. How she planned to retire. If she had investments or savings. All the things *sane* Charlie would have thought about, obsessed over; instead he'd convinced himself he was in love and happy and that all those things he'd *known* were important would work themselves out.

That was for other people. People who could ignore reality. People like Dell, who could follow a dream. Charlie had never been that way. Too practical. Too smart.

Yes, he felt so damn *smart* right now.

He'd never even discussed living arrangements with Meg. No further talk of marriage, of what the baby's last name would be. He'd been sucked into some vortex of ignorance and he'd been so very stupid to think he ever belonged there.

"Would you like to talk about the Collier details? I'll always be available if you have a question, of course, but my job hunt and the subsequent job will really have to be a priority."

"Charlie, don't be upset," Cara said, worrying her hands together.

He lifted an eyebrow, an expression he'd honed in his teenage years when Dell berated him for not caring about the family land, perfected in his time as a boss at Lordon. *Were you under the impression that I care or think we're equals?* "Do I appear to be upset?"

Cara glanced at Mia, who only shrugged.

"It's funny, actually. I thought I was doing you all a favor, and you thought you were doing me one. Well, now it's time to stop playacting and move on with our lives."

"Charlie." Now there really was no missing the hurt in Mia's expression, but just because he saw it didn't mean it was his problem. He'd built a life that couldn't hurt him for a reason. He couldn't *stand* this feeling, so he'd ice it out.

And he'd make sure from here on out he remembered exactly what he got for being a stupid dreamer.

"If we're not going to discuss business, I do have other things to do today, ladies."

Cara sighed. "Let's go to the kitchen." She walked into the hallway, and Charlie waited for Mia to follow, but she stood by the couch, her back to him, surreptitiously typing something into her phone.

Charlie walked over to her, put his hand directly

over the screen. It took every ounce of control to keep the anger deep, deep down.

"Whatever you think you're doing, do not text my brother assigning some hidden upset or emotion to this. I am simply choosing to do what's best for all of us."

Mia raised her chin, fixed him with her best challenging glare. "Well, I don't agree with your best."

"You would be wrong, and if you think Dell is going to run to your aid and apologize profusely, you're only wasting everyone's time. I have a real life to lead. So does he. So do you."

"What would ever make you think the life you've been living for the past month isn't *real*?" Her voice had gone soft, and maybe if pity wasn't laced all through it, it would have had more effect. "It was your life, wasn't it? It was you *living* it," she continued, steel returning to her voice.

"I was doing you all a favor," he said, making sure his voice was flat and final. "That's all." Because if that life could hurt him like this, he didn't *want* it to be real.

She shook her head, disgust turning her mouth into a scowl. "I hope you lie better to Meg."

"Mind your own damn business, Mia."

"Excuse me," Wes said from the doorway, his voice dark and authoritative. "It's time for you to leave, Charlie."

He wanted to laugh. He wanted to throw a punch. He wanted to do a lot of stupid things with all these stupid, ridiculous *feelings* rioting through him.

Instead he smiled his best businessman smile. "I think you might be right." And he walked right out of the Stone cabin and didn't give a flying leap where he ended up.

# CHAPTER TWENTY-FOUR

MEG WORRIED. IT WAS probably silly, but it was there nonetheless.

He should have been home an hour ago. He should have at the very least texted her about food. But there was nothing. No responses to her texts, and he didn't answer when she called.

She paced the kitchen, trying to decide between calling him incessantly and being *that* kind of woman, and going out and seeking solace with her goats.

She glanced at the clock. It'd be time to milk them in about twenty minutes, and she was doing better at stomaching it in the evenings. She could do it on her own, even if she got a little nauseated, but she'd liked sharing the chore with Charlie.

Where on earth *was* he?

She heard the car before she saw it, which was odd. Charlie's sleek sports car didn't make much noise. She peered out the window, and when the vehicle came into view, it wasn't his black sedan, but a big black SUV.

Her stomach pitched. She could only think of

bad news accompanying a vehicle like that. And Charlie wasn't answering...

Oh God, what if something had *happened* to him? What would she do? What would Seedling do? What—

But those thoughts came to a screeching halt because no uniformed bad news bearers stepped out of the car.

It was her parents.

She thought she might pass out. Spots danced at the edge of her vision because she was hallucinating. She had to be hallucinating. That was *her* parents. *Her* parents getting out of the SUV, walking across *grass and gravel* to her...

"No. No, no, no." Meg ran through the house to the front door. It was bad enough they were here. The worst, absolutely the worst, but they would *not* set foot in her home. They would *not* spew their poison in her sanctuary.

She flung open the front door and ran out onto the porch, almost tripping. Which was enough to force herself to take a breath. To try to find some calm in the panic. She didn't need to take a stumble and hurt the baby because her parents were here.

Here.

She muttered a prayer she'd heard her grandmother say a thousand times over her grandfather's failing body. The words didn't penetrate the fog in her head. They didn't even make sense; she probably messed the whole thing up, but it centered her, it anchored her.

Against the storm that was coming ever closer.

"Margaret," Mother said, primly clutching her purse to her stomach. "I have no idea what to say about this place."

"I'd venture to guess the condescension in your tone says it all, really," Meg returned before she could stop herself. She had to find a line here. A line between cowering and panicking—because she had no idea what they'd do with that on *her* turf—and between being the abrasive teenager trying to piss them off.

She had to find some essence of Charlie's calm and detached dismissal when he was irritated. She took a breath and stood on the stoop. A silly thing to have this height leverage over them, but it made her feel powerful. Anything that gave her that right now was fine.

"Does it always smell this bad?" Dad asked, holding a handkerchief to his nose. He was dressed in his normal business attire. A well-tailored suit and shiny black shoes.

"Eau de goat," Meg said, trying to be cool and calm, and failing so very miserably.

"Well," Mom said, waving her hand in the air. "That's sort of beside the point, I guess." She turned her head to Dad, speaking out of the corner of her mouth as though she was trying to keep it between her and him. Of course, she was loud enough for Meg to hear every word perfectly. "Though I can't imagine raising a baby in this squalor and stench is in any way fitting."

"Why are you here?" Screw being *calm* or *cool*, she needed them gone before they filled her head with more doubts, more insecurities. Where was Charlie? Why wasn't he *here*, when she needed him?

"Well, you having a baby changes quite a few things."

Meg placed both hands over her stomach. It was such a futile gesture, but it always made her feel stronger. Like she could protect this growing thing inside her.

"It doesn't change anything for you," Meg said, finally finding the cool, dismissive quality to her voice she'd been seeking.

Of course, the terror on her face and the protective gesture probably gave her away, but it was a step.

"This child will be our grandchild. Whether or not it has the Carmichael name legally, *being* a Carmichael comes with certain responsibilities." Dad grimaced as he lowered the handkerchief. "Is Charlie here? I think he'd be far more amenable to this discussion."

"Charlie is none of your business."

"Oh, honestly, Meg. You are too old to be this difficult. If you care at all about this child, you have to think about the opportunities we can offer it."

"I can support my child on my own. And more, I will *love* my child, and that is far more important than the opportunities our last name can offer."

"I told you she wouldn't listen," Mom said acidly.

"That baby is a Carmichael," Dad insisted, clearly just *confused* she might think of that as a curse rather than a blessing.

"This baby is *my* baby."

"I told you we needed to talk to Wainwright," Dad muttered, as if she weren't even there. As if she didn't matter.

It was funny, but it didn't cut quite as deep as it used to. It was almost as if telling Charlie they didn't love her, verbalizing that thing she'd always known, telling him the truth, had taken some of their power away from them.

How could they hurt her? She already knew they didn't see her. This was not new. So it very surprisingly didn't cut her in half. It shockingly didn't turn her into a blubbering mess.

There were people who *could* love her through all her mistakes, all her failures. People who could see the woman she'd made herself into. People who wouldn't look at her and see a *mistake*. Not just Charlie, his family, Dan and Elsie. She had found a *family*. She had found love, and knowing Mom and Dad couldn't take it away gave her all the strength she needed.

She stood taller. "I'd like you to leave now. Stay away from Charlie. He has nothing to do with you."

"He's the father of my grandchild," Mom said, her ownership sending a cold shiver down Meg's spine.

She swallowed down the bile that rose in her throat. This child was *their* nothing. She wanted to believe that. She wanted… But she couldn't get that wrapped up in what she wanted. She had to think about what was *best* for Seedling.

It wasn't these people. It wasn't. Their money, their influence, oh, it could move mountains, but not if it was crushing you under those mountains while it did.

"What is it you really want? Let's cut through all the posturing and 'my grandchild' nonsense and be clear and honest." She barely bit back the *if you know how* on the tip of her tongue. "Why did you come *here*?"

"Obviously," Mom said, gesturing to the cottage and the goat barn, "we made a lot of mistakes with you, but we don't want the same fate for our grandchild."

Meg closed her eyes. It was going to be a war. Inevitably. There was no way around it. They would view Seedling as part theirs. Always. Forever. A chance to make up for their embarrassment of a daughter.

It was hard to fight back the black wave of futility that threatened. She didn't want to spend the rest of her life fighting her parents. She wanted to spend her life away from them, cut off from them. She thought she'd managed to do that, and now...

But no matter how many dark thoughts threatened, no matter how her stomach clenched, it didn't matter. Because she would work tirelessly for her entire life if it meant making sure Seedling was safe from this.

"I'm sorry you feel that way, but I will raise this child as I see fit."

"Obviously Charlie will have a say in things."

She gritted her teeth at Dad's insistence that Charlie was somehow different than her, better than her. "He doesn't think any more of you than I do."

Dad raised an eyebrow. "You think so?"

"I *know* so." Charlie would never betray her that way.

They all turned as the sound of another car entered the conversation, Charlie's black sedan coming to park next to her parents' vehicle.

*Thank God.* She wanted to run to him, but that would give her parents access to her front door, and as paranoid as it might be, she felt she had to protect it. Protect the cottage and any chance of them entering.

"Well, this is a surprise," Charlie said, his tone bland as he walked across the yard. "Is everything all right?"

He looked at her as he asked it, but she noted something very weird. He didn't come to stand next to her. He didn't make a move to block the door or her. He merely...stood there. All three of them on the ground, her still on the stoop.

"They showed up. I'd like them to leave."

"Now, Meg, no use overreacting. Charlie is a man of sense. He'll want to hear this." Dad clapped Charlie on the back.

Charlie didn't slap the hand away. He didn't even move. He merely looked at her dad's hand on his shoulder with a quizzical frown. "I'll want to hear what?"

"What the Carmichael name can offer your child."

"Our child," she said. "It can offer *our* child nothing. We don't want your offers. If, at some point, you're interested in this child as a human being, maybe we can discuss that. But this isn't a business acquisition. I won't let you treat it like one."

Charlie still didn't look at her. He hadn't brought food. He was hours late, and her father's hand was resting on his shoulder.

Something had happened.

It chilled her to the bone to see him looking at her father with a certain kind of consideration.

She'd spent so much of her life feeling alone, so much so she'd gotten used to it. She'd come to accept alone was the best version of her. Feeling alone around her parents was certainly no new thing. She'd always felt that.

But feeling alone with Charlie standing next to her was so painful she could scarcely catch a breath.

What had happened? What on earth did it mean?

"Charlie," she said, so carefully trying to keep her voice from trembling. "I need you to back me up here."

He finally looked up at her, nothing but a flatness to his expression. Not one emotion she could read anywhere in his eyes or the way he held his mouth. Everything was so blank.

"Charlie. Please."

He blinked, then looked back at her parents, standing there in their designer clothes, sneering down their noses at the things she loved beyond measure. The things that had given her a life beyond their incessant need to "fix" what wasn't broken inside her. The things that had saved her from alcohol and drugs and hating herself as much as they did.

"She's right, of course," Charlie said, and she could finally take a breath. "Opportunities are important, but not at the cost of our child's well-being. Unfortunately I'm not sure your involvement would be for the best."

He took a step then, away from her father's hand, onto the stoop with her. Finally, *finally* taking a step to her side. "You should probably go."

Her mother sniffed and huffed away, but her father stood there, eyeing Charlie in a way that made Meg want to step in front of *him*, to protect *him*, but that was silly. Charlie didn't need any protecting.

Without another word, Dad turned and walked back to his car, where Mom was already seated inside. The car started, backed out and away. They were gone. Gone.

Thank God. She leaned against Charlie, relief coursing through her so quickly she felt light-headed.

But he didn't put his arm around her. He didn't reassure her. He didn't do anything except let her lean, and her chest tightened again.

They might have dodged a bullet, but she had a very bad feeling something just as bad was coming.

# CHAPTER TWENTY-FIVE

CHARLIE STEPPED INSIDE Meg's cottage feeling as though his skin were suddenly made of lead.

"Where have you been?" Meg asked, stepping in behind him.

It wasn't accusatory. Not really. It was a simple question, gently asked. She probably pitied him too. Maybe love was nothing but fucking pity.

"I had some phone calls to make. Took longer than I expected." He knew he should touch her. Reassure her somehow that what had happened outside with her parents wouldn't happen again, but of course he couldn't do that. He had no doubt that last look Jeffrey Carmichael had given him had not been the expression of a man ready to give up on whatever he had it in his mind he had to do.

"Are you all right? You seem very different than the man who walked out of here a few hours ago."

He shrugged. "You know, I had a bit of an epiphany when I was going over business with Cara." That was all it was, really. A realization that all the playacting in the world didn't make him someone else. No one ever saw who he really was because it was a lie, and the fact that he'd thought Meg saw it had just been…delusion.

"Why do I have a feeling it isn't the kind of epiphany you left with?"

"I have an interview in Chicago on Friday."

"Excuse me?"

"I spent the past few hours calling all the contacts who'd offered me job interviews that I'd declined because they weren't here. Most were filled, but there was an opening in Chicago. I'll fly out for the interview and be back the same day." Sense. Responsibility. Surely not a failure.

And if it had taken him over an hour of staring at his childhood home to convince himself that those were the steps he'd needed to make, that didn't make him wrong.

"You're…interviewing for a job in Chicago?"

The incredulous note to her tone did nothing to stop him. "It hit me, you know, how little I was making. How little I'd thought about things like insurance and retirement. College savings and diapers. We haven't thought about this from a financial aspect at all. We don't have a plan." That a fantasy life was never going to be meant for him.

"*We* might not have thought of those things, but *I* have."

Her. Alone, because she didn't really need his help either, did she? She had everything handled without letting him into *any* of it. He was still the outsider he'd always been.

Hell, at least that man knew how to void out the pain, freeze it away. "You really think you can accomplish all that without your father's help?"

"No, I don't think that, Charlie. I *know* that." She curled her hands into fists, and he sighed, not wanting to fight her. He was tired of fighting *feelings* today. He wanted his gone, and he'd mostly banished them. If she picked at him, he'd lose that control. It was why he'd ignored Dell's texts. He was done with emotion, with hurt.

He was *done*.

"I know that whatever scrimping and saving I have to do to give my child everything that will give him a good life, a life full of opportunity *free* of Carmichael strings, is what I will do."

"That's foolish."

"Foolish," she echoed, shock and hurt and anger twisting into one simple repetition of his word. "You're talking about moving to Chicago and *I'm* foolish."

"I'm talking about *us* moving to Chicago."

She made a high-pitched sound. "I hope you're drunk, because that isn't funny."

"It isn't meant to be funny." Just a cold, rational plan of action. "We'll move to Chicago. We'll be able to offer the baby a nice life there." It would get him away from this fictional world he'd created for himself. He wouldn't hope for things there; he wouldn't be constantly searching for a place to belong.

It made sense.

"A nice life there? And what do you suppose I'll do with, oh, this?" She waved her hands around the house, and he assumed she meant the goats, as well.

He shrugged. "Sell it. I should make enough to support all three of us without you working. You know, studies show stay-at-home mothers—"

"Stop. Stop talking. You've lost your mind, and I can't *listen* to any more without crying. So I need you to stop."

He ignored her. He had to ignore her, because she was wrong. She should see how wrong. "I haven't lost my mind. I've found it. My mind, my sense, my reason. We can't sustain this life with a baby."

"Says who?"

"Sense, reason—"

She whirled away from him, disgust in every movement farther into the cottage. "Go sleep it off, Charlie."

"I'm not drunk, Meg. You don't have the first idea about how this really works. You said it yourself. Your grandmother made this for you while you were off drowning your sorrows. I don't think you understand the reality of finances."

She whirled again, taking a few threatening steps toward him. "Don't I?"

Her tone was a dangerous thing, full of land mines. He shouldn't go any further. He shouldn't keep pressing. He should hold her and tell her the truth of what happened.

Instead he hit where it would hurt. "Your father isn't evil."

She sank onto the couch, as if he'd shot her where she stood. Hell, he might as well have. He knew what he was saying. He knew what weapons he was using. He couldn't parse out why exactly.

Because he was a jerk, he supposed. To think he'd ever be anything but had been a laughable exercise in idiocy. Heartless, hard, uptight Charlie. That was *him*. Everyone saw it except Meg.

*Meg.* Something about that thought hurt even deeper than Cara saying she'd pitied him. That Meg saw who he'd always wanted to be but hadn't found a way to be.

But he couldn't dwell on that, or the ice would melt, the hurt would win, and then what would he be left with?

"You need to tell me what the hell happened," she said, those blue eyes boring into his. Her hope that there was some explanation was a terrible thing to crush.

But he had to. "Nothing happened."

"My ass, Charlie. My *ass*. You left here happy

and sweet and, if I'm not totally mistaken, *excited*. And now you're…you're… I don't even know what this is."

"It's reality."

She shook her head, not bothering to hide her disgust. It was like at the diner again, when he'd suggested marriage, except this time…he knew. He knew he was being a jerk. He knew he was being the absolute last thing she needed or deserved. He deserved her disgust.

But he didn't know how to be anything else. That way led to stupid dreams and *pity* and a pain he didn't know how to fight. "Do you keep your finances organized? We should go over them. It will give me a good idea of what salary bracket I'm looking for."

"Charlie. Stop." She shook her head, and her blue eyes were full of tears. But they didn't fall. They simply pinned him where he stood. "Stop the robot act, I know it isn't you."

It was his turn to feel shot. Because it *was* him. Everyone thought it was. How did she think there was anything more to him?

"So, tell me what happened." Her voice implored, her expression implored. It coaxed, it whispered promises he couldn't believe. Not now.

"I was discussing some financial information with Cara, and our discussion underscored how important it is for me to get a real job."

"That *was* a real job."

He wanted to laugh. Everyone thought it was real, but they didn't seem to understand reality included bills and opportunities that *required* money. "Do you know how much college costs?"

"Charlie, that's no reason to move to Chicago! Or anywhere. I'm not selling my business. It's my *heart*." She fisted her hand at her chest.

He chose to ignore her, ignore how he'd heard Dell say the same about the farm. It might feel like their hearts to them, but sometimes you had to do what was sensible with no thought to your damn heart. "And that's completely ignoring the fact that we could live in a better school district."

"We could live in a worse one too. You are a product of this school district, and you're brilliant."

Was she trying to kill him? Compliments and seeing this fictional version of himself? He couldn't stand it.

"You can't milk goats forever. I can't go around giving advice to farmers' market booths forever. Eventually this fad will pass, you know. They'll die out again and people will buy their food at the grocery store just like they do mostly anyway, and they'll order their weird soap on the internet. This is temporary."

She hopped off the couch, temper rising as clearly as the color in her cheeks. "Don't patronize me. I know what the market looks like, and I know its potential for being volatile in terms of supply and demand. *That's* why I was thinking of expanding, but beyond that there is this magic thing called *adaptability*. Where you change and grow and bend because you can't ever make the world this safe, sensible place. There will always be potential for failure and success and getting knocked on the ass. Didn't you learn that when you lost your job?"

"No, I learned hard work is bullshit and luck favors the lucky. The end." *And I am not the lucky.*

"I've worked very hard, and it's paid off for me."

"This is not reality," he threw at her, losing those last grips on patience and control. "It's *fantasy.* I want nothing to do with it. It was a nice vacation, but that baby giving you a *bump* deserves one of the people in his life to be rational. To be real. To acknowledge that opportunities are important. What happens if *adapting* doesn't work? What happens when this turns into another mistake? Another failure? Do you keep *adapting*, or do you go back to what got you here in the first place?"

"And what was that?" she asked, her voice a dangerous piece of steel.

"Drugs. Alcohol. When the *pain* of failure grips you again—because it *will*—do you go back to that?"

She reached out and slapped him right across the face. Hard.

He barely felt it, though he felt the shame of what he'd just said. "I deserved that," he said, his voice as calm and even as it had been outside.

"You're damn right you did," she seethed, but then she did something that stoked the rage he couldn't quite eradicate.

She placed both hands over her stomach.

Maybe he was being mean, but he was right. He was being rational. She didn't get to... No.

"Don't do that. Do not put your hand over your stomach like you have to protect that child from me."

"Seedling *should* be protected from you right now. I know what you're saying. I know what you mean by connections. So, that's exactly what I'm doing, Charlie. Protecting us both from your crap. You don't get to suggest my father has something to offer, and more important, you don't get to stand there and paint me as the villain in parenting this child. Something climbed up your ass and rattled around in your brain, and you want to be—" she waved a hand up and down his front "—this. Get out."

"Meg—"

"I am too hurt to be *rational* right now. So get out. Get. Out. Don't come back until you're willing to do it on your knees."

He could argue. He could apologize. There were a million things he could do, but quite honestly… he didn't want to be here. He didn't want to hurt her and he didn't know how to stop.

So, he did what she demanded and left without another word.

MEG STOOD THERE frozen for she didn't know how long. He'd…been someone else entirely and then left as though it didn't matter at all.

Not a word. Not a goodbye. Just turned and walked out the door, and she didn't know how to process that even a little.

Something had happened—something far more than an epiphany. Something far more than suddenly out of nowhere becoming obsessed with *reason* and finances.

Part of her felt sorry for him. But part of her was too livid to let that other part grow. To insinuate she might fall back into drugs, to say her father wasn't evil and act as though they might need her father's connections.

No, her father wasn't *evil*, but he wasn't good. He wasn't nice. He wasn't father- or grandfather-worthy, and the worst part was Charlie knew that. He knew it.

What on earth had *happened* while he was gone? Why wouldn't he tell her what was really bothering her? Acting like nothing had happened except he'd come to his senses. She wasn't stupid, and she wasn't that easily fooled. How dare he leave with words like love on his lips and return with that…whatever that was.

She stomped around the house, gathering her boots and gloves and everything she would need for tonight's milking. Which was now off schedule. She grunted and cursed all the way to the goat barn. She opened the door in the front and the back, hoping some of the sweltering heat would be alleviated with a decent cross breeze.

She took a few deep breaths before entering the barn, both to ward off the sick feeling but also to try to calm herself. Grumbling and swearing at the goats as she milked them wouldn't do any good.

It helped—the breathing, the sitting down and methodically milking each goat. It calmed her, soothed her, in a way very few other things would.

Oh, she was still angry with him. Still seething with fury if she thought too much about it, but in the end…in the end, she was, well, hurt. Which she didn't want to analyze too closely, and that was probably her own failing. Not his.

She simply felt raw and hollowed out now. Alone. A little antsy for a drink, though thankfully pregnancy gave her something concrete to fight that urge with.

"I won't be going down that road, Seedling. Not

ever again. That's a promise I'm going to stand by, no matter what your daddy says."

At the thought of Charlie saying that, and the word *daddy*, all Meg wanted to do was curl up and cry. But she couldn't. She went through processing the milk, feeling exceedingly exhausted and in no condition to work on any soap molds tonight. She just wanted to sleep.

*Alone. You are utterly alone.*

"Well, that simply isn't true, is it?" she said aloud, giving her belly a little pat as she locked everything up for the evening. "We'll always have each other."

She'd sink herself into the comfort of that for as long as she could.

For the third time that night, the sound of a car interrupted her; for the third time, her heart leaped in the hope that it was Charlie.

For the second time, she was disappointed, though she shouldn't be. She should be glad it wasn't like Charlie to rip out her heart a little harder so he could actually stomp on it instead of leave it there kind of bruised and hanging out, bleeding all over the floor.

Mia and Cara stepped out of Mia's farm truck, and Meg should have been pleasantly surprised and happy to see them. If she could get a handle on all this metaphorical bleeding.

"Hey, guys. I wasn't expecting you. Unless pregnancy brain really got to me."

The sun set behind them and she shaded her eyes against the fiery orange glow. She thought it might be symbolic, but she was afraid of the symbolism. Of that fiery end to this crap of a day.

"No," Mia replied kindly. "We're sorry to stop by unannounced. I could have called or texted. We've just been… I'm sorry. Is Charlie here?"

"He left," Meg replied flatly. *Just left.*

Mia blew out a breath. "I feel terrible. We made a mess out of everything."

"It was my fault. I had to open my big mouth." Cara rubbed her finger behind her ear. "He was weird, wasn't he?"

"If you consider being a cold asshole weird, then yes."

"Well, it *is* Charlie." At Mia's glare, Cara sighed. "In that…I think cold asshole might be his weird default. Look—"

But whatever she was going to say was interrupted by Mia giving her a little jab in the arm, both of them so sweet and pretty with their larger baby bumps and concerned expressions.

"He left, but he *was* here?"

Meg blinked, tried to find a blasé calm. "Yes."

"And he was cold *to you* in particular?"

Meg sighed. "Yes." Cold, total 100 percent asshole, and the worst part was some little part of her wanted to go after him, wanted to hold him, comfort him through whatever it was that had shaken him up so badly. But he didn't want that.

"It was our fault. I hope you know that. We... well, we asked for his help with our businesses because he was so lost with losing his job and everything. He was acting *so* strange, and I was worried about him, so I forced them all into—"

"Oh, don't martyr yourself over him," Cara interrupted her sister. "They were pity jobs. But I'm the idiot who said that to his face, being all surprised he'd actually done a lot to help me this past month."

"His pride was hurt," Meg murmured, understanding a little too clearly where all his talk of reality had come from. Reason. "Oh, that idiot."

"My sentiments exactly," Cara murmured, earning herself another little jab from Mia.

"The point is, we need to find him and talk to him," Mia said. "Apologize. Explain—"

"It won't work," Meg said, not even sure why she was so certain, only that she could feel it. His pride was hurt, but more than that she thought...

She thought of all the times she'd thought she was clean for good only to fall off the wagon. Because something bad had happened, because someone had said something that hurt her.

Maybe Charlie wasn't the same as her, but she couldn't shake the feeling that, well, he was actually a *lot* like her—if a little more straight and narrow when he imploded. He thought he'd had it all the past few months, finally found himself and his joy, and then they'd told him they'd done it out of pity.

It *shouldn't* matter, but Meg figured Charlie's pride and his desire to fit in with his family would make that a pretty shocking blow.

Mia looked so stricken, so Meg mustered a reassuring smile. "Apologies won't work because he doesn't want to hear them, you know? He's hurt, I would guess. And, unfortunately, I think that means he shut it all down. Apologies and explanations won't fix this lame epiphany he thinks he had."

"Then what can we do?" Mia asked, her eyes looking suspiciously bright and full.

"I think we wait."

"Wait? For what?"

That was a good question. "I think we let him have his little tantrum, then see what decisions he's ready to make once he's done stamping his foot."

Mia smiled, though her eyes remained a little watery. "Well, I think you're a few steps ahead on this whole motherhood thing."

Meg reached and offered Mia a reassuring if slightly awkward pat on the shoulder.

"You seem better," Cara said. "Your hormones must have settled down."

That. Maybe partly. Or maybe it was as simple as facing the things she'd been so sure would fell her, and realizing they didn't have that kind of power.

# CHAPTER TWENTY-SIX

CHARLIE FELT LIKE…Charlie again. He was wearing a suit. His laptop bag was arranged carefully at his feet, copies of his résumé enclosed should they be necessary. This was what he knew. Business. Even if he was in Chicago. Even if he checked his phone every five seconds to see if Meg had texted or called.

It didn't matter, because this was the man he knew he could be. The only man he was, really. He had no doubt at all that he would walk into that office and charm the interviewer. That he would make his case, talk of his accomplishments, and it would be *impressive*.

*So, why do you feel so damn depressed?*

It was the uncertainty. Realizing he'd wasted the past few months on things that weren't ever going to be permanent or give him what he needed. Give his *child* what he or she would need.

He or she. Anytime he thought that—the inevitability of having a *boy* or a *girl*, an actual child, a baby who would grow up before his eyes like

Lainey had done—he missed Meg more than he'd ever missed his job, his suits, his old life.

He missed her with a sharp pain and an ache that stuck there, in his chest, just...constant. But he wasn't apologizing—especially on his knees—considering that even though he was being a dick, he was being a smart one.

"Mr. Wainwright? Mr. Oakson will see you now."

Charlie stood and smiled, then followed the receptionist into Mr. Oakson's office. It was an overused thought in his head, but it really was like coming home. To sit and greet and smile and charm. To talk business and sales strategies. He could tell the very moment Mr. Oakson decided to hire him. There was a little smile, just like that little smile customers got before they agreed to your terms.

"We have a few more candidates to interview, and then we'll decide if we need to conduct second interviews," the man said, standing and shaking Charlie's hand. "But you've got an impressive résumé and an impressive character, Charlie. I think any second interview might be a formality at this point."

Charlie shook the man's hand. Smiled. "Thank you, sir. I look forward to hearing from you." That had to be what he felt. *Excited.* Or happy and secure. It didn't really matter.

This was good. This was where he belonged. The issue of a move would be a challenge, but maybe somewhere new would… Maybe it would be good for both of them. To get away from New Benton and the fictional life they'd been leading for a month.

They could pick out a house *together*. Research schools for Seedling. Be away from her parents, but not so terribly far from his that they'd struggle to visit or vice versa. This was the right choice.

He told himself that, over and over, on the ride to the airport. As he waited for his flight to board. Everything he'd done the past few days weren't just the right choices, but the *only* choices. He pulled the ultrasound picture out of his wallet and stared down at it.

He was doing what was right. For this. He'd been ridiculous to think one curveball in his life should make him jump on one after the other. He should have gone with that first instinct. Control. Manage. Get married and get organized before the baby was born. Not get lost in things like belonging and love.

He needed a real job, a real life. Even if he was irritated with Meg and she was furious with him, they did love each other. They would build a life together. A good life.

*Are you so certain this is love?*

That thought hit him right in the center of his

chest, strong enough to feel like a physical blow. Almost simultaneously with his phone going off.

He didn't recognize the number, but it was a St. Louis area code and he answered it immediately, before worry and fear and the possibility of bad news could take root in his mind.

"Hello."

"Charlie. Jeffrey Carmichael."

Charlie tensed. He might have told Meg her father wasn't evil, and he might still have some thinking to do about how his connections might help their child, but that didn't mean he particularly *liked* Jeffrey Carmichael, and he most certainly didn't trust him. Even a little bit.

"Hello."

"I was hoping you might have some time this weekend to sit down and have a little chat."

"Without Meg, I'm assuming." It didn't come out quite as condescending in his head. No, he sounded downright agreeable. Maybe an after-effect of the interview and saying everything he knew the interviewer wanted to hear.

"I think that'd be best, though if you'd want her there, that'd be fine. Just fine. But this is about business. Carmichael Grocery business."

Charlie stared down at the picture in his hand. It seemed somehow less real than it had that day, than it had the other morning when he kissed Meg's stomach and felt a soaring kind of…

*Insanity. That stupid feeling was insanity.*

"All right. I'm actually going to be near the airport around six." It wouldn't be the worst thing in the world to meet with Jeffrey. After all, the man had something up his sleeve. Something he was trying to do, and there was no way he'd gotten to where he was in business by ignoring what other people seemed to need.

So Charlie was protecting Meg, all in all, by agreeing to meet with her father. Figuring out just what the Carmichaels were after with their sudden attention on him and Meg and the baby.

"Let's meet for dinner."

If it was a dinner with the devil, well, he knew enough to guard himself against it.

"IT'S MY TURN to wait on you, girly girl," Elsie said, clucking her tongue as she fussed around Meg in the kitchen of her cabin.

"I'm pregnant, not an invalid."

"And I'm cancer free, not a sick old woman. Guess we're even."

Meg laughed. Elsie had a way of putting things that brooked absolutely no argument, and though Meg's nausea seemed to have faded mostly to the wayside the past few days, she was finding herself more and more exhausted.

It was nice to sit at the kitchen table and be waited on. Plus, she was starving. Pretty much all the time. Elsie's dinner spread was fancier than their usual to-go from Moonrise. She'd shown up with a bag full of fresh fruit, brownies from a new bakery and the ingredients to make a stir-fry, which she was currently working on at Meg's stove.

It smelled amazing, and only the fact that Meg was avoiding caffeine and couldn't have an ice-cold soda with it took away the pleasure.

*Liar.*

Okay, yes, she'd take Charlie in a heartbeat over a soda, but she'd tell him that precisely never.

"So, do we tiptoe around the fact that your man isn't here, or do you tell me what's going on?"

Elsie set a plate heaped with food in front of her, along with a large glass of ice water. It felt like love, and Meg wanted to dwell in that mushy feeling forever.

"I'm not sure 'your man' is particularly accurate," she said with a sigh, immediately shoving a bite of food into her mouth—both because she was starving and because she didn't want to say any more than that. She wanted to enjoy Elsie's surprise visit.

"So you did have a fight?"

Meg thought about that. It *had* been a fight. A nasty one at that, and she still didn't understand it. Even with the insight into it after Cara and Mia's visit…she didn't understand why he wouldn't tell her. Why was he so afraid to explain his feelings had been hurt?

"I'm not sure men are worth the trouble, Elsie."

Elsie snorted out a laugh. "You say that to me again when you haven't gotten any for a few months."

Meg let out a shocked little squeak. "Elsie!"

"I'm just saying, chemo knocks it out of you. Then you get it back and—"

"Oh, I love you and Dan, I do, but I want to hear zero about your sex life."

Elsie laughed, something close to a cackle, tickled pink with herself. Meg smiled, happy to have made this friend, to have this woman who *cared* and laughed, and she couldn't wait to tell Charlie...

Oh, damn him.

"Go on now. Tell me what's what." Elsie took the seat across from her, where Charlie had sat most mornings for the past month, smiling at her over his coffee, pretending he wasn't looking forward to milking the goats when she'd *heard* him starting to talk to them last week.

Not like she did, the long, rambling conversations that made her feel less alone when she was feeling sad and isolated, but a few encouraging words, a few directions.

He didn't love the goats the way she did, but she'd started to entertain the fantasy he might *learn* to. Much like she'd entertained the fantasy he might love her always, as easily and happily as that month.

"I don't really know. He's…" Meg blew out a breath. *He* was like a hangnail. It pretty much always hurt when he wasn't there. Pretty much always hurt that he hadn't called or texted. It was this constant, nagging pain that she knew he was in Chicago interviewing for a job that would take him away from her.

Because she loved him. Even this jerk-off version of Charlie, she *loved*. But she wouldn't leave her life for him—not for his "reality" or "reason" or whatever else. Maybe, if it was for something important. If she hadn't seen firsthand the difference between businessman Charlie and the Charlie of the past month.

"Something happened that hurt him, I think. With his family. So he's got it in his head he has to go back into business and take a job in Chicago and I'm just supposed to hop on that and go with him."

"And leave your goats?"

"Thank you!" Meg shoveled another few bites of food into her mouth. See? Elsie saw it. How important this place was to her. How leaving wasn't an option—easy or otherwise, *best* or otherwise.

"So. What happened?"

"I told him I wouldn't move, and I told him he needed to tell me what on earth had gotten into him, and then…" Meg took a deep breath, then let it out. Her hunger left her in an instant. Suddenly she was too full. Too everything. "He looked me in the eye and told me my father wasn't evil—which I get. I do. He isn't *evil*, but Charlie stood there lecturing me. Wondering if a failure would send me running back to drugs. Just like…"

Just like her parents always had. She was the foolish little girl. He was the smart, responsible adult.

Meg closed her eyes against the wave of pain. She'd been ignoring this. Trying to drive it deep beneath being angry with him, but the fact of the matter was…yeah, it hurt.

Elsie reached across the table and rested her hand on Meg's. "He lashed out, then?"

Meg huffed out a breath. "Oh yes. At first he was so calm and flat and *reasonable*, but he lost it when I argued with him. I told him to leave. And not to come back unless it was on his knees." The memory of that bolstered her. She'd been strong. She'd stood her ground.

Elsie patted her hand. "Good on you."

"Yes, good on me."

"But you're still miserable."

She rubbed her hand against that frustrating ache in her chest. "I love the bastard. I hate that he's hurt. I hate that he hurt me. I hate…all of it."

"Well, if that isn't love, I don't know what is."

"But he hasn't apologized. Or called. He hasn't done anything." She glanced at the clock. "All I can think is he's in Chicago or he's already on his way home and he thinks he's right. And I can't do anything except wait." Or did she give up? She didn't know.

Elsie was quiet for a long while, and the words *give up* echoed in Meg's head. Was that the only option? Because she wasn't going to pine after him. No way. Her pining days for love were over. Her parents didn't love her. She was done wanting them to. Elsie loved her. And even if he was being a stubborn pain in the ass, Charlie loved her too.

But was love enough?

"I hate to always bring Hannah up, I do," Elsie began carefully. "It's just…when you've failed such an important relationship, it's a constant. You play it over in your mind, again and again, trying to make sense of it. Find a cause, a blame, a reason. Sometimes there isn't one, and sometimes the reasons you come up with are silly, but let me tell you this. I let her go. She stormed out and I didn't go after her. I didn't fight for her. I clapped my hands together and decided she had to figure it out on her own."

"But we do. You know." Meg turned her hand so it grasped Elsie's, wanting desperately to give the woman some comfort. The stories of her estranged daughter always pulled at Meg's heart.

"When you're addicted, well and truly, no one can swoop in and fix you. Not a loving family member, not the right person. The addiction is in *your* head and *your* heart—and no one can erase that. Ever. My grandmother stood by me through three setbacks. No matter how much she believed and gave—it didn't make me clean."

"Would you have ever got clean if she hadn't been there all those times?"

Meg could only sit there and stare. She'd never thought of it quite like that, but it hit a soft spot. Because…hadn't it been Grandma's steadfast love even in the face of her failures that had well and truly broken the cycle? That she'd come to accept, even when she failed, she could do better?

That was partly her. Partly accepting she was in control of her feelings and her life, but would her mind and soul have been able to get there without knowing she had someone supporting her?

Maybe. It was possible. Recovery had been all about personal responsibility and accepting you were the master of your own actions. So it wasn't magic. Grandma's love hadn't *healed* her.

But it had given her the foundation on which to heal. Just like giving her this place. Meg had been the one to make it successful, to care for it day in and day out, but Grandma had been the foundation.

"I thought fighting drove her away, and then I

was convinced letting her be was what kept her away, and in the end you know what the real problem was?"

"Life blows?"

Elsie smiled indulgently. "Part that. And part that none of us…said it. That we loved each other, that we needed something from each other. I tried tough love and unconditional love and no love at all. I tried everything. Except the truth."

"I demanded he give me the truth, to be the man I know he is. He wouldn't."

"So you're giving up, then?"

"He has to come to the realization on his own. He has to realize he has to tell me on his own. I can't make him."

"No, but you can let him know you're here. You can, I think if you really love him, you can give him a few times where you stand up in the face of him being a *man*—translation, idiot—and tell him you're here. You're here when he's ready."

"I don't want to be a doormat."

"Do you love him?"

"Yes, but—"

"Do you believe he loves you?"

"I do, but—"

"Will he make a good father to your child? A good partner in your life? Because if the answer is yes to those too, you aren't being a doormat for fighting. You're being the strong, amazing, caring woman I know you to be at your heart. I know that's you, Meg. Once you stop doubting those voices in your head telling you you've done it all wrong, you'll look around and you'll see all you've built, and you'll fight for more. Because that's what women do."

"What are you doing to fight, Elsie?" She said it gently, because Elsie was right. Every last word was a firework of epiphany and right. But she wasn't the only strong woman who needed to fight sitting in this kitchen.

"I just kicked cancer's ass. Isn't that enough?"

"It'd be easier if you believed that, but we both know you don't. Hannah's the thing you turn over and over in your mind. Then you need to fight too. For her. For you. And any way I can help, anything you need—you tell me. I've been there. I can help."

Elsie reached her other hand across the table, and they held on to each other, both a little teary and neither willing to admit it enough for a tear to fall over. "Believe it or not, I've stood where you stood and had to knock a good man over the head to see his future was with me. So I've been there. I can help."

Meg swallowed and nodded because she didn't

trust her voice. Nodded because she thought she would really need that help.

But she'd always been a fighter. It was time she believed it.

# CHAPTER TWENTY-SEVEN

CHARLIE MADE HIS WAY toward Jeffrey Carmichael in a dimly lit restaurant. He wondered if this was what people in those shark cages felt like being lowered into the water. Surely he was safe, because he was in control of his own life and Jeffrey wasn't going to *eat* him.

But he was still a shark.

"There you are, son," Jeffrey greeted genially enough. He held out a hand and Charlie shook it warily.

The strangest thing happened. He got a flash from that scene in *It's a Wonderful Life* where George shook Mr. Potter's hand and came to his senses...

Which was crazy, because Charlie's life wasn't a black-and-white Christmas movie. Charlie's life didn't have guardian angels and finding out what would have happened if he'd never been born. Because he lived in *reality*.

Reality.

So, why did he feel so shaken?

He ignored it. Ignored the clammy feeling in

his hand. He was just tired, and drained from the stress of a job interview. He'd let Jeffrey say what he had to say, then go home and get a good night's sleep.

*Where is home?*

"I'm glad you agreed to speak with me alone."

"Well, you upset Meg."

*And so did you, way to go.*

He shook that thought away. He'd fix it. Fix it like he always fixed things…

Except he couldn't think of a single *personal* relationship he'd ever fixed. Everything that had healed between him and Dell had been done pretty much because Dell had been the one to bend.

All the other meaningful relationships in his past had been terminated. The thought of anything with Meg *ending* left Charlie feeling even more off-kilter. Sick, down to his soul.

"Yes, well, Meg has done a lot of upsetting us over the years." The corners of Jeffrey's mouth went a little sharp, but it didn't stop him from *smiling.* "Which is why I'm glad you agreed to talk with me. My wife and I are sincerely worried about the welfare of our grandchild."

Charlie laughed. He couldn't help it. "Why on earth would you be worried about that?"

"Addiction is an ongoing thing. If Meg's told you differently, it's a lie. My wife and I, we did all sorts of studying up on it. Every book, every therapist, everyone says the same thing. There's no cure."

"She didn't need to be *cured*, she needed parents who loved and supported her." And those words, said so easily, made Charlie even more shamed that he'd thrown that possibility of her failing and going back in her face.

He'd deserved her slapping him. He deserved worse, quite honestly, and she deserved better than him. Better than practicality and realism. So much better than all he could offer.

Wasn't that what it always boiled down to?

"Meg is an addict," Jeffrey said as though Charlie just didn't understand. "Drugs. Alcohol. You name it. She spent numerous months of her life in rehab facility after rehab facility. She was— and possibly *is*—a compulsive liar, a thief, a—"

"Enough," he growled. There must have been enough rage in his tone—a rage Mr. Carmichael must not have been used to, because he snapped back in surprise, jaw shutting with an audible click.

"That is enough," Charlie repeated, slowly, carefully. Because if he wasn't careful, he thought he might fly over the table, and then he wasn't even sure what he would do. Only that it would likely get him arrested. "I did not come here to listen to you disparage the mother of my child."

"Then why did you come here, Charlie?"

Funny that it would take Jeffrey Carmichael asking him that question to get him to realize how *stupid* this was. How pointless. He wasn't ever going to hurt Meg by using this man's connections or influence—not for Seedling, not for "stability."

He couldn't betray her *that* way. He'd already betrayed her enough.

"I'm realizing it was quite the mistake." Charlie stood. He wasn't going to eat dinner with this man who thought his daughter—his vibrant, beautiful, *strong* daughter—was a mistake.

No, he wasn't spending another minute here.

"We won't rest, you know? That baby is a Carmichael. That means something in St. Louis, and it's a chance for us to make up for all the embarrassment Meg caused us. That baby will be our recompense."

Charlie felt physically ill. That a man could think of a child as *recompense*. A child who hadn't even been *born* yet. He wanted to hurt him—physically, yes, but more than that, he knew he needed to end this. Here. Now. Before Jeffrey could touch Meg or Seedling any more than he already had.

And standing there in the middle of this fancy restaurant he'd entertained clients in more times than he could count, talking to a man he'd done business with indirectly, Charlie realized the answer didn't exist in this world.

But it existed in his other world. The one that had never understood him, the one that had pitied him. That world suddenly gave him the exact thing he needed.

"I know what you did to Peterson's," Charlie said, realizing just how much damage that could do. The inherently underhanded ways Carmichael had crushed the tiny grocer in New Benton. It had happened when Charlie was in graduate school, and he'd heard about it only because he'd been high school buddies with the Petersons' son.

Charlie had forgotten all about it, and while it certainly couldn't threaten what Carmichael was as a successful store, it could hurt Jeffrey Carmichael's reputation—the threats he'd personally leveled at the Petersons.

Charlie had the suspicion that Meg's father cared *only* about his reputation, and that gave Charlie quite the leverage. Didn't it?

"You'll stay away from Meg, or I will wage a war against everything you are."

Jeffrey didn't flinch, didn't pale, but there was a tightening around his mouth that spoke to at least a little concern over the threat. "You're unemployed, Wainwright. A nobody. What could *you* possibly do to *me*?"

Charlie smiled, the same sharp smile Jeffrey

had leveled in his direction in the beginning. "I sincerely hope you'll find out."

He left on that note, because his best bets were vague threats and a call to Casey Peterson before he started shooting off his mouth. But Charlie knew enough, and enough people, that he couldn't destroy Jeffrey Carmichael, but he could make his life a little tricky. It would be enough to keep that man on his toes, and away from *his* family.

His family. Meg and Seedling. He stalked to his car, trying to make sense of the past twenty-four hours, the past week. Trying to make sense of *himself.* He had to go back to his parents' and change and try to figure out what the next step was.

A plan. The right apology. The right words. He needed his head on straight, and he wasn't any-where near there.

He drove back to New Benton, half tempted to screw it all and just go to Meg—on his knees, just as she'd demanded. But she deserved better than an exhausted and half-cocked apology.

He drove up the dirt path, past Dell's warmly lit cabin, up to the old farmhouse. It was late enough only his parents' bedroom light was on. Charlie got out of the car wondering how everything had flipped in such a period of time, how he could have been so wrong and convinced he'd been so right.

He loosened his tie and collapsed onto the old

rocking chair that had rocked on the planks of this porch for at least his entire lifetime. The sky, dark and vast, sparkled with stars. Every sound— the crickets, the occasional animal rustling, that rhythmic squeak of the chair as he set it rocking— the sound track to his childhood.

Rare that he'd listened to it. Rare that he'd ever sat still enough to *see* it. He'd always been so busy moving forward, striving for bigger and better. Following that plan. Ignoring every feeling, every beat of his heart, with the hope that if he could just *achieve* enough it would stop feeling like this.

Like he didn't know who he was, or what he wanted. Like he didn't fit anywhere. And this past month hadn't felt like that, but…how easy it had been to be knocked back into that place of not belonging. Of not being sure of *anything*.

"Saw your car drive up," Dell said, stepping onto the porch.

It was dark, so Charlie could only make out the vague outline of his brother in the faint glow of the houses and starlight.

His brother, who he'd *always* been envious of, because Dell had always, *always* known what he wanted. Who he was.

"Mia told me Cara let it slip about why we hired you."

Charlie shrugged, looking away. "Not quite the crux of my issues right now."

"Oh, trust me, I know the look of a man who has woman problems."

"See it that much in the mirror you can tell just by a look, can you?" It was his default, that slap back. Charlie opened his mouth to apologize, but his words were all jumbled and confused.

Dell ambled up the porch, took a seat on the railing. "You know, about five years ago, I—"

"If you tell me the story of how you and Mia worked things out, I'm going to throw up. Right here on this porch."

"Suit yourself. But your problem has always been, Charlie, that you refuse to see anyone else might have an answer for you. You're so determined to find all the answers yourself."

"Maybe that's because no one sees me for who I really am. And suggestions to 'unclench' or not be such a hard-ass aren't exactly helpful."

"That isn't us anymore. It hasn't been for a while."

Dell said it so quietly, so earnestly, Charlie couldn't do anything with it except feel ashamed. No, things had changed. It probably wasn't fair to act as though they hadn't, but he was feeling so damn raw.

How much more could he give? How much more of his heart did he show people only to have it *hurt*? He knew how to fix things. Dwindling sales numbers and obstinate customers.

He didn't know how to fix…hearts.

"You're a pretty hard guy to read, Charlie. Did you know that?"

He might have heard that a time or two.

"It's a little worth considering that while you're sitting there assuming no one sees you for who you are, it's because you've never *let* us. And, before you get pissy about *that*, consider we learned from the best on that score." Dell nodded toward the house, which no doubt meant Dad. "I include myself in that."

Because, yes, Dad was a good man, but he wasn't exactly an easy one to read or understand. None of them ever had been—so busy protecting themselves and trying to get the upper hand. So busy trying to be better or righter.

It *had* changed the past few years. Having a kid had mellowed Dell, and in the presence of his kid, Charlie had mellowed and it had allowed for a kind of friendship. The past month of bonding over significant others growing babies and whatnot had developed into a kinship.

*Based on pity.*

"You could have all told me you were offering me jobs out of pity."

"We could have, but you would have told us where to shove it, and then none of us would have realized how good you are at it. What good instincts you have when it comes to growing partnerships. I knew you were a good businessman, Charlie, but I didn't know what that entailed. You impressed us all. So I'm not sure sulking like Lainey when it wasn't for the reason you wanted it to be for is really all that sensible of you."

"Did you come here to start a fistfight or…"

Dell chuckled. "If you want to take a few swings at me to make yourself feel better, feel free. Do you know the kind of female attention I'll get for a good shiner?"

But Charlie didn't move. Mostly because as irritating as Dell's words were, Charlie still couldn't muster anger. He didn't have the energy or the foolishness running through his blood to want to move and punch his brother.

He wanted to brood. He wanted to drown in this feeling because drowning would be a hell of a lot better than all this hurt.

It made sense to him then, in a way that he hadn't thought of before. That Meg had buried her parents' awful treatment in drugs and alcohol, until it had poisoned *her*. It seemed everything about today was set up to make him feel terrible for throwing it all back in her face.

How did he fix that? He wouldn't even blame her if she never forgave him, so how did he go over there and…hurt all over again?

Dell sat there, not saying anything. But Charlie

supposed he'd said enough. He'd said the truth. And now he was going to sit it out.

Charlie was going to have to analyze that at some point. The fact that he'd run, but his brother wasn't doing so.

"I don't want to be a salesman anymore." Charlie said it aloud. Carefully. Clearly. Truthfully. That world fit in its own way, but…he still didn't want it. He didn't want an office, or to be on the phone all day. He didn't want to cleverly maneuver around people.

It had been hard to see because he was good at it, and because there were parts he enjoyed. He liked seeing what he could do with a fixed budget. He liked figuring out the best angle to take when it came to getting a customer the right item.

But so many parts he'd grown frustrated with, or allowed to permeate him, and he didn't want that anymore.

He wanted to give more to his budding family than he did to a company that could get rid of him simply because they'd been bought out.

Maybe Dell and Kenzie and all the in-laws and what-have-yous thought he was *hard to read*, but he'd done nothing but give himself to Meg—over and over again, make sacrifices for his comfort to show pieces of himself, to offer love.

And then he'd stomped it all to hell in an immature blink.

"I'm going to reiterate what Mia and Cara have been trying to tell you. You were good at what you were doing for us. No, we can't pay you what you made being a big-shot sales guy, but we don't have to be your only clients. There are farmers' markets all around, and, sure, some people are pretty darn good at the business side of things. But some people could use some help. You know enough of both worlds to be a lot of help."

"That's…" *Not for me. That's not for me.* "…a huge risk."

"A lot of things are possible with a little luck and a lot of work. But more than all that, taking the chance makes more things possible than sitting there thinking you can't have it."

Well, perceptive points to Dell. But Charlie wasn't ready to give up that…fear. "I have a child on the way."

"And a family and friends who would step in to help you if you needed it. Also, a mother of that child. The thing is…could my kids have more stuff? Sure. Is Lainey going to pitch a fit someday that I won't buy her some overpriced piece of clothing? We'll see. But I didn't have any problems with how we grew up. Did you?"

"This isn't about us. I want my kid… I want…" He couldn't find the words. How did he verbalize this giant thing that lay in front of him. Raising another human being, bringing him into the world and navigating him through it. He wanted to be better. He wanted to be more. For that child.

"You want your kids to have it all," Dell said, leaning forward so his elbows rested on his knees and his gaze was on the night that stretched out between the porch and his little house down the way. "Trust me, I get it. Been there. But getting it all and having it all aren't the same things. You can't be a good parent if you're pissed off all the time, or never there. You...you have to have something for you too. We're lucky we have the opportunity to do it."

"Remember when you were the screwup?" Charlie muttered irritably.

"I do. And I had to swallow a little bit of my pride and put a lot of my heart on the line to work it out. Guess what, buddy? You're up."

"But I..."

"Screwed it up? I believe that's a Wainwright family tradition."

"I was an ass."

"Well, surely Meg's used to that."

Charlie scowled, but Dell grinned. "The shitty thing about love is it has the power to hurt you. And sometimes, because we're human, we use our love as a weapon, or a shield, or any number of things—anything but what it is."

"Which is?"

"A gift." Dell slid off the railing. "One you have

to be brave enough to give and accept." He was silent for a beat before he clapped Charlie companionably on the shoulder. "And if you tell anyone I said that, especially my wife, I'll end you."

Charlie only grunted, and he sat there on the porch, long after Dell left, long after the night went cool.

And he tried to figure out how to give a gift that Meg had every right to reject, and accept a gift he didn't deserve.

# CHAPTER TWENTY-EIGHT

MEG STRUGGLED TO force herself out of bed. It was a market day, and she had a million things to do.

Elsie's words about fighting had stuck with her all night, and she hadn't slept well at all. But she felt...strong. Physically exhausted, wrung out, but *powerful*. She'd suffered something of a heartbreak, and she hadn't reached for anything to numb the pain.

She'd talked to a friend. She'd talked to her goats. She'd talked to the growing baby inside her. All of that added up to trusting the people— and animals—in her life with her pain, and it had made a world of difference.

She was clean, not broken. Strong for getting this far, not weak for falling in the first place. A work in progress *and* a success. Struggling and overcoming.

She made mistakes, inevitably would again. But she *wasn't* one.

Which was somehow terrifying and wonderful all at the same time. Like pregnancy. Like love. Heart-stopping fear. Heart-soaring amazement.

With renewed energy and strength, she pushed through her chores and getting ready for the market. Exhaustion threatened, a slight headache pulsed along her temples, but as she clambered into her truck—soaps stowed safely in the back—a giddiness wrapped around her.

Would Charlie be at the market?

Would he be miserable? Would he be apologetic? Would he avoid the market simply because he knew she'd be there?

She all but vibrated with the questions. With trying to figure out what she would do in the face of each possibility. Mixed with trying to navigate the desire to go home and hide under her covers.

But she was a fighter. A *fighter*. She'd come too far to give up now. If he wasn't there, she would darn well find him. She would take Elsie's advice and let him know that she would be there, standing right there, when he was ready to put himself back together.

Because that was what they'd been doing. Putting together the pieces of themselves side by side, *together*, and it had been silly to ever think that would be easy or smooth sailing. There would be bumps and stumbles and setbacks, and they had to stand with each other through them. Even when they'd rather throttle each other.

She parked her truck behind her usual booth at

the market, nerves dancing along every surface of her skin. Fear burrowing deep inside her.

But business came first; she couldn't look for Charlie until she was certain she was ready to face the morning of customers. Setting up her table and her soaps, pretty and inviting. *Not* throwing up from nausea or nerves or whatever was currently battling its way out in her stomach. Probably both.

The market opened and the crowd was a little thin, though it would no doubt pick up soon.

Despite that, she couldn't see the Pruitt Morning Sun booth from her stand without maneuvering around her table, and that seemed far too obvious.

"What are you so afraid of?" she muttered to herself, craning her neck to try to catch a glimpse. It was a rhetorical question, obviously, and yet she wondered if she shouldn't consider that.

What was she so afraid of? She knew she had to fight, she knew she had to give. She understood those things in her bones, and yet…

She didn't *want* to. It sounded hard, and more… What had her grandmother gone through sticking by her? Seeing her fail over and over again. What would that have been like to keep standing there, supporting her?

Awful. It had to be awful. To watch someone fail and promise and fail and lie and…

*And you were an addict, not a guy having a
hard time with his pride.*

Why did this have to be so *hard*? She gave herself a second to sulk and pout, and then she straightened, placing her hand on her belly for strength.
Stepping out on a limb, obvious or otherwise, it
wasn't just for her.

It was for Charlie, and it was for their child.

*It's for you.*

Yes, it was important enough to put on that list.
She wouldn't ignore trying to find some kind of
acceptance and forgiveness for something when
said things would be so good for *all* of them.

Determined, and customerless, she took a step
to skirt the table and march right down the line
to Mia and Dell's booth and see if he was there
and—

There he was. Nowhere near the Pruitt Morning Sun booth. Almost looking like he was purposefully trying to blend in with the sparse crowd
and avoid her.

It was like that first day she'd laid eyes on him
all over again. Heartsick over Grandma, pouring it
all into this job, this thing that had kept her afloat.
And there he walked, a little across the way, but
right in front of her booth.

As though she didn't exist. She wanted to throw
something at him, but all she had within reach
was soap and she wouldn't waste her product that

way. So she yelled something he couldn't walk away from.

"Columbus Day is just around the corner!"

He stopped dead in his tracks, though his head and gaze stayed forward for a few humming seconds. Then he shook his head faintly and turned. "Columbus Day. Really?"

"Well, what else is there?"

"Fourth of July, Labor Day, possibly—"

"Oh, shut up and come over here."

"I'm—"

"Move your feet over here. Now."

He scowled, but he did as ordered, taking a visible deep breath and presumably steeling himself. *Jerk*.

"I'm not buying any soap today," he said gravely, grave enough she wanted to laugh. "Last time I checked, people don't give gifts for *Columbus* Day."

"I don't want you to buy any soap." *I want you.* That was…it. The bottom line. Under all the insecurities and the fear. She wanted *him*. They couldn't both exist—having him and giving in to that fear. Not happily.

So she had to trust. And she had to believe.

*You have to fight.*

"I saw your father last night," he announced, so completely out of nowhere she could only blink at him for a humming few seconds.

Then she went cold. "I thought you had an interview in Chicago. I thought—"

"He called when I was in the airport. Asked to meet me for dinner."

She couldn't read his expression. It wasn't the flatness of the other night when he'd blown everything up, but it wasn't *love* either.

"I apologize for anything remotely *not negative* I said about him or his presence in our child's life."

"Oh, Charlie." She stepped forward, nearly forgetting all the reasons she was mad at him. She reached out, figuring he'd need to feel supported after a dinner with her father. A soft place to land. Reassurance. Those things she'd always wished for and never received. "What did he say? Are you all right?"

"You would..." He shook his head and ran an agitated hand through his hair. "Why should you care after I've been such a..."

"Heartless jerk?"

"Yes, that."

"Because I love you." Simple as that. Strong as that. She loved him, and she would always care that he was all right.

"Meg." Finally, *finally* his expression evolved. It crumpled a little, looked hurt, baffled, frustrated— but at least it was *real*. Nothing blank or cold about it.

"Tell me what happened."

His gaze met hers, his eyes looking haunted. Like a man who'd made many mistakes and didn't know how to fix them.

Well, she'd give him some time to fix them; she'd give him support. Just like Grandma had done for her once upon a time, like Elsie had done all these months. This time she was going to be the one to stand up, to be someone else's foundation.

"I shook your father's hand, and I realized something very humbling and simple. I don't want that life. It's comfortable, it might even suit me, but I don't want it."

It was her turn to be humbled. Humbled that he'd figured it all out on his own.

"Then come home, Charlie. You know it's home."


THIS WASN'T GOING according to plan. He had been trying to sneak over to the flower booth, and King Bread. He had a whole *plan*, but she'd seen him and started yelling about Columbus Day of all things, and just like it had been in the beginning, Meg had busted his plans all to hell.

Now she wanted him to come home. Simple as that.

But before he could take that leap of faith, give her the apologies he'd practiced all morning, before he could get down on his knees and *beg* her to forgive him, some woman stepped up to Meg's table and began chatting away about soap.

Soap.

Charlie frowned at the woman and her terrible timing. He repeated the expression for the woman who lined up behind her.

"Stop hovering and scowling and scaring away my customers," Meg hissed under her breath after the first woman vacated her spot, pounds of soap in a bag, and before the second woman stepped up to the table.

"*You're* the one who insisted I come over when I—"

She reached across the table and jerked his arm so he had to either sidestep the table or crash right into it.

He sidestepped and she pointed to the back of her truck, which faced the back of the table. "Sit."

The customer giggled. "Well, you have that one on a leash," she said cheerfully.

"Not nearly as much as I'd like," Meg replied pleasantly before she and the woman had an interminable discussion about the merits of goat milk, and how much Meg enjoyed caring for her goats.

Charlie didn't want to sit. He didn't want to be ordered around. He *wouldn't* be. Except he could see all of Meg now, no table hid that slightest of slight curve where *his* child was slowly, slowly growing. Day by day.

*Their* child. *Their* life. Home.

The customer finally left and Meg turned around to face him, hands fisted on her hips. Her hair was pulled back, but strands fell out around her face, and her pale eyebrows drew together to nearly form a V.

It wasn't so much that *love* slammed into him, because he always loved her—every second of every day, with every breath—whether he wanted to or not. Love was this constant thing in his chest. Always present and beating just as his actual heart, but there were moments when it could hit so clearly, so distinctly it was overwhelmingly, painfully there.

Painful because he knew, no matter how he fixed it, there would still be mistakes and disagreements ahead of them. Fights and anger and hurt. Always. Love *meant* people could be forever hurting you, missing all the things you didn't know how to tell them. And it meant always wanting more.

She straightened and glared down at him. "All right. Now…"

She trailed off as he stood up. He had no doubt he looked angry and menacing. He *felt* angry and menacing as he closed the distance between them. He wanted to punish the both of them for being so stupid for falling into this trap that would only hurt them forever. Over and over again.

And he wanted to thank her forever for opening this up inside him.

So he kissed her. He didn't know what else to do. He didn't have the words, a way to fix things. He just wanted...*her*.

EVERYTHING IN HER went limp. She wanted to be stronger than a girl who'd melt the second a guy touched her, but the guy was Charlie and there was such relief that he would touch her, kiss her, before they'd figured anything out. Before he'd agreed to come home. But this was agreement, wasn't it?

He held her up, his mouth crushed to hers, his arms banded around her like he would always be that strong pillar to hold her up. She found her footing because she wanted to be that for him too, to stand with him to be that for their child.

"Oh, Charlie. I missed you. I *miss* you," she murmured when he ended the kiss, each of them leaning against the other a little breathless.

"Meg." He said it with an exasperated sigh, but his palm smoothed down her spine—a physical *I miss you too*.

"I don't know what we're doing," she muttered into his chest, wishing she could bury herself there. But she had a stand to run. She had things to do. They didn't have time for this.

Because *this* was so much more complicated

than kiss and make up—no matter how much she wished otherwise.

"It's quite a club we've got here, then."

She wanted to laugh, but she heard the sounds of the market buzzing around her. This was her livelihood. *One hour off won't kill you.*

Then Charlie let her go, and she thought *that* might.

"I have…customers," she said weakly.

But he strode over to her table and pulled the little cord that kept the front flap of the tent up. "You're closed for a little bit."

"Charlie, I—"

"I'll buy all the soap you want. Let's just have this out. *You* called me over here."

"*You* walked by as though you didn't know this was exactly where I'd be."

They squared off, and she was certain by the way his mouth firmed and he didn't say anything that it had *not* been accidental.

"Can we go back to kissing?" Meg asked hopefully.

His mouth quirked, his stance softened. "I don't even know how we got away from that."

"You turned into a zombie businessman Charlie jerk?"

"The goats made me do it?"

Why his ridiculous joke made her want to cry

was absolutely beyond her, but tears formed. Even as she laughed.

"I was going to buy you flowers. I was going to buy you bread. I was going to…shower you with every token of affection I could find."

"I only want you."

He closed his eyes as though she'd hurt him, and when he opened his eyes, there was a whole mix of emotions in them and Meg didn't feel so much like joking or kissing anymore. She wanted to take away all the hurt, all the confusion.

"I don't know how to fix this. I don't know how to put it right. How do we…?" He shook his head. "You know, my brother keeps saying these obnoxiously insightful things."

"Terrible man."

His lips quirked just a hair. "He said that sometimes people use love like a weapon, or a shield, and I've done both. With my family. With you. It always comes with caveats and carefulness. And fear. I never knew *how* to let that protective shield down, not until I met you. I didn't know how to trust that, not when I thought, well, I thought I'd finally found all the things I wanted, and I had, but the process to get here was so…different, so alien to me, I didn't know how to trust the results. I didn't know how to not be hurt. I don't know how to *hurt*."

"If love can be a weapon, and a shield, it can

also be a comfort. A salve for all that hurt. I didn't know how to hurt either, Charlie. Not for the longest time. I had to numb it, and I had to use something outside myself to do it, but love was always the thing I could count on instead of drugs or alcohol. It just took me some time to trust that love, wholeheartedly. Because love can be a foundation too. The thing we stand on when we don't understand each other, or the world. When we're hurt or afraid. It's the thing we're supposed to lean on, to believe in. Most *especially* when it hurts."

"Dell said love was a gift—that you have to give, and receive."

Meg smiled. "I like that. I think…maybe, it's all those things. I know it's the thing I've been missing. And I *know* it's what I feel when I'm with you. Sometimes it will be as perfect and easy as the past month, and sometimes it will suck as hard and awful as the past few days, but we have to keep getting back up."

"Keep giving."

"And receiving," she said pointedly.

He crossed to her then, took her face between his palms. "I love you, Meg." He looked so grimly serious a tear slipped over her cheek, then another. "I'm sorry for everything I said. It was fear and it was… It was wrong. You're the strongest woman I've ever known, and you did so much of that on your own. I've been jealous of people so much of my life without realizing it, but I think I finally get that leaning on those people, loving those people, is a lot better than wishing I could be them."

She placed her hands over his, trying to blink back the tears and failing.

His thumb brushed one off her cheek. "You're the only person I've so gladly put my heart on the line for. It was jarring how easily it came, how good it seemed. I've never been very trusting of things that seem too good to be true, because, quite honestly, my life has been easy. I can handle easy. It makes hard stuff seem that much more…insurmountable. So, I never put myself or my heart on the line. I never invested in what I knew would be a gamble, because I didn't want to lose."

"Love isn't ever going to be easy, maybe not even a sure thing. It can't be. Plus, we have a baby. Which makes things even harder. But it also means you're going to have to surmount it. And if you're scared, or unsure, I'll stand here being brave and sure. Because I love you. And I know— I *know* you're going to do the same when I falter."

"What if we both falter at the same time?"

Somehow that only made her feel stronger. She wasn't the only one who was scared, unsure. She wasn't the only one who might screw up. In fact, screwing up was a given, but the couple that screwed up together…stayed together? She could hope.

"We'll always have Columbus Day," she said.

He dropped his hands from her face only to scrub them over his own as he laughed. "You are…" He shook his head, hands dropping to hover between them. Then he reached out, gently placing each palm over her slight bump.

"You are both everything I want, and…I guess I had it in my head the only way to get what I wanted was to work so hard at it that everything else fell away. Being with you has never felt like work, even when it has felt like I've lost my mind, falling into a bizarre universe of goats. It has never felt like something I *earned*. But it's something I want. Something I love. So, I guess I'll have to go backward and earn what I've already got."

"You don't have to earn me. Or us. You just have to be here. And we both have to be honest, and open. Even when we'd rather, oh, rip our tongues out and grind them into meat."

"Okay, you can stop talking now."

"Tongue meat was too much, huh?"

"Meg."

"What?"

His mouth hovered close to hers, his hands still above the child they'd created by accident. "Shut up," he said, before a grin flashed over his face and his mouth touched hers.

She would gladly shut up and be kissed, and be loved, and be trusted. Because it wasn't about what she'd earned, or what had been held against her in the past.

All that mattered was that Charlie was here, and they had a whole future ahead of them.

# *EPILOGUE*

A WAINWRIGHT-PRUITT Christmas was truly something to behold. It didn't matter that Meg had now partaken for three years—that it was all her babies had ever known for Christmas. Each year she walked into the barn where she'd gotten married—just like Mia and Dell, and Cara and Wes—and her jaw dropped at what these two families could do when they came together.

Even with her own family crawling all over her, a sleepless night behind her, all she could feel was awe. Awe that she got to come to this. That her life, and her children's lives, were free of the Carmichael brand, that stifling pain, all thanks to Charlie and the secrets he'd known about her father that kept the Carmichaels and their obsession with appearances far away.

But that was the last thing Meg wanted to think about on Christmas. She wanted to think about love, and family. Not just her babies, not just the Wainwrights and the Pruitts.

This afternoon at Dan and Elsie's had been a nice reminder too. Every year she was awed by the way they'd taken to her children like grandparents. Each year, little by little, the ways they'd made inroads with their daughter, who'd now been clean for almost a year.

Christmas had become awe and wonder and light. Warmth and hope and happiness. Family. Love. All things she'd never really had before, Grandma aside.

She rested her palm on Daniel's head as he wriggled in the wrap against her chest. Even at only three months old he seemed to be determined to be mobile at all times. Little May, tiny and wiry even at nearly three, tried to climb Meg's leg the better to find her pals.

"Mama," she whined, her big dark eyes taking in the whole room as she looked for her cousins. The three girls, each only a few months apart, were a nearly inseparable threesome at any family gathering. Usually following Lainey around with barely contained awe and reverence.

Poor Daniel, terribly outnumbered by the older girls. She brushed a gentle kiss across his fuzzy head as Mia walked past, hand pressed to the small of her back, the still-small swell of a baby more noticeable these past few weeks. "Well, fourth cousin might be the charm, sweetie," Meg murmured.

Lainey rushed over and came to a skittering halt in front of Meg. "Hi, Aunt Meg," she said breathlessly. "Daddy said we can open a present when Uncle Charlie gets here." She gave a little hop.

"He's bringing in the present wagon."

Lainey squealed, then took May's outstretched hand. "Come on, May. Grandma Pruitt is letting everyone have one gingerbread man."

The two girls bounded off to the kids' table, where Mia's mother was huddled with Grace and Violet. Meg smiled, glad her little girl had something very close to sisters in her life.

Meg shifted with Daniel, trying to decide where the best place would be to sit so she could feed him soon, but as she surveyed the room, it hit her, as it did every year. This...*this* was her family. *Hers.*

She had learned Mia and Cara's father wasn't much of a talker, but he indulged any child who climbed onto his lap. Their mother fretted over the kids, the table, her children, but she seemed to have a knack for quelling fights and kissing scrapes that no one else possessed.

Mrs. Wainwright and Kenzie were as ruthlessly efficient in getting the meal served as war generals, and Mr. Wainwright was always adept at keeping everyone's glasses full.

When they weren't chasing after their ever-increasing broods, the adult children could be found all but slumped over in holiday exhaustion, trying to maintain some semblance of conversation with each other.

They invariably failed.

It was Meg's absolute favorite day of the year, and every year, without fail, she cried. It was magic, in all its exhausted, stressful tinsel-laden madness. Family and joy and coming together.

"Meg." Charlie's exasperated voice came from behind her, but she didn't bother to turn around fully. He would come up and put his arm around her, like he always did. Kiss her temple, and tell her there was no reason to cry.

"There's no reason to cry."

Her lips curved and she used the back of her hand to wipe away the stray tears. "I'm too happy not to cry."

He kissed her temple, and his arm wrapped around her shoulders. "I'll never understand that."

But he didn't have to, because he was here. Finding him had given her love. Family. A place to belong.

Some days, drowning in diapers and lack of sleep and business stress, it was hard to find her gratefulness. That was life. But so was this.

All she'd ever wanted. Perfect in its imperfection. Joy and pain and hope and fear. All wrapped up in love.

All she'd ever wanted. All they'd ever need.

* * * * *

*Be sure to check out the other books in
Nicole Helm's* **A FARMERS' MARKET
STORY** *miniseries!*

*ALL I HAVE
ALL I AM*

*Available now from Harlequin Superromance.*

# LARGER-PRINT BOOKS!

## GET 2 FREE LARGER-PRINT NOVELS PLUS
## 2 FREE GIFTS!

**HARLEQUIN®**

*Romance*

### From the Heart, For the Heart

# LARGER-PRINT BOOKS!

**HARLEQUIN**

*Presents*®

PASSION
GUARANTEED
SEDUCTION

## GET 2 FREE LARGER-PRINT NOVELS PLUS 2 FREE GIFTS!

**YES!** Please send me 2 FREE LARGER-PRINT Harlequin Presents® novels and my 2 FREE gifts (gifts are worth about $10). After receiving them, if I don't wish to receive any more books, I can return the shipping statement marked "cancel." If I don't cancel, I will receive 6 brand-new novels every month and be billed just $5.30 per book in the U.S. or $5.74 per book in Canada. That's a saving of at least 12% off the cover price! It's quite a bargain! Shipping and handling is just 50¢ per book in the U.S. and 75¢ per book in Canada.* I understand that accepting the 2 free books and gifts places me under no obligation to buy anything. I can always return a shipment and cancel at any time. Even if I never buy another book, the two free books and gifts are mine to keep forever.

176/376 HDN GHVY

| Name | (PLEASE PRINT) | |
|---|---|---|
| Address | | Apt. # |
| City | State/Prov. | Zip/Postal Code |

Signature (if under 18, a parent or guardian must sign)

### Mail to the **Reader Service:**
**IN U.S.A.:** P.O. Box 1867, Buffalo, NY 14240-1867
**IN CANADA:** P.O. Box 609, Fort Erie, Ontario L2A 5X3

**Are you a subscriber to Harlequin Presents® books and want to receive the larger-print edition?**
**Call 1-800-873-8635 today or visit us at www.ReaderService.com.**

* Terms and prices subject to change without notice. Prices do not include applicable taxes. Sales tax applicable in N.Y. Canadian residents will be charged applicable taxes. Offer not valid in Quebec. This offer is limited to one order per household. Not valid for current subscribers to Harlequin Presents Larger-Print books. All orders subject to credit approval. Credit or debit balances in a customer's account(s) may be offset by any other outstanding balance owed by or to the customer. Please allow 4 to 6 weeks for delivery. Offer available while quantities last.

**Your Privacy**—The Reader Service is committed to protecting your privacy. Our Privacy Policy is available online at www.ReaderService.com or upon request from the Reader Service.

We make a portion of our mailing list available to reputable third parties that offer products we believe may interest you. If you prefer that we not exchange your name with third parties, or if you wish to clarify or modify your communication preferences, please visit us at www.ReaderService.com/consumerschoice or write to us at Reader Service Preference Service, P.O. Box 9062, Buffalo, NY 14240-9062. Include your complete name and address.

HPLP15

# REQUEST YOUR FREE BOOKS!

## 2 FREE WHOLESOME ROMANCE NOVELS IN LARGER PRINT

## PLUS 2 FREE MYSTERY GIFTS

### HEARTWARMING™

*Wholesome, tender romances*

**YES!** Please send me 2 FREE Harlequin® Heartwarming Larger-Print novels and my 2 FREE mystery gifts (gifts worth about $10). After receiving them, if I don't wish to receive any more books, I can return the shipping statement marked "cancel." If I don't cancel, I will receive 4 brand-new larger-print novels every month and be billed just $5.24 per book in the U.S. or $5.99 per book in Canada. That's a savings of at least 19% off the cover price. It's quite a bargain! Shipping and handling is just 50¢ per book in the U.S. and 75¢ per book in Canada.* I understand that accepting the 2 free books and gifts places me under no obligation to buy anything. I can always return a shipment and cancel at any time. Even if I never buy another book, the two free books and gifts are mine to keep forever.

161/361 IDN GHX2

Name _____ (PLEASE PRINT)

Address _____ Apt. #

City _____ State/Prov. _____ Zip/Postal Code

Signature (if under 18, a parent or guardian must sign)

### Mail to the **Reader Service:**
**IN U.S.A.:** P.O. Box 1867, Buffalo, NY 14240-1867
**IN CANADA:** P.O. Box 609, Fort Erie, Ontario L2A 5X3

* Terms and prices subject to change without notice. Prices do not include applicable taxes. Sales tax applicable in N.Y. Canadian residents will be charged applicable taxes. Offer not valid in Quebec. This offer is limited to one order per household. Not valid for current subscribers to Harlequin Heartwarming larger-print books. All orders subject to credit approval. Credit or debit balances in a customer's account(s) may be offset by any other outstanding balance owed by or to the customer. Please allow 4 to 6 weeks for delivery. Offer available while quantities last.

**Your Privacy**—The Reader Service is committed to protecting your privacy. Our Privacy Policy is available online at www.ReaderService.com or upon request from the Reader Service.

We make a portion of our mailing list available to reputable third parties that offer products we believe may interest you. If you prefer that we not exchange your name with third parties, or if you wish to clarify or modify your communication preferences, please visit us at www.ReaderService.com/consumerschoice or write to us at Reader Service Preference Service, P.O. Box 9062, Buffalo, NY 14240-9062. Include your complete name and address.

# LARGER-PRINT BOOKS!
## GET 2 FREE LARGER-PRINT NOVELS PLUS
## 2 FREE GIFTS!

**⊕ HARLEQUIN®**

# I N T R I G U E

## BREATHTAKING ROMANTIC SUSPENSE

HILP15